THE ART OF KILLING

C. R. CLARKE

Matador
Unit E2 Airfield Business Park,
Harrison Road, Market Harborough,
Leicestershire. LE16 7UL
Tel: 0116 2792299
Email: books@troubador.co.uk
Web: www.troubador.co.uk/matador
Twitter: @matadorbooks

ISBN 978 1805140 122

British Library Cataloguing in Publication Data.
A catalogue record for this book is available from the British Library.

Typeset in 10.5pt Adobe Garamond Pro by Troubador Publishing Ltd, Leicester, UK

Matador is an imprint of Troubador Publishing Ltd

For Zoe, who is always there for me,
taking the loneliness out of life's
equation and filling my world with
joy, love and companionship.
For that I am truly grateful.
I love you…

'I will execute great vengeance upon them with furious rebukes. Then they will know that I am the Lord, when I lay my vengeance upon them.'

Ezekiel 25:17

PROLOGUE

Transcribed telephone communication – Sunday, May 3rd
Time – 7:27am
Duty operator – Helen Cope

'…Emergency services. Do you require Fire, Police or Ambulance?'

'Police. P-Please.'

'Hold the line. Putting you through now…'

–Ringing–

'Gloucester Constabulary. What's the nature of your emergency?'

'… I-I-I f-f-found, a b-body.'

'You've discovered a *body?* Where?'

'In Stroud. I'm in Stroud.'

'Could you try to be a bit more precise for me, sweetheart?'

'Under the bridge, N– the viaduct I mean, near Dr Newton's Way.'

'*Under* the viaduct…? Dr Newton's Way…? Is that the A419, my love?'

'Erm? Yes. I– I think so.'

'And how did you discover the body?'

'Walking my dog. I'm– I'm out, walking my dog.'

'And… are there any signs of life?'

'No.'

'You've checked? Are you sure?'

'Oh. Fuck me, yes. Dear Jesus!'

'All right. That's all right. The police have been informed of your call and are on their way now. I can hear you're shook up. Are you still there, at the location? Is this your mobile?'

'Yes. Yes, it is.'

'And what is your name, my love?'

'Janet. Janet Dando.'

'And, the body, is it lying on the ground, or—?'

'No. It's– it's suspended, on wires.'

'*Hanging?* Do you mean a suicide?'

'No. N-No. Oh Jesus! Oh sweet Jesus!'

'Okay. Try to keep calm for me. Can you tell me if it's a man or a woman?'

'It's– it's a child. I *thhhink* it's a little boy, but I can't really be sure. The body, it's– it's been– oh dear God in Heaven, help me!'

ONE

DETECTIVE INSPECTOR GUTTERIDGE lurched from his slumber with a jolt like he'd taken a hit from a defibrillator, jewels of sweat mottling his brow. It took a moment to recognise where he was, shuffling to the edge of the buttoned leather armchair he'd flopped into on his return from work.

The fire he'd lit earlier had gone out, and the room felt chilled and unwelcoming.

He cupped a despairing hand to his forehead and sagged. The old dream was back. The *nightmare,* was back! Visions of Jerry Masterson's incomprehensible crimes taunting his sleep. But he was awake now, and safe.

But the image of his deceased wife – Cynthia – remained, emblazoned on his memory like a branding iron, her dead, lifeless eyes peering into his soul from across the room, watching his arrival and the heart-crushing horror galvanising his face.

His tear ducts itched with a compulsion to cry, but he fought it back with a clench of the gut and a pursed exhalation of pent-up sorrow.

The fingers of his right hand momentarily gravitated to his ring finger to twirl the band of gold, but he'd long ago ceased wearing it in an attempt to force the moving-on from such a painful chapter of his life, and his fingers fell on nothing but skin.

Ewelina's face flashed his thoughts like a subliminal cut, and guilt manifested briefly in his churning stomach. But *why* should he feel guilt? Was his own happiness worth so little that he had to abstain from any concept of inner peace and contentment?

But the loneliness was eating him, and it only seemed to be getting worse. He needed a new life companion, a new soulmate, since the love of his life had been so cruelly and needlessly taken from him. But was Ewelina Kaminska truly eligible to fulfil that role?

His mind turned to thoughts of a warm shot of whisky, and a long, neatly chopped line of coke – the idea momentarily appealing to his struggling inability to handle the grief – but the notion was instantly expunged by one of the Rolodex of bad memories of previous times he'd relented to *that* urge, those memories that had finally allowed him to remain sober.

'Throw yourself into your work,' he muttered into the soft dawn light warming the drapes and the solitude engulfing the room, turning resolute. 'Just throw yourself into your work...'

DS Keaton's angelic face – her soft features and warm smile – emerged through the swirling fog of his sorrow. He allowed himself a smile, because that woman had saved him, given him back his ability to give a shit.

He checked his watch, sighed, and rose to shower...

TWO

1997

THE DEEP, GRAVEL-THROATED, Munster accent coursed through the child's fear of his father's hair-trigger fury.

'You wouldn't be a faggot now, would yer? No O'Leary has ever raised no faggot. Now… pick up the bastard gun, and kill the beast, before yer make me ashamed to be yer father.'

The air in the barn reverberated to the baritone threat, the child hanging uneasy in the haze of his unwillingness to take a life, his ten-year-old fingers repelling from the captive bolt pistol slammed onto the fold-out table before him.

The mud-caked radio in the background crackled with news of a possible Northern Ireland peace deal, but the atmosphere – at that moment – felt anything but optimistic.

The child's father fixed him a stare harder than any he'd drilled him with before, and ten minutes earlier, the boy would have sworn that an impossibility.

'P-Please, Daddy. I don't w-w-want to,' appealed the boy.

The quaking fume returned to the man's broad yolk, his

work-hardened, forearm muscles flexing like cables beneath a tarp.

'Tek the fuckin' gun, before I'm forced to thrash yer,' he seethed.

The heifer penned into the narrow stall began to sense the swelling agitation polluting the fresh, autumnal air, and started padding about for an escape.

'But… why? Why do I have to?' the child stammered, his eyes beseeching, his confusion genuine.

The man stooped his face towards the boy's, the sky behind burning vermillion to the tune of a low-hanging sun. In the halo of the broiling backdrop, he looked every bit the devil he was.

'Because… I feckin' said so,' he seethed, before turning a look over his shoulder towards the fireball rising in the east. 'Roit now, there's a lion tearin' a gazelle apart in the Serengeti. It's the way of the world we live in, child, and yer have ter face dat, sooner, or later… I choose *sooner*!'

His wiry beard began munching his loathing for the child's pathetic display of compassion, spits of rage-saliva clinging to the coarse doughnut of salt-and-pepper fur encircling his grinding jawline.

He raised mocking brows. 'If yer a bum-boy, just feckin' say so, and I'll disown yer now. Else, pick up the bastard gun, and kill the beast.' He leaned further in, his nose now just an inch from the boy's. 'An' if yer don't, al tek off me belt, and al beat yer arse till it bleeds!'

The stench of cheap whisky on the devil's breath forced the child into retreat. The man twisted an ironic look into the boy's shrinking pupils. 'But you'd probably loik dat, wouldn't yer, yer queer. Now *pick* yer poison!'

The devil took up the pistol without his eyes ever leaving the child's, and gently placed it in the kid's upturned, sweat-glazed palms. 'Tha gun does the haard work, all *you* got ta do, is pull the bastard trigger. Now. *Do* it!' he insisted.

Reluctantly, the boy took it, fumbling the weapon in his tiny fingers, trying to make sense of his adolescent hands' unwieldy attempts to operate the device's adult proportions.

'You can climb up on the gate to get a clear shot,' the devil suggested, flicking a glance towards the pens. 'A've made a mark for yer, roit between its ears. Put the gun to its head, aim towards the spine, and pull. It's easy. A girl could do it.'

The boy barely recognised his father anymore. He'd always been a hard man, an uncompromising man, his potential for aggression matched only by his physical size. But the grief and the drink had changed him, drowning any suggestion of love that may once have existed.

The kid stumbled clumsily up the holding-pen fence, using the rungs as a ladder. The stun-gun clattered against the railings.

'Be feckin' careful wid dat, it cost a lot of money. More than *your* sorry arse is worth to a man loik me!'

'Sorry. I'm sorry,' the boy sobbed, the clueless heifer's big, black eyes reflecting his soporific progress.

He reached the fourth rung and leaned his thighs against the top railing. He leant out unsteadily, his reluctant hands shaking, attempting to find a comfortable grip on the killing machine.

The doe-eyed heifer shuffled back from the looming figure invading its space, but the devil leaned in and shoved it forwards again.

A spot of red floor-marking spray above the beast's eyes foreshadowed its doom, beckoning the boy to take aim.

'Will you get it done, before the cunting animal cottons on,' he spat. 'Just *feckin'* do it. *Now*!'

The boy's facial pleas continued to fall on deaf, disinterested ears, and the stern look of adamance returned to a front that was never going to accept a 'no'.

Tiny arms extended tiny hands. Tiny hands extended the cylinder of death towards its next victim.

'Now, remember, yer have ter angle it towards the spinal column, else it won't be a clean kill. You'd risk giving it a painful death, and I know a soft shite loik you wouldn't loik dat.'

The cow turned serine, seeming strangely resigned to its approaching fate, or simply confused by the close proximity of the polished-silver embellishment to its personal space. But either way, it stood static, its puppy-dog gaze mirrored by the boy's, mesmerised by what was unfolding.

A reluctant finger hooked the handle and leaned against the trigger on the textured grip. The boy tried to come to terms with the feelings of foreboding torquing his stomach into a fist.

His face grimaced. He panted through his disinclination to succeed, trying to squint the impending horror away to some convoluted form of detachment.

His tiny finger continued to lean on the trigger, fluttering reluctant attempts to pull harder.

'*Shoot... the fuckin'... ting!*' his father barked.

His slender arms grew fatigued with the weight of the pistol.

'Hold it up, keep it straight!' the devil screamed.

'I'm trying,' the boy sobbed. 'It's heavy, it's too heavy.' Lactic acid flooded his arms and stung like fire, his shoulders now an inferno.

The heifer began padding again. Panic set in, and the boy tugged desperately at the trigger.

With a *crack* that echoed around the surrounding countryside, the pistol kicked in his tiny hands. The bolt fired, smashing through the cow's skull with a hollow, sickening thud, and retracted again. But the shot was angled high, missing the spinal cord.

'What did ya do? You were holding it too feckin' low, ya stupid wanker!' the man growled.

The heifer's legs stiffened, splayed, and it dropped to the soil like a rock. It began kicking violently on the floor of the pen, tongue lolloping from a salivating mouth.

The boy just watched in horror at eyes rolling independently in a head gushing a cocktail of blood and cranial fluid. The creature spasmed for what felt like an hour, before finally falling still. Silent. Dead.

The boy's face crumpled, and tears loosed from his regretful eyes. He felt sure an overtly Catholic, fire-and-brimstone God would come for him for what he'd done, for what he had been *forced* to do.

His father stepped in and took the pistol. 'Well done, son... you fucked it up a bit, but well done.'

He helped the shaking boy down from the gate, but the child's tear-glazed eyes never left the results of his sinning.

'Next time, it'll be easier. Trust me,' the devil said.

The boy turned panicked, pinprick pupils up to his father's words, then back to the cow carcass lying inelegantly on the floor of the pen.

The man placed the gun gently back on the table, and walked backwards from the child, unhooking his buckle.

The *swiff* of leather whipping from belt loops dragged the boy back into the shed, and he turned to see his father removing his belt.

The boy's saline face widened. 'But I did what you said? I did it. I killed it. I killed the cow?! Oh God, *pleeease*!' he wept, his malnourished limbs and beseeching eyes shrinking away from the knowledge that he was to receive yet another beating.

The crotch of his soil-stained corduroys darkened as amber fear emptied from his flimsy body, the taste of tears filling his mouth. 'I didn't do anything wrong! I didn't! I did it! I did what you said! *Whyyyy*?' he wept.

The man snapped the folded belt in the void between his livid fists, the crack of the leather shocking the air between them. He looked strangely excited. 'Because… Yer cried…'

THREE

Present Day

'ANOTHER ONE APPEARED LAST NIGHT, on the side of Lidl, above the entrance,' DS Keaton said, sitting in the passenger seat of the black Saab 9-3, scanning the tabloid she'd swiped earlier from the greasy spoon where they ate breakfast. Not her usual read, but she harboured a kind of morbid fascination for the working-class appeal of its trashy content.

DI Gutteridge allowed his attention to drift from the road long enough to crane a look. 'Where? Let me see.'

Keaton turned the paper towards him. He had to squint. 'I haven't got my reading glasses on, what is it this time? Apart from overblown shite,' he scoffed.

'Not an art lover then, Pat?'

Gutteridge took mild offence at the slur, however light-heartedly it may have been delivered. 'I *am*, and I *do*, appreciate art. But I'm not sure that this... what's he calling himself? Tick-Tock...?' Keaton nodded. 'I'm not sure this Tick-Tock's particular brand of vandalism constitutes art.'

'Well, what else would you call it?'

'Exactly what I just said – vandalism.'

Keaton considered the photo again. 'Well, the critics seem to accept it as art,' she said, 'and that one on the side of the newsagent's, on the farthest side of town, the owner cut that out of the wall and it sold at auction two weeks ago for £127,000. If that isn't art, God knows what is.'

'But that's what I don't get,' Gutteridge said, signalling to join the main carriageway. 'The shopkeeper gets *that* money, not the daft sod that made the unilateral decision to vandalise his store. So how does that work?'

Keaton shrugged. 'I don't know. Maybe he—'

'Or it could be a "she",' Gutteridge interjected.

Keaton see-sawed an acknowledging head. 'Or she... but whatever their gender, maybe *they* see it as giving back to the community.'

Gutteridge scoffed for the second time in as many minutes as he turned into the drive-through lane of McDonald's. 'Who the fuck would feel a desire to give back to a shithole like Gloucester? And why has it always got to be some animal-rights bollocks? It's just plain, old-fashioned attention-seeking. Nothing more. Nothing less. Same old.'

Keaton realised Gutteridge had been cursing more than usual. His swearing tended to increase exponentially with his levels of frustration. It had been slow in CID for months; it could have been that. But Keaton suspected it more likely to be something in his personal life that was troubling him. She considered asking, but quickly changed her mind. She had her own personal frustrations to cope with.

Gutteridge leaned his face out of the side window to address the speaker. 'Can I have one of those double bacon burger things you've got on the menu at the moment. As a meal please, with tea. Oh, and six chicken nuggets with a tub of barbecue dip.'

He turned a defiantly smug face towards Keaton. 'There's your animal lover... What do *you* want...?'

*

They sat in the core of an aroma of cooking oil, rhythmically machine-gunning oversalted fries, before tucking into hastily stacked burgers that looked nothing like the poster.

'It can't be attention-seeking,' Keaton said, jabbing the air with a fry to accentuate her point, 'no one knows who this "guy" is? And it probably *is* a guy, judging by the aggression in the sweep of his handwriting.'

'That's bollocks, someone must know.'

'Go on then, "Detective", who is it?'

'Well, I don't bloody know, do I? But are you telling me this narcissist hasn't let on to *anyone* that they're the cause of this – what is it now? – two-year frenzy of interest in his ineffectual daubing?'

Keaton smirked at his use of the word 'daubing', old-fashioned and indicative of his age. In fact, she liked the art, but didn't want to cause a rift by admitting it to someone she had to spend a majority of her day with. She may have found his incessant griping amusing at times, but not when she was on the receiving end.

'I don't call a hundred and twenty-seven grand "ineffectual",' she said.

Gutteridge shuffled in his seat to face her. 'Just because some chinless Hooray Henry from the crime-ridden cesspit that is London is willing to part with a ridiculous sum of money to own that pile of crap, doesn't make it relevant.'

'I think you'll find it does.'

Gutteridge held the look. But Keaton feigned ignorance of his efforts to stare her down.

Keaton broke from the pressure of the stare. 'Come on then,' she chirped, stuffing burger wrappers and emptied waxed-paper cups into the bag the food came in, and swiping crumbs from her lap, 'let's go over and take a look at it. A *proper* look, I mean. There's sod-all we can do with the Gurney-Combes case until the report from pathology lands, so let's see if we can't enlighten your grumpy-old-bastard arse to new forms of culture.'

Gutteridge considered if he could be bothered, while Keaton checked her make-up in the sun-visor mirror.

Keaton then realised – as usually happened – that when things in the department were slow, her awareness of rank seemed to evaporate, and her interactions – especially with Gutteridge – took on a far mateyer air, and she feared, one day, stepping across the line. But Gutteridge seemed to enjoy the banter that passed between them, and that hadn't happened… *yet.*

Gutteridge watched Keaton fixing herself in the mirror. He thought she possessed a pretty face, in fact, *no*, it was beautiful – an opinion also shared by most of the men in the department, especially the younger recruits with their fizzy dicks and chemical-warfare hormone imbalances. She had a pert mouth, and striking, electric-blue eyes that often came in useful on the job. A disarming quality that loosened the tongues of suspects and witnesses, including the straight women. Her features were slight, but well defined. 'Sharp' was the single word Gutteridge would use.

'Ahh, sod it. Go on then, I'll bite. Lidl, you said?' grumbled Gutteridge, twisting the key in the ignition.

'Yep, Lidl,' she confirmed, as she skillfully wiped a lipstick smudge from the corner of her mouth with her pinky. Her hands were petite, delicate, like a child's, but they moved with an adult elegance.

Gutteridge pulled out from the parking space. 'And I'm forty-fucking-four. That's not old. You're just young…'

FOUR

THE PIERCING SQUEAL of school-bus brakes announced its arrival to all within earshot of the desolate country road it struggled along.

The long slab of door hissed open, and 'the boy' dropped off the cliff-edge step onto the verge, brandishing a painting that had earned him the highest mark in class.

He turned to wave his muted thanks, like he had every single day, of every single week, of every single year he'd attended Adrigole Primary School. But again – and not for the first time – the driver thought it seemed like some coded cry for help. But his hands were tied by a minefield of procedures and protocols.

He'd noticed the bruising just shy of the cuffs and the neckline of the child's sweater, and the limping, the flinching, the tentative way he took to a seat. But what could he do, in such a tight-knit community, that wouldn't threaten to fuck up his social life?

'Moind how you go, little fella,' the driver said, leaning on the wheel.

Again, the boy fixed him an outwardly emotionless, but eerily desperate stare, hanging static in the frame of the door, until it hissed shut, and once more, the view through the window abandoned him.

The boy walked the long, mud-track lane to the farm on reluctant legs. He could feel the throb of the thumb print bruising beneath his rucksack straps.

The sun hung low, the sky fiery, as fiery as his father's temper. He wanted to turn and run – like the voice said. But to where?

The calls of the cows grew louder in the still evening air as he rounded the corner of the grain-barn, and saw his father in the yard brushing mud from the blades of the tiller.

The man turned to face his son's tentative approach. 'What ya got dere?'

'A painting, I did it in class. Mr Cullock said it was the best one.'

'*Aaart!*' he slurred in a mocking, dismissive tone. The boy could already smell the peaty fumes of his father's breath from ten feet away. *Run*, said the voice. *Just run!*

'Yes. Art. I… I like art.'

'Let me see,' he chewed, extending an insistent hand to take the rolled-up baton of paper.

An image of the heifer, tongue lolloping from its swinging mouth, flashed the boy's thoughts.

The man slid the rubber band off the roll, flicking it across the courtyard, and unfurled the painting. He turned it this way, and that. 'What the fuck is it supposed to be?'

The boy didn't want to answer. He'd already read the room and knew his jokes would bomb. 'It's supposed to be a rep… representation of how I feel.'

'Yer feckin' what?'

'Erm… of– of how I feel.'

The devil held the painting up again, considering the image of a distorted face, vivid slashes of colour cutting through its wide-open mouth. 'Is dat supposed to be a feckin' joke? Is this the feckin' ejication moi taxes are payin' fer?'

His face reddened, a white-knuckled fist wielding the screwed-up painting, looking about the courtyard. 'How the fuck is *dis* supposed to pay fer this feckin' farm?' he seethed. 'This... this– *shoite*!'

He lunged and lashed out at the boy, but the child was ready, and the stumbling, pissed-up attempt failed to land. But the boy's fleetness just riled the alcoholic, and he chased him towards the house. 'Go and get your fecking work clothes on, yer shite, and come and do some real work. Proper work! *Man's* work!'

The boy stumbled into the unkempt farmhouse, his father turning back to carry on his unfinished job.

The boy ambled through the entrance hall, past the boot-cupboard and into the heart of the living room.

Dust particles sparkled in the rays streaming through the window. He could still smell his mother; even through the musty stench of dereliction, her scent remained, engrained into the fabric of the brick and the cloth, even after all that time.

She'd passed away just eighteen months earlier, and he hankered for the soft, protective embrace of her arms, the pillow of her bosom, and the calming effect that her words had on his father's rage. A rage that had always existed, but that now was unchecked.

Run! came the voice, again. The voice in his head. The voice that had arrived shortly after the fifth or sixth beating. *Run! Run away. Run far...* it hissed. *Else kill himmm!*

FIVE

GUTTERIDGE WALKED OUT OF LIDL brandishing two waxed-paper bags. He handed one to Keaton. 'Toffee yum-yums. They're nice. Help clear the taste of that bloody dog-burger! I got you just three because I know you're on one of your diets.'

She took one from the bag, studied it with suspicion, and took a cautious bite. 'Mmmmmm… oh my God!' she enthused. 'They… are… amazing.' A reminder in sugar form of just why she had to work so hard to maintain her pert physique.

He joined her on the bonnet of the car and leaned out to consider her figure. '*Another* diet,' he sniggered, 'Christ knows why, you look good to me. *Better* than good.'

Keaton's eyes remained locked on the artwork looming high above them. 'Shouldn't be looking,' she said, her tongue scooping stray flakes of yum-yum from the inside of her cheek.

'It's not illegal to look, not yet anyway.'

'Nor is it illegal to report you for harassment,' she responded, taking another bite. She loosed a wry smile. 'Go on then. Give me that one about, "If I were ten years younger".'

Gutteridge smirked, then laughed, and followed her locked gaze up to the mural emblazoned high on the wall above them.

He'd not been partnered with Keaton long, a little less than a year, after his previous partner transferred to a Scottish division to be closer to family – his father having contracted stage-three cancer.

From day one, she'd grown on him. She didn't react to his shit like the others had, and actually tempered many of his deeper flaws simply by existing. He liked her, and respected her, and not just because she was good, but because she made the job bearable again.

'Come on then, "Searle", tell me what you think,' she asked.

'Who the hell is Searle?' Gutteridge replied.

Keaton turned to address his ear. 'Adrian Searle. The art critic from *The Guardian*?' She turned back to face the painting again. 'Jesus, Pat, we have to get you to read a newspaper sometime.'

'Newspapers are full of opinions, none of them my own. The only opinion I care about, is mine.' He realised too late what he'd said. 'And yours, of course… but only if it's a match to my own.'

'Yeah, yeah,' she sneered, nodding towards the new embellishment to the store's brickwork facade. 'So, come on, tell me what you think?'

Gutteridge's eyes swam over the details of the mural, absorbing it like it was the scene of a crime – which, in his old-world mind, wasn't too removed from the truth.

Like all the others, it appeared to have been done using pre-prepared stencils, he assumed to make the process quicker, and avoid getting caught, threatening to break the media-fed frenzy that went arm in arm with the anonymity.

A depiction of an overhead conveyor, delivering a stream of chickens hanging helplessly by their feet to a forked neck-slicing device, stretched wide and loud above the words 'MURDER MOST FOWL' painted in colours more usual to an abattoir.

'I feel guilty for eating that sodding burger now,' Keaton said.

Gutteridge flashed ironic brows and huffed a snigger. 'I know what you mean. If he's trying to breed guilt, it works.'

He lifted a yum-yum to his waiting mouth, and his chin to the wall. 'What do you reckon that bit means?'

'Which bit?'

'The kid?'

'Eh? What kid?'

'You're joking, right? Third chicken along, *isn't* a chicken. It's a child.'

He was right – there it was, large and loud. The third victim in line from the waiting blades was indeed a child, suspended by its ankles like the rest of the cull, arms hanging, slotted in with the other unfortunates. Its skin was depicted as bloodless and pasty white, making it blend in with the confusion of wings and feathers.

Keaton's face buckled with repulsion. 'Oh fuck. I didn't see that. What the hell!' she slurred. 'That's sick.'

'So, go on then, "*Searle*",' Gutteridge mocked. 'You studied psychology. Unpack *that* particular glimpse into a fucked-up mind.'

Keaton chewed a lip. 'Well, I can't, can I? I mean, why bring a kid into it?'

Gutteridge's whole face squinted. His brows flickered. He lunged from his perch on the bonnet and stepped in, leaning pinched eyes up towards the artwork high above them.

'What is it?' Keaton asked.

'I don't know…'

He dropped a half-eaten yum-yum into the bag and tossed it onto the bonnet. He rounded the car, wiping sugar crystals from his fingers on his trousers, popped the boot with his fob and unzipped his camera bag.

A crescent of shoppers had gathered behind his vehicle, marvelling at the new addition to their city, swapping eclectic opinions.

He took out his most powerful lens, clipped it onto the body of his Nikon, and made his way back around to the front of the car.

He pocketed the lens cap and presented the camera to his open eye, twisting the barrel of the lens to focus on the writing.

'What are you looking at?' Keaton asked.

'I'm not sure,' he said. 'The words, they're moving.'

'Moving?'

'Yeah. Moving…'

Gutteridge's unsquinted eye widened. 'Flies!'

'Did you say "flies"?'

'Yes,' he said, passing the camera to Keaton. 'Look.'

She fumbled at the old-school contraption. The weight surprised her. Her own camera was a point-and-shoot affair, modern and idiot-proof. She felt like an idiot.

She finally managed to offer it up to her eye, and after a few wild swings, found the heavily exaggerated writing looming large in the viewfinder. It moved with a strange munching quality, reminding her of how *everything* had looked to her the first and only time she'd ever tried magic mushrooms. But *this* movement wasn't a trip, it was insects, congregating on the taste of decay, attracted by a coppery tang drifting on the wind.

'That's real blood?' she said, turning her surprise from the viewfinder.

Gutteridge was already nodding. 'I know. The crazy bastard's bled himself and smeared it all over the wall. Fucking freak!'

'Well, you know,' Keaton interjected, 'it's not unknown for an artist to use their own bodily fluids in the creation of their art.'

Gutteridge turned his disgust towards what he felt was an attempt to excuse the outrage. 'You fucking what? Is that true?'

'Yep,' she chirped, lifting the camera to take another look. She felt strangely superior for knowing, and could feel herself welling at how good it felt.

She rarely felt superior in the company of Gutteridge; he'd been on the job so much longer than she had. And despite his grumpy overtones, he was considered the best foot-soldier detective in the division. So, when she was presented with an opportunity to feel superior, she wore it, gladly, with style and a measured lack of pomp.

'Well, I think it's disgusting, and any la-di-da that feels compelled to part with hard-earned cash to own this tosser's defecant, is welcome to it,' bemoaned Gutteridge, taking the camera back from Keaton, and firing off a few shots for posterity and his own morbid interest.

He rounded the car again, dropping the assembled equipment back into the bag and slamming the boot shut.

They pulled away from a now sizeable gathering of spectators that had accumulated around the car, interests sparked by their own viewing of the 'masterpiece'.

'I gather you're still not a fan, then?' Keaton smirked.

'Nope! Crap.'

Keaton laughed out loud. 'I love you,' she smiled, 'you joyless git.'

'Yeah, yeah. It's too weird for me. All that *cutting yourself for your art*. I mean, really…!'

'It's not *really* his blood. I was just agreeing with your assumption to freak you out. The sheer amount on that wall would have killed him to draw it, unless he did it over a number of days. It's probably animal blood he's used.'

Gutteridge's expression brightened. 'Ahh, yeah. You're probably right.' He felt concerned that he hadn't figured that out himself, but the recent spell of inactivity in the department had transpired to detune his finer instincts. He allowed a weak laugh to mask his concern.

His brows fluttered again. He checked the mirrors and spun the car in the road to head back.

'What the hell are you doing?!' Keaton complained, peeling herself off the side window.

'Going back.'

'Back? Why?'

'To take a sample.'

Keaton looked confused. 'Of the writing? What for?'

Gutteridge swung into the entrance of Lidl and pulled into a vacant space. He shut the engine off and turned to look Keaton square in the eye. '*Because*... no one so outwardly "animal rights" would ever use animal blood in a painting. It would go against *every* principle they seek to champion. Wouldn't it? So... what the *hell* did he use?'

He popped the door and rose from the car. Keaton followed suit. 'Besides, beats getting morbidly obese on fast food, doesn't it?'

'I guess so,' she had to agree.

Gutteridge slammed the door. 'I'll go and see the manager, see if they've got a ladder we can use. You bring the kit from the boot.' He tossed her the keys.

Keaton still looked bemused, but felt a pop of excitement in her belly. 'Okay, boss. I'm on it...'

SIX

HIRED BEARERS carried the coffin respectfully to the graveside and fumbled it onto batons spanning the waiting hole. Seven feet, by three feet. Six feet deep.

To the congregation of six, it had a hungry look, ready to swallow it down into the pit of hell where it belonged, and despite their saddened facades, none of them could wait to see the back of the 'old cunt' inhabiting such an undeservedly opulent casket.

Five hung in the background, a sea of suits and black netting. Extraneous family members there only out of a misplaced sense of duty, and to make up the meagre numbers.

But the sixth – 'the boy', now eighteen – stood on the edge of the precipice looking in.

His face wore a mixture of satisfaction and insincere regret that didn't sit right, and that none of the eyes behind the dipped brows, or the ghostly faces resolving from beyond the midnight lace, could fathom. But now that 'he' was gone, none of them cared enough to question what was behind it.

The priest stepped up to the graveside and opened his book. He looked about at the congregation, but he had seen enough over the years to tell none of them cared to be there.

Himself, he could find no sincere words to say about the unwelcome addition to his sacred soils that hadn't already been said during the heavily redacted service: one hymn; one reading; and a seventy-two-second eulogy about a hard-working man. The first service in his twenty-seven-year history that wasn't graced with a single mention of 'love'. So, unhypocritically, he bypassed the Lord's prayer, and cut straight to the committal.

He lifted a nod to the bearers who stepped in with straps, hooked the casket, drew the batons, and began lowering it away from memories keen to forget.

The priest turned eyes to his good book. He knew the words by heart, but his faith, at that moment, waned.

'We therefore commit Conor O'Leary's body to the ground. Earth to earth. Ashes to ashes. Dust to dust. In sure and certain hope of...' The priest paused, choking on the words. 'In– in sure, and certain hope of– of– of resurrection, to eternal life.'

The boy didn't notice the stutter; all he heard through the monophonic bleat was the word 'ashes', bringing forth visions of Dante's inferno, and the three-headed Satan who resides there, all three mouths abandoning their eternal torment of Brutus, Cassius, and Judas Iscariot, and turning their attentions to his father's soul, tearing it apart limb from limb as skin boiled from his hateful bones.

The whip of the straps leaving the hole carried the boy back to reality with a flinch. The crack of the leather belt rang loud in his memories. The strange look of pleasure he would see in his father's eyes when a beating was coming.

He wanted to spit on the grave but held it fast in the floor of his mouth. He smiled, and nearly laughed. It had been so easy. *Too* easy? Just one push...

Had God presented the opportunity, he wondered, to be behind his father, just at the moment he was checking the grain silo? Had *God's* hands even been behind his own when he pushed his father in? And had God even stood on his shoulder as they watched the man struggle, flounder and drown in the dust and the kernels of the cereal quicksand? Had the voice that had urged him on; urged him to run; urged him to hide; urged him to *Do it! Push him! Push him now!* actually *been* God's all along?

The mock-mourners disbanded, stepping in to place heartfelt touches to the boy's shoulder. He turned smiles to their displays of affection, expressing a desire to be alone, just with a look. They and the priest acquiesced, turned, and left him.

They all heard the sound of a kicking foot, and the spatter of soil on wood, and the hock, and the spit, and the 'good riddance, you *fuck*!' but they all pretended they hadn't.

The boy pondered what he would do. The farm was his now, but it held too many memories, too many shadows, too many beatings.

The cuts and bruises to his body were gone, replaced by scars. But the bruising inside remained. Lacerations to a psyche that could never heal, and he wanted to run, run away, run far, like the voice had said all along. The voice that remained. His only friend?

He would sell the farm, the land, the equipment and the cows, but only to a dairy that promised to give them a good life, and he would leave Ireland forever. Once his home, but now just a bad taste in a mouth that hankered for the flavour of the England he'd read about. A land of polite society. A land of ladies and gentlemen. A land two countries distant from the emerald hell, and the spitting hatred that would always, in some way, colour him…

SEVEN

DCI BRYANT STOOD AT THE HEAD of the incident room, holding printed and stapled sheets of paper at the ready like a conductor's baton, looking out over a sea of semi-interested faces and slouching sitters holding half-hearted pens to disinterested pads in readiness.

He had a clean-cut, corporate, almost office-jockey look that belied his rank. But after eight weeks without a single serious case to oversee, his look had deteriorated: top button undone; tie loose; comfortable shoes for the office. He would now save his smartest look for the press packs and the cameras he hadn't seen in months.

'The report from pathology *seems* to concur with DS Keaton's idea that the Gurney-Combes case was an accident,' he said. 'The contents of the stomach and the tox report show a fatal quantity of Tramadol in her system.'

He lifted a look across to Keaton who was sitting near the back, attempting to not look smug. 'Now, as many of you will already know, she was taking Tramadol as part of her prescription for pain relief. But according to her GP, she has a history of accidentally overdosing her meds.'

He folded the top sheet to the back and scanned the notes through glasses perched on the tip of his nose.

'Tramadol – as you're probably aware – is an opioid, not *that* far removed from heroin, and *can* cause memory loss as a side effect. She *may* have dosed multiple times as a consequence. It's been known to happen, and a lack of any signs of trauma around her mouth or throat, or traces of the substance in her glass or food, *seems* to discount the probability of forced consumption. The report also says that the addition of alcohol can cause respiratory problems and seizures, which seems to support the witness statements.'

A phone rang out at the back of the room. DI Gutteridge drew the device from his pocket and ducked from the meeting, lifting an apologetic wave to those looking back at the distraction.

Keaton watched him leave and considered following. The Gurney-Combes case was obviously dead in the water, and she knew what the call was likely to be. She was equally curious about the outcome as Gutteridge.

*

Gutteridge quietly pulled the door to, tapping the phone symbol flashing on the screen. 'Gutteridge.'

'Pat. It's Carl. I've run that sample. Where did you get it?'

'Why? Is it something interesting?'

'You *could* say that. I thought you said it was animal blood?'

'I said it *might* be animal blood. Why, what is it?'

'It's human.'

Gutteridge hung silent… He had it wrong, which didn't happen often. He didn't like the feeling that he was losing his touch, a feeling that seemed to be manifesting with increasing frequency the further he got from his famously messy fortieth birthday.

'Are you still there?' Carl asked.

'Em. Yeah. Sorry. So, it *is* human,' Gutteridge muttered. 'It came from that Tick-Tock painting on the side of Lidl. Apparently, this freak's been cutting himself and using the blood in his art.'

It was now Carl who hung silent on the end of the receiver. 'Well… it *is* standard form, whenever detecting human blood, to run it through DNA as a matter of course,' he explained. 'Pat… that blood… it came from a child that's been on the missing person list for over four weeks!'

The door behind Gutteridge crept open, and Keaton slipped from the voices to join him. 'Is it pathology?' she mouthed.

Gutteridge held serious eyes and nodded.

'And?' she asked.

'Carl, can I call you back? Oh, and we obviously need to do a full forensic sweep of the site. If you could arrange things your end, I'll clear it with Bryant? Can you forward me those details so I can look up that report from MP, and I can organise letting the family know.'

'Of course. I'm on it. Sorry to the bearer.'

'No. It's fine. Thanks for getting back to me so quickly. I'll call you later.'

He dropped the phone from his ear, and his gaze to the floor.

'Are you going to tell me?' Keaton pressed.

'It came from a kid. The DNA matches a missing-persons case.'

'What? No!'

'Yep. Four weeks ago, and it turns up smeared all over the wall of a bastard supermarket.'

'Oh shit!' Keaton exhaled.

'I'd better let Bryant know, and we need to check out the rest of this fucker's *art*.' He lifted grim eyes to meet Keaton's, his brows wilting regretfully. 'Looks like we have a possible, or more likely *probable*, murder on our hands...'

The door behind them opened, and a stream of detectives exited the room.

'Are we done in there?' Gutteridge asked.

DC Leech nodded. 'That case is dead. It's being passed off to mortality review to deal with.'

Gutteridge ducked his head inside the door to see if Bryant was still in the room, but he'd gone. He turned to Keaton.

'I'm going to go and find Bryant. Can you call Sotheby's, find out who bought that section of wall?'

'How do you know it was Sotheby's? It could have been Christie's, or Bonham's?'

'Because I already looked, after you told me about the sale.'

Keaton was surprised he'd taken an interest in something she'd only mentioned in passing and felt strangely honoured. 'Okay. Leave it with me.'

Keaton watched him stride with conviction in the direction of Bryant's office. He stopped and turned back. 'Oh, and as long as Bryant agrees, me and you'll go out after and take a proper look at the other paintings. And then we'll organise taking a team over to wherever that section of wall ended up, to swab and dust it for prints.' He folded his bottom lip between his thumb and forefinger, his brow racking with contemplation. 'Oh yeah. And after you've talked to Sotheby's, could you make a list of all the known locations where these things have sprung up, and try and make it in chronological order, so we can visit the most recent ones first – there'll be a better chance of finding usable evidence there.'

He set off again. Keaton watched, fascinated. When he wasn't afforded time to gripe, he was like a machine. A problem-solving machine. She admired that side of him, and wished she had the exact same qualities, in the same amount of spades.

'Sotheby's,' she murmured, turning on her heels and making for her desk...

*

Gutteridge drove, while Keaton cradled the list she'd made of all Tick-Tock's known locations.

The arrival of May had brought with it fine weather, which should have infused the air with swelling optimism. But the feeling in the Saab was anything but.

'Capper from missing persons is informing the family,' Gutteridge said. 'Boy, would I hate that fucking job.'

Keaton acknowledged the information with a single nod.

'And pathology are doing a full toxicology on the blood. They're pushing anything else aside. Priority one. Oh, yeah, and the blood, it's from a girl.'

Again, a nod. 'How old?' Keaton asked.

'What?'

'The girl. How old is– *was* she?'

'Twelve.'

'Jesus...!' she slurred. 'Do you think she's dead?'

Gutteridge drove, leaning into the wheel, chin nearly resting on hands sitting at twelve o'clock on the rim. He peered through the screen at the road unwinding before him, swimming in a surreal transitive state. The situation didn't feel real. 'I don't know. There's no way of telling. But like you said, the sheer amount of blood on the wall, I think, would suggest...'

Another nod, this time, the 'knowing' variety, but she didn't want to accept that particular truth. 'Okay,' she whispered, clutching an involuntary hand to her womb. 'Stop the car!' Keaton cried.

Gutteridge sat back from the wheel, snapped eyes to the rear-view mirror and pulled the car over to the side of the road.

'What is it?' he asked, but she was already out of the door, and running back towards the newsagents on the corner.

Gutteridge sat twisting in his seat, watching through the rear window, waiting for Keaton to re-emerge.

She trotted back moments later brandishing a newspaper, the click of her heels growing louder, rebounding off the open door until she appeared in the opening, and hopped back in.

She had to take a moment to catch her breath. 'Look. Another one,' she swallowed, handing the paper to Gutteridge. 'I saw a headline on the *Gloucestershire Echo* sandwich board outside the shop.'

Gutteridge flicked through the pages, until they fell open on a grainy black-and-white picture of yet another mural. This time, emblazoned on one of the retaining walls of Llanthony Lock, a disused section of historic canal on the west side of the city.

'Llanthony Canal. I know it,' Gutteridge said, 'it's not far from the College. It's just up the road here, about five minutes.' He looked at his watch. 'Let's go now and take a look, before too many interested fingers contaminate the scene.'

Keaton picked up on his use of the word 'scene', as in, 'scene of the crime'.

Gutteridge leaned a look into the passenger footwell. 'We'll need to go on foot, so break out your sensible shoes.'

EIGHT

THE GROUND ON THE APPROACH was blanketed with a thick carpet of grass that felt boggy under foot, the original puddle-clay linings of the old canal still effective at retaining moisture, even after all those years out of service.

The weather was fine but came at the tail end of a two-week spell of rain that had raised Gloucester's already high water table to flood-warning levels.

The engineering-brick walls to the lock were surprisingly free of graffiti, and Keaton spied the latest addition to the lock's long and extensive history file just beyond the footbridge that arched between the walls high above them.

The new embellishment looked out of place in its antiquated surroundings, screaming its New Age vibrancy defiantly amidst the relative gloom.

They stepped carefully towards it, negotiating the overgrowth, until they were both standing shoulder to shoulder facing the anomaly.

'It's the same as the last one!' Gutteridge complained.

Keaton scanned the image. 'Why's he done that?'

'I don't know!'

The image confused them, an apparent exact copy of the

one on the side of Lidl, the only painting out of Tick-Tock's series that had been repeated. All the rest had been drastically different to each other, the animal-rights subject matter the only common ground they shared. It just didn't seem to fit.

'A copycat?' suggested Gutteridge.

'Might be, but why do that?'

Gutteridge shrugged. 'Why does anyone do anything?' His searching eyes squint, then brightened. 'No. No it's not! Look again.'

'What? Where?' Keaton asked, rescanning the mural.

'The child.'

Keaton's eyes snapped to the end of the conveyor, searching for the anomaly, and there it was. The kid, still hanging helplessly by its ankles, but this time, the *second* in line from the waiting blades.

'It's moved!' she barked.

'I know, one position further on. But what does *that* mean?' Gutteridge said, his voice dripping with ominousness.

The words scrawled beneath were different too. 'DEATH OF THE INNOCENTS!', scrawled in the same deep, sanguine, terracotta red as before, but somehow, the colour had more vitality, more verve. A far less coagulated hue.

'Blood again?' Keaton asked.

Gutteridge loosed a resigned sigh. He'd seen enough blood in his working life to recognise its grisly hue. 'I think so. Looks the same. Fresher though, don't you think?'

Keaton found herself clinging to a hope. 'Maybe… and if it tests the same, *came* from the same girl, the freshness could indicate that she might still be alive?'

Gutteridge see-sawed his reluctance to seed a hope that could prove fruitless. 'You never know. Did you bring the kit?'

'Yes,' she said, lifting the bag to prove her foresight. 'I'll glove up and take a swab.' She twisted a look about the walls surrounding them. 'We should cordon the area off and call in forensics to do a proper sweep.'

'Yeahhh,' he sighed, 'we should. I'll get uniform over to keep the public away. If word gets out, everyone'll be down here, traipsing through the evidence to gawp at it.'

His mood was sombre. He had one of his feelings, the kind he hadn't had in a long time, not since the Masterson case in the mid-noughties when he'd first made a name for himself. Like a positive charge that fizzles in the atmosphere when a thunderstorm is imminent, the feeling that a storm was coming churned in the deepest recesses of his gut. Things were beginning to feel unnervingly inevitable.

NINE

DCI BRYANT STEPPED UP to address a room of concerned faces, while Tamara – his PA – unobtrusively dealt stapled A4 photocopies to eager hands like a croupier.

Gutteridge perched on a desk behind and to the right of Bryant, eyes to the ground, compiling words that would set the right tone.

Bryant widened his eyes to cue the room to listen. But he already had every ear. No one slouched. No one blinked, and Bryant's top button was fastened tight, his Windsor knot symmetrical and neat.

'I guess most if not all of you have already heard, but events have come to light, events of concern, events that can only be classified as extremely serious in nature, and I'm putting all available detectives on it forthwith… Now, I know many of you here are on other cases, and you *still* are. But I'm bringing you in on this meeting to keep you in the loop, just in case you might see, or hear something, *anything*, of relevance on your own investigations that may, in *any* way, help to bring this to an early conclusion…' Bryant's brows wilted. 'Children are involved, and this is time-sensitive…'

He held a look out into the room, granite eyes the only things moving in a face galvanised with concern, daring anyone not to take the situation seriously. For once, he looked his rank.

He began pacing the invisible stage. 'An incident room is being set up in the adjoining office as we speak, and copies of all relevant case pages are being passed to all concerned. I *can't* express enough that this stays in the department, at least for now. The press – at this moment in time – aren't aware of the situation, and I want it to stay that way, at least until *I* decide otherwise. We may, down the line, need their assistance. But I *don't* want this out, not yet.' He threatened the room with the look again…

He took a breath and softened his gait. 'I will, of course, be heading the investigation – but only in an official capacity. I want Detective Inspector Gutteridge to take the lead on this, so *he'll* be the SIO. Without him, we wouldn't even be here talking about it. He'll keep me informed of any leads and new information, but for time's sake, *he'll* be the go-to.'

He turned invitational eyes and a smile subtly laced with gratitude over his shoulder to Gutteridge. 'DI Gutteridge will take you through what we already know, and as I say, it's only down to *his* foresight, *and* DS Keaton's, of course, that we're here, today… DI Gutteridge.'

Bryant stepped aside, and Gutteridge rocked forwards from his perch, addressing his colleagues with a regretful smile.

'So, this is what we know at present. I'm aware news of the blood evidence from the Lidl mural has already burned through the department, so I've no need to say too much about that that isn't already known. CSI have run their eyes over the scene, under the cover of a backstory that we're attempting to find the culprit, citing vandalism as our main concern. But they were unable to find anything of use. No hairs. No prints. No fibres. Nothing.'

Gutteridge raised aloft the sheets he held in his hand. 'The results from Llanthony Lock landed this morning; you have copies near the back of the pages Tamara has just handed to you.'

The room erupted with the sound of brushing paper, and all eyes dropped away from Gutteridge.

'It's a hard thing to say, but *unfortunately*, the blood from *that* writing – and it is blood, make no mistake – did not match that found at Lidl… It *is* human, and we *did* find a different DNA match on file…'

Gutteridge lowered morose eyes to his own set of pages. 'Thomas Leinster, aged eleven, from 13 Beaumont Road, Gloucester, reported missing roughly three weeks ago on the 10th of April.'

Half of the room shifted in their seats. Gutteridge noticed that most who did were those with families. He turned back a page. 'The *Lidl* blood evidence came back as a Sally Tweets, aged twelve, also from Gloucester – 5 Barnwood Avenue. Reported to MP on the 25th of March. Now I know some of you will have already worked out that those two addresses are within spitting distance of each other, but we don't – at this time – think that's anything more than a coincidence, but keep it in mind, and keep that mind open.'

Gutteridge began to feel comfortable addressing the room, but it didn't come naturally, not the way it did to Bryant.

Bryant looked on. He held a level of respect for Gutteridge that he didn't for anyone else in the division. He was the only detective he would step back to make way for. He'd done it before with success, and as long as it worked – and kept on working – he would do so again.

He was also astute enough, and humble enough, to be aware that Gutteridge was an infinitely better detective than he ever was, before he'd been elevated to DCI status, and that it was only because he possessed an easy manner, and a more media-friendly persona – more so than Gutteridge – that *he* was kicked to the top, and Gutteridge was passed over. And besides, in his logical mind, it would be criminal for a detective as competent as Gutteridge to be taken off the job and locked away in an office.

A smile played on the corner of Bryant's lips as he watched Gutteridge addressing the team. Gutteridge had lost it three years back, turning to drink and, Bryant had also suspected, coke. But he'd personally identified Keaton – and her no-nonsense attitude – as a potential remedy, and it had worked. She had pulled Gutteridge back from the brink, and he seemed to feed off her youthful interest in the job. And besides, she was herself a good and insightful detective, with knowledge of all things young and on trend that had left Gutteridge behind the times, and together, they made a good team. Their partnering could be seen as Bryant's greatest success to date as a DCI.

Gutteridge continued… 'Forensics are looking at the other eight locations where these "things" have gone up. But they don't hold out much hope of finding anything useful. There's been too much weather pass over each of the sites to have any real hope of finding anything of use. Our best hopes are in the two recent additions – Lidl and the Lock – which have been tented off to try to preserve them – and the one sold at auction, which by a miracle, we believe had never seen rain before it was removed and sold. It *will*, of course, have had a lot of finger-fall during its removal and transportation, but any DNA evidence should still be present, and traceable – at least that's the hope.'

He shuffled his sheets until he found the next page he was looking for. 'The buyer… is in Knutsford, Cheshire… a Toby Jackson, a tech-millionaire who uses his new-found wealth to buy up art.' Gutteridge couldn't hide the cynicism from his voice, and Keaton – sitting near the front – couldn't help but laugh. Gutteridge noticed and dropped the resulting smirk to his sheets to hide it. But he was glad of a moment of levity to lift his mood.

'Myself and DS Keaton are driving up there after we're finished here, mainly to try to get his permission to work the section of wall he now owns. But it'll be difficult; he's forked out a lot of money to own this thing, and without actually letting him into our confidence as to *why* it's so important that we do, he might not let us. The vandalism story alone might not cut it, so we *may* have to take him into our confidence, and *hope* that he doesn't talk, but only if upon inspecting the section of wall we think there could be even the remotest of possibilities of finding something of use to the case. We could, of course, get a court order to allow us access, but that would just raise suspicions as to our real motives, and we'd almost certainly lose all cooperation from Mr Jackson. I'm also certain Mr Jackson has a fairly impressive legal team to hand, so we're trying at all costs to avoid that avenue.'

Gutteridge twisted and tossed the file onto the desk behind him; he turned a sullen facade back to the front. 'We *don't* know at this point if the children are still alive. The volume of blood present at each site would suggest not, but we don't know that for sure. But *assuming* they're not, and *assuming* the perpetrator didn't know the "victims", then we have the prospect of a potential serial killer on our hands, and we need to work fast to stop him. *Or* her. But we're pretty sure at this point that it's a man.' He darted a look to Keaton, who returned a weak smile. 'I'm going to break the six officers we have available into three teams, and I'll be talking to each of you in person after we're done here about how I want you to use your time. Are there any questions?'

The room sat silent, the odd head spinning to see if they were alone in not having a query to push forward.

Keaton looked on with a certain level of awe, and a warm, swelling feeling of pride that she was deemed good enough to work with such a man. She admired him, and his irrefutably daunting track record.

'Okay,' Gutteridge said, 'let's do our best work. Thank you for your time.'

He turned from the room and caught Bryant's eye. Bryant nodded his approval, his thoughts in a place where Gutteridge would make a fine DCI. Better than him?

TEN

'TAKE THE M5 until you see signs for M6 north, then we stay on that until junction 19,' Gutteridge said, looking down at the open map book on his lap. 'I'll give you directions from there.'

Keaton drove, smirked, and simply nodded, one eye on the road ahead, one eye on the satnav facing her from its cradle.

She turned a look his way. 'So. How have you got the troops deployed?'

He lifted his eyes from the map and checked the mirrors like he was driving. 'I've got Stanton and Banks revisiting the missing-persons cases. They're going to reinterview the friends and family of the Leinster and Tweets kids, see if they can't find anything new that was missed.'

'Good call,' Keaton said, 'especially Banks. He's got a keen eye for body language.'

Gutteridge slow blinked and nodded. 'He's good, and I think Stanton has that same disarming quality you do in interview; she puts them at ease, the way you do. Together, they should find anything that's been missed. *If* it's been missed.'

Keaton had a welling feeling, like a warm hand pressing gently against her diaphragm, at hearing Gutteridge compliment her abilities. She knew he thought her capable, mainly from second-hand information passed to her by others. But she rarely ever heard it straight from the horse's mouth.

She released an unsteady breath to clear the feeling and allowed herself a smile. 'Who else?'

'Erm…? Corbould is liaising with forensics, and getting handwriting analysis done on the paintings, while Koperek compiles an exact timeline of this Tick-Tock's art, to see if it might correspond to any other missing-persons cases that currently remain unsolved, so she'll be liaising with Stanton and Banks. She's also going to be our logger for the HOLMES system during the investigation, so everything goes through her.'

Keaton nodded.

He shuffled to get comfortable, bedding in for the long haul, stowing the map book by his leg and tossing his folded jacket onto the back seat.

'McWilliams is scouring the web: Facebook; Instagram; chatrooms; stuff like that, to try and see if anyone claims to know who this Tick-Tock is. And Parker is looking through CCTV.'

Keaton considered his decisions. She thought them sound. 'Why's he calling himself Tick-Tock?' she asked.

'Yeah. I've been asking myself the same question. It must mean something.'

They sat silently for a couple of miles, pondering the name, the cabin humming to the drone of tyres slapping tarmac at eighty miles an hour.

'Do you know the nursery rhyme "Humpty Dumpty"?' Keaton asked.

Gutteridge huffed a laugh. 'Of course. Go on?'

'Well, the only way you know it's an egg, is because someone drew an egg. But there's absolutely no mention of the fact that it's an egg in the rhyme itself.'

Gutteridge ran the words through his mind. 'Oh yeeeah. I've never realised that before. What's your point?'

Keaton reran her thoughts to check they made sense. '*Because*... if no one knows who the guy is, and he's never written the words "Tick-Tock" on any of his paintings—'

'—then how does anyone know he's called Tick-Tock!' Gutteridge interjected, finishing her thought.

'*Right!*' Keaton said. 'If *he* penned the name – which I assume he did – then *he* must have put it out there at some point in history, and that could possibly be traced?'

Gutteridge took up his phone from the centre console and scrolled to McWilliams' number. He rang it...

'Ian... Gutteridge... I've got something else for you to check...'

He turned a look to Keaton, hand clamped across the mouthpiece. 'Clever girl!'

*

Knutsford town centre typified the word 'quaint'. A mixture of red-brick and black-and-white timbered frontages lining streets that were once wide enough to accommodate the horse-drawn carts that passed through its chocolate-box lanes, but that now felt cripplingly tight to those more used to Gloucester's wide-open roads.

Keaton could tell by the shops that the town's inhabitants had money. Staggered rows of boutiques and antique emporiums, interspersed with turn-of-last-century tea shops, all periwinkle porcelain and doilies.

Gutteridge directed Keaton to take a road that travelled north from the town. The highlighted route on Keaton's satnav concurred...

Keaton turned the nose of the Saab into a driveway, moments before Gutteridge instructed her to do so, passing through overtly majestic, gaudy wrought-iron gates that had a distinct air of new money about their indelicate proportions.

The car crunched along the peach-coloured gravel towards a timber-framed barn conversion that had more glass than brick filling the voids in the interlocking beams.

An island – tightly planted with tulips and primroses – created a roundabout in front of the house. Timber stables to the left, with a grey, dappled horse watching their arrival with head-nodding interest, and the nose of a lime-green Lamborghini peeking from the adjoining triple garage.

'How the other half live, eh?' Keaton muttered.

Gutteridge leant forwards and peered up at the house as they parked in front of the main door. 'It's a bit Essex for me, but I wouldn't say no.' He sat back. 'What's this guy done to earn this then?'

Keaton shut the engine off. 'He's got a few apps under his belt. But the one that made him his money is an app where you upload photos of you and your partner, then photos of your and *their* parents, and then it shows you what your kids will look like. I tried it on my friend once. It's frighteningly accurate, and very popular. Et voila, a multi-millionaire.'

'And *that* made all of this? Whatever happened to working for your money?'

'Old news, Pat. Things are different now.'

'I'm gathering that. Thank fuck I have you here to keep me informed. I sometimes feel I should be wielding a club and shaking my fist at volcanos.'

Keaton chuckled, fondly.

The door to the house opened. Gutteridge didn't turn to look. 'Is it him?'

'I think so.'

'Is he wearing a baseball cap, and jogging bottoms with some expensive brand name plastered up the leg?'

Keaton sniggered, popped the door, and rose from the car. She leaned her head back in. 'Yes!'

*

'Thank you for agreeing to see us, Mr Jackson,' Gutteridge said, following the trendy thirty-something into the confusing mix of old and new. 'Is that an original Strat?' he asked, lifting his chin towards a heavily worn guitar hanging high on the wall. A ploy to break the ice and create a bond, but as an occasional guitarist, he was also genuinely interested.

'It is,' Jackson said, with a strange kind of pride. 'Apparently, it used to belong to Pete Townsend,' he bragged.

Keaton turned a who-the-hell-is-that look to Gutteridge.

'One of the ones he *didn't* smash up,' Gutteridge said. 'Does it sound good?'

Jackson shrugged. 'I don't know. I don't play.'

Gutteridge had to stop himself from rolling his eyes. He leaned into Keaton. 'The lead guitarist from The Who,' he whispered.

'Ahhhh,' Keaton exhaled.

'So, what's this all about?' Jackson asked, leading them out into the rear garden through patio doors. 'The phone call intrigued me, something to do with my Tick-Tock?'

The garden was larger than even the house's sizeable aspect would have suggested. Heavily landscaped, and smattered with random pieces of art, no two alike.

'Yes. Your Tick-Tock,' Keaton confirmed.

'I'll show it to you in a minute. Do you have time for tea?' Jackson asked, extending an invitational arm to a cluster of patio seating on a lower terrace.

Keaton looked to Gutteridge for a lead. She looked weary from the three-hour drive.

'Tea would be lovely, thank you,' Gutteridge agreed.

Keaton smiled and mouthed, 'thanks'.

'Perfect. I'll just find Asha. Won't be a sec.'

He climbed steps to the house, calling Asha's name.

They descended the handful of steps to the terrace and sat. Keaton leaned in. 'Servant?'

Gutteridge shook a discrete head. 'Probably his partner, or wife, by the soupy way he forms her name.'

Jackson lolloped down the steps again with a carefree swing of the arms and plopped into one of the chairs opposite. 'She's on it. Won't be a sec.'

'Are you married?' Gutteridge asked, flicking a look up to the house.

Jackson turned a look towards the kitchen. 'Not yet, but we will.'

Gutteridge flashed brows to Keaton. She huffed a smile.

'Your mother, is she Polish?' Gutteridge asked.

Jackson's brow buckled. 'How did you know that? Have you been looking me up?'

'No,' Gutteridge said. 'Just a guess.'

'A guess? How would you guess that?'

'You have a very subtle accent, a barely perceptible Polish twang when you pronounce your vowels. Not strong enough to suggest you ever lived there, but certainly strong enough to suggest you spent time in conversation with someone who had. So, I'm guessing you must have been very close to your mother, and spent a lot of time with her.'

Jackson laughed, then quelled it, his face tight with interest. 'It could have been my father that was Polish?'

'Maybe, but I doubt it. You're very well mannered, and your diction is good. Suggests a stable home, a *wedded* home, and your name's Jackson, not Kowalski. English surname, Polish twang, et voila, you were close to your mother – who was Polish.'

A smile stretched slow and wide across Jackson's face. 'He's not shit, is he!' he said, darting a look to Keaton, who was equally impressed but trying not to show it. 'I love that stuff. But yes. You're right. Mother's name was Zuzanna. She was from Kokoszkowy.'

Clicking footsteps approached from the house. A long, beautiful girl with supermodel looks, carrying a tray of cups on saucers, made her way gingerly down the steps towards the waiting visitors.

Jackson rose to help, but she dismissed the offer with a temperate smile.

'Hello,' she beamed, lighting up the garden.

'*Czesc. Dziekuje*,' said Gutteridge.

The girl lengthened her face with theatrical amazement and gave a funny sort of courtesy. 'Wow,' she said. '*Prosze*.'

Jackson grinned beneath a frown and shook his head at Gutteridge's display of intuition.

Gutteridge leaned forwards and took up one of the cups. 'Asha... grey eyes... and we're all supposedly looking for someone like our mothers.'

Jackson held the look directed at Gutteridge, then broke from it with a laugh. 'What an insight,' he enthused, leaning back in his seat with the tea. 'Would I love to make an app with you sometime. Something that would really fuck with people's heads.'

The girl joined them, Jackson taking her hand in his.

She reminded Gutteridge of Ewelina, more beautiful for sure, but not so much that it tainted his fascination of his own Polish muse. He hadn't called her in a while, and this girl gave him an urge to correct that.

'How did you meet?' Keaton asked – a girl-interest question.

'At a club. The old way,' Jackson said, beaming disbelief at his luck across at the girl's sultry features. She returned the look. She obviously loved him and wasn't all about the money.

Refreshing, thought Keaton. It gave her hope.

Jackson broke from his ocular embrace. 'So. The Tick-Tock. What do you want to know…?'

ELEVEN

GUTTERIDGE HAD BEEN SO ENGROSSED in the exaggerated limbs of the mile-long angel and how much she reminded him of Ewelina, that he'd forgotten all the prep he'd done on the journey up, and now wondered how best to present the information.

Jackson *seemed* to have a good heart and wasn't the self-satisfied arsehole he was expecting. But he had to tread carefully. If *he* ended up being the cause of the story hitting the newsstands, if *he* became ground zero, he would lose a trust from Bryant that had taken him years to re-earn.

Keaton watched Gutteridge's attempts to stutter into the conversation and stepped up to the plate. 'Have you seen anything in the news about Tick-Tock's recent work?'

'Of course,' Jackson replied. 'I don't think any of it is as good as the piece I own, but he's definitely interesting. *Intriguing*. Don't you think?'

Keaton stumbled around the subject. 'Well, yeah. I... um... I like it,' she said. The smiling photo of Sally Tweets she saw in the case file on the way down flashed into her mind. She could no longer appreciate the art, not in the way she once had.

Gutteridge finally remembered which avenue of lies he'd decided on earlier and interjected. 'The thing is, Mr Jackson—'

'Please. Call me Toby.'

It felt wrong, but Gutteridge thought the gesture suggested some kind of friendship offering, and with friendship, comes candour.

'Okay, *Toby*. The thing is, we've discovered some of the paintings, murals, *art*, whatever you want to call them, have been created using substantial quantities of blood, and public health has voiced concerns as to whether this is hazardous to the public or not. So, we've been assigned to the case to make the necessary checks.'

Jackson squinted at Gutteridge's offering. 'So, what do you need from me?'

'We'd *like* your permission to process the work you own. Check it for prints, blood evidence, and to make sure it isn't a danger to you, or indeed, Asha. And maybe find the identity of the artist, to request he stops using bodily fluids.'

Jackson tilted a curious look past his shoulder to the mile-long beauty curled up by his side. 'Is this for real?'

Keaton took up the baton. 'It would be unobtrusive, causing absolutely no harm to the piece. In fact, the Met have an Art-and-Antiquities crime unit; we could make sure one of their team is present to oversee the process, make certain that nothing untoward happens during the procedure.'

'Are you telling me that you drove – what is it, two and a half, three hours – just to come and ask about my Tick-Tock because public health have concerns?'

'Yes,' Gutteridge replied, holding a look directly into Jackson's eyes.

Jackson rolled an indecisive head, taking up his phone from the table, and began fiddling within the screen. 'I'm not sure,' he slurred. 'What assurances would I have that your guys wouldn't fuck it up?'

'Well, our word, and of course, you can be present during the entire process.'

Keaton piped in. 'And as I said, Art and Antiquities would be present. You'd have absolutely nothing to worry about.'

Jackson sat looking at his phone. 'So, he uses blood in the art, does he?'

'It seems so.'

'His own?'

'Must be,' Gutteridge said. 'Who else's?'

'And public health sent you?'

Gutteridge frowned. *Was this guy stupid?* he thought. 'We're here on their behalf.'

Jackson paused for a moment, then stood. 'Why don't we go and take a look at my fabulous section of wall while I think about it,' he said, inviting them to follow with a matador-esque swing of the arm. 'We'll talk more there.'

Keaton pulled peculiar eyes at Gutteridge; he shrugged.

They placed their cups on the table and followed Jackson up the steps.

The mile-long Polish beauty remained in her seat, pulling her knees up and folding in on herself. She smiled up at their departure. '*Czesc*.'

Gutteridge spun a parting look back at her angelic face. '*Czesc*...'

*

'So tell me, what do you think?' Jackson asked.

They were faced with a section of wall encapsulated in a welded and bolted box-section frame, roughly twelve feet long, eight feet high.

'Jesus!' Gutteridge slurred. 'This thing's huge! Wouldn't it just have been cheaper to buy the shop?'

'It weighs three tonnes,' Jackson said, with a strange sense of boast in his voice.

The section of wall showed a depiction of men in tweed, firing shotguns into fans of airborne grouse and pheasant. Upon closer inspection, each man had a tail, horns, manes, and overhanging canines, salivating to the tune of their merciless killing.

The words 'ANIMAL CRUELTY' had been scrawled beneath as before, but this time, it was unmistakably written in paint.

'It's not the same,' Keaton said, not sure if she should be happy about that, or not.

'In what way isn't it the same?' Jackson asked.

Gutteridge stepped back from the painting he'd moved in closer to examine. 'This one doesn't seem to have blood as a key element in its creation.'

'Are you sure?' Jackson asked. He sounded disappointed.

'Not a hundred per cent. But it looks unlikely. Why?'

'Because it would be worth a damn sight more if it could be proven to incorporate the artist's actual plasma. Like the others do, right?'

'Right,' Gutteridge said.

'The others that contain *his* blood.'

'Yes?' Gutteridge repeated with a furrowing brow.

Jackson checked his phone again. 'Mr Gutteridge. Do you know what it is I do?'

Gutteridge could hear a strange tone that seemed intentionally woven into Jackson's voice. 'Yes. You made an app, showing people what their kids would look like.'

'Yes, but that's just one of many. Do you know what my third bestselling app is?'

Gutteridge didn't know where he was going with this. 'No.'

‘It’s this,’ he said, presenting the screen of his phone to Gutteridge. ‘It’s a voice-stress analyser-based lie-detector app, and although you’re good, so good you nearly fooled it, it indicates to me that you’re not being completely honest with me.’

Gutteridge looked across to Keaton for telepathic advice. She flashed eyes and shook a tilted head.

Gutteridge loosed a sigh and turned to face Jackson head on. ‘We have a situation.’

Jackson’s eyes pinched. ‘And it’s not public health, is it?’

‘No.’

Jackson tilted his searching gaze. ‘Is it serious?’

‘You have no idea, and I’m trying desperately to keep it that way, for the sake of the case and those involved.’

Jackson swung a look across to Keaton, trying to gauge her reaction to Gutteridge’s words.

‘*Is* it blood you’re looking for?’

‘...Yes.’

‘Tick-Tock’s?’

‘...No.’

Jackson cocked a curious eye, absorbing the gravity burning from Gutteridge’s face. ‘Human?’

Gutteridge hung in pregnant silence, wondering if his estimation of Jackson’s character was sound. He took a breath. ‘Yes. It’s human.’

Jackson’s interest flitted between the concerned faces pleading back at him. ‘Aaaare people in trouble?’

Gutteridge held the most serious look his eyes could muster into Jackson’s, and nodded reluctantly.

Jackson lingered in the moment, absorbing the seriousness emanating from both Gutteridge and Keaton, and slow-blinked. ‘Then call your team. It’s all yours.’

TWELVE

'HERE ARE SOME MENUS. Maybe I can take an order for drinks while you're choosing?'

The mother directed kind eyes up to the young man hovering in readiness, while her husband took up one of the menus, and leaned his shoulder against his son's with a clandestine stoop of the head, trying to draw the kid's attention by some convoluted form of osmosis.

'What would you like, Jayden? Come on, help me choose.' But the kid seemed too wrapped up in his phone to take any notice.

'Tea for two, please, and probably a Coke? Jayden?' the mother asked.

The kid nodded, without his eyes ever leaving his phone.

'Yes. And a Coke.'

'Diet?' the young man asked, darting a look laced with disapproval towards the overweight child.

The kid pulled a face like he'd swallowed something bad, then shook his petulant head. 'No. Full fat,' he blurted, again, not looking away.

The mother lifted eyes crimped with a subtle he-is-what-he-is apology up at the young man and smiled. 'Regular please.'

But she wasn't sure he'd heard her. The young man seemed to be staring at her son, a fixed, blank expression on his face, but she fancied she saw mild contempt behind the poker visage. 'Regular. Please?' she reiterated.

The young man broke from his stare. 'Um. Sorry,' he said, shaking himself clear of the moment. 'Regular it is. I'll be back in just a moment to take your orders.' He delivered a corporate smile, and turned, jotting on a palm-sized notepad.

The husband flopped back out of the clandestine huddle, looking to his wife to try to get a rise from the child.

'Jayden. What do you want?' she insisted. 'The man'll be back soon to take your order. Have a look at the menu, sweetheart, and choose what you'd like.'

'I want sausages,' the kid barked.

The mother sagged into the briefest of looks of weariness, before pulling herself back from her display of weakness, rebooting her forced and well-rehearsed chirpy nature. 'Sausages? Is that all you want? I'm not sure they'll have just sausages.'

The kid erupted from his social-media trolling. 'I don't know! Sausage sandwich, breakfast, anything. I'm trying to do this,' he moaned, lifting the device into the path of his rebuke.

The father loosed a barely audible sigh, pondering what he would do differently if he was given a chance to raise the 'petulant shit' all over again. He lifted the menu to his own eyes, using it to cut the fruit of their bad decision-making from view. He scanned the list of options several times over. 'I don't think they *do* sausages. *Or* full-English.'

'Let me see,' the mother said, extending an impatient hand.

The father withdrew the menu from reach, not appreciating the assumption that she could succeed where he'd failed.

'There's another one there,' he said, pointing to the table with his nose, his voice dripping with agitation.

She took it up, and scanned it, then turned it in her hands to look at the cover page with a scowl. She twisted on her seat to drink the place in. 'I think it must be one of those veggie or vegan places… I can't see anything that's meat on the menu.'

The news pulled the kid from his phone. 'You what? No sausages? Or bacon?'

The young man arrived with a tray laden with pots, cups and a glass of Coca-Cola and began doling out the drinks. 'Have you picked?' he chirped, looking about the table. 'And would you prefer cow's milk, or soya?'

'Don't you do sausages?' the kid complained.

The young man paused from his cup dealing and lifted his gaze to meet he child's. 'Um. No. This is a vegetarian cafe. We don't do any meat… We have *veggie* sausages. They're made with soya mince; you really can't tell.'

The kid had a face like the man had pissed on his plate. 'What the crap are we in a place like this for!'

'*Jayden!*' the father snapped. 'What have I told you about swearing?'

The kid rolled his head in frustration at being corrected. 'Sorry… but why are we in here? I want bacon or sausages, not that gay stuff,' he said, nodding aggressively towards the menu.

The mother could see the stare had returned to the young man's face, but this time, the contempt was less well hidden. But she couldn't bring herself to blame him; her kid was a 'right little shit', and since hitting his teens a year ago, only seemed to be getting worse.

'Look, we can order some toast and jam for now, then we can go somewhere else after,' she said.

'Why can't we go somewhere else now?' the kid asked, kicking a leg of the table.

The cutlery and condiments leapt in the repurposed milk-bottle basket, landing with a crash.

'Because the drinks have arrived, love,' she said, lifting another apologetic smile to the young man. 'Come on. Let's have some toast, or tea cakes, and we can go to McDonald's after. Okay? That's your favourite.'

The kid didn't answer, just turned his sulk back to his phone.

The father slumped in his seat, exhausted by the boy. 'Just... erm... just three rounds of toast, and jam please.'

'Any specific flavour you'd prefer, or should I just bring a selection?' the young man asked.

The mother could just make out a very faint Irish twang in his voice, especially in the way he formed the word 'flavour'.

'A selection would be fine, thank you,' she replied with another smile, another crimp of the eyes. She was getting used to apologising without words.

She watched him leave and roll his back against the swing door into the kitchen. Then she turned hardened eyes to her husband.

'What?' he fizzled. 'I didn't know it was a bloody vegan place. There wasn't anything in the window or the sign that suggested it was.'

The mother spun on her seat, looking for evidence that he was wrong, so she could take her frustration out on him. But her search came up empty.

The decor *did* have a distinct 'artisan' feel: mismatched furniture; shelving made of scaffold fittings and rough-shorn planks; exposed brickwork and images of healthy living frescoed by someone with considerable skill on the walls and ceiling, like a Pre-Raphaelite church for the animal loving. But nowhere, the word 'vegetarian'.

'Shhhhh...!' the mother hissed, lifting a finger into the delicatessen-scented air to draw her husband's attention. 'Listen... They're arguing.'

The father listened, trying to work out what was being said, but the voices were too quiet to make out complete sentences. 'I assumed he was here alone,' he whispered.

'Me too,' she agreed; until then, the place had been deathly quiet. 'What are they arguing about?'

'Don't know. But I thought I heard someone say, "my child"?'

The voices stopped, and moments later, the door to the kitchen relented to the young man's shoulders as he pirouetted back into the room wielding another tray.

He placed plates of seeded granary toast carefully on the place mats, then two pots, one with individually wrapped pats of butter, and one with a selection of blister-packed portions of jam.

'Everything all right?' the husband asked in a playful voice, to the wide-eyed abhorrence of his wife.

She turned to face the young man with a please-excuse-him gleam in her eye. 'We thought you were alone here,' she said.

The young man turned eyes racking with confusion towards her comment. 'What?'

The husband took up the baton. 'Here. Alone. We thought you were alone. It's just… it's so quiet, it was easy to imagine you were.'

The young man darted a confounded look in the direction of the kitchen, then turned frowning eyes back to the family. 'Erm… It's just someone I have in to help now and again.'

'Burn the toast, did he?' the husband quipped.

'*Roger!*' the wife snapped. 'Sorry, he thinks he's funny. Take no notice.'

The young man looked lost and confused. 'No… No, that's all right. Nothing wrong with levity…' His face suddenly brightened. 'Oh, yeah,' he said, reaching to take something from the back pocket of his jeans. 'We're having a draw, for a weekend break in a country cottage. It's free to enter. Are you interested? You're local, right?'

'Yes. Stroud. Not far.'

The young man placed a printed slip of paper and a pen on the table. 'All you have to do is give feedback, and then fill in your details: name; address; email, and we'll contact you if you win.' He turned a brief look to the kid, and then towards the kitchen, and then a beaming smile back to the diners. 'You may as well, it's free.'

He turned, hugging the tray in his folded arms, and left.

The father pulled his toast in closer and began unfolding a pat of butter.

The mother took up the sliver of paper and the pen, and clicked the nib out with her thumb…

THIRTEEN

GUTTERIDGE LOWERED HIS MOBILE from his ear, lightly dabbing it off with his thumb.

'Okay…' he exhaled, nibbling a lip. 'Forensics are sending a team up tomorrow; they'll liaise with Cheshire. Full analysis, and Jackson said he'll make sure he's in.'

'Do you think he'll talk?' Keaton asked.

'Not sure? He *said* he won't, and I have to confess, I believe him. But we've all been down *that* particular road before and got stung with our ventures into the world of trust.'

'I know, but I agree, I don't think he will.'

'Let's hope we're right about him.'

'Are you going to let Bryant know we've confided in Jackson?'

'Probably, yeah. I'll *have* to. He'll understand. And it's not "we", it's "me". If this turns out to be a bad decision, I'm not having you wear any of it.'

Keaton smiled at the display of gallantry, then turned her attention back to the road.

The 2.3-litre Viggen-spec engine chased the rolling horizon. Keaton began rerunning the key points of the case over in her mind to pass the time.

Gutteridge glanced furtively across to Keaton, who seemed lost in her thoughts, then lowered his eyes, but not his face, to his phone.

He quietly opened his contacts and scrolled through the flickering alphabet of friends and work colleagues until it arrived at 'P', then slowed the scroll until it landed on 'Pizza' and stopped.

His hesitant thumb hovered above the thumbnail. He thought of the girl, Asha, and her impossibly long legs, and the smile, and the accent, and softness in her eyes and her voice. He dabbed the file open, tapped the envelope symbol, and typed…

'Are you free tonight?'

He quickly closed his contacts and scrolled to Phone Settings – Sound Options – Tone Setting and tapped – 'Silent'. He lifted his eyes again and let the phone slip quietly between his thighs.

A sign for 'Norton Canes Services' flashed by. 'Costa Drive-Thru?' he suggested. 'On me? Take the sting out of the drive?'

Keaton checked the mirrors and signalled left. 'Well, I can't very well turn down an offer like that now, can I?'

*

Gutteridge handed Keaton his card. She took it and tapped it on the reader before handing it back. 'Thanks, Chief,' she smiled.

'Got to keep the troops happy,' Gutteridge said in an exaggerated voice, slipping the card back into his shielded case, spreading his legs a little while he was looking down to see if there were any new notifications flashing on his phone. There weren't.

The girl in the window handed across an Earl Grey, a flat white coffee, and two Wiltshire-ham and cheese toasties, which were all routinely stowed in cup holders and recesses that had witnessed the same actions a hundred times.

A fistful of slim wooden stirrers and packets of sugar were passed across the daisy chain of grateful hands to Gutteridge, and they pulled away to find a space to sit and sugar their drinks.

'So, what's happening between you and this Tony guy?' Gutteridge asked, as he tore open the ends of three packets of sugar.

'Tony? Why do you ask?'

'Well, there's obviously something wrong. You haven't spoken about him for days, and I've noticed you checking random men out – like Jackson – asking him how he and Asha met, in some hope of finding out what works. So, what's happened?'

Keaton lightly frisbeed the still wrapped toastie onto the top of the dash and slumped back in the seat, leaning her head on the rest. 'I don't bloody know. Maybe I try too hard.'

'Was it you, or him?'

'Him, mainly. It's the hours we keep.'

Gutteridge took a cautious sip of his tea. 'There's a good reason why coppers date coppers.'

'I know. But I don't want to end up married to the job – metaphorically speaking.'

'You'll find someone,' he assured her. 'You're a nice girl, and funny with it, not to mention beautiful to look at, not that that's really important in a relationship scenario, but it helps.'

Keaton rolled a smile his way. 'So, you think I'm beautiful, do you?'

Gutteridge held his gaze out of the window. 'I don't *think* anything, you are. You must notice the guys at the station staring at you.'

'And if you were ten years younger?' she asked.

Gutteridge lifted his sandwich into the air between them. 'I'd be all over you like the cheese on this toastie.'

She laughed and rolled her head to peer out of the side window. 'Why aren't you married?'

'Because I never met your mother?'

Another laugh, this time, from the belly. 'Moron!' she chuckled. 'But seriously, I know you're pretty private about this stuff, but don't you have anybody?'

Gutteridge paused from the conversation for a moment and held a pensive silence.

Keaton's mouth widened with an exaggerated intake of breath. 'There *is* someone. You dark horse! Who is she? Or is it a "he"? Or an "*it*"?'

Gutteridge turned his head away and shook a despairing smile. He sometimes felt like a teenager when talking to Keaton, a feeling he didn't wholly object to. 'It's no one. Just someone I see from time to time.'

'Who is she? Have I met her?'

'Nope. And it's going to stay that way.'

Keaton huffed her body petulantly into the seat. 'You're no fun!'

'Yeah, I am,' he grinned, then turned sombre. 'It's difficult though, isn't it, *life?* Don't you sometimes feel guilty for talking about your own pursuit of happiness, when there are parents with kids that are missing?'

'Of course. But like you've drilled into me on many occasions, we can't always wear their pain, or you'd end up a gibbering mess.'

'And you would. It's true.'

'So, we need to partition that off, right?' Keaton said. 'Live parallel existences, isn't that how you put it?'

'Exactly. But those are just words. *Mine*, and *wise*, for sure, but they're much harder to be guided by when there are kids involved.'

Gutteridge parted his legs slightly and lowered a look to

his phone. A white light blinked on the top left of the screen. Ewelina's face flashed into his thoughts. 'I need the bathroom, won't be a sec, then we can get on our way.'

He popped the door and rose into the temperate but fresh spring air, furtively pocketing his phone.

'Say hi from me,' Keaton sang through the opening. 'Send her my love. Tell her I look forward to meeting her someday.'

Gutteridge laughed. 'Arsehole,' he slurred, slamming the door.

He made his way into the main building, through the bustle of weary travellers and excited teenagers dipping fries from fast-food bags. He lifted the phone from his pocket and dabbed 'Pizza'...

FOURTEEN

MOTHER – displaying all the signs of caring – stepped from the vestibule of their Victorian semi and scanned the street for her son. Father was in the kitchen loading the dishwasher.

'Jayden, it's getting late,' she called into the softening light, 'just half an hour more and you need to come in, okay, sweetheart?'

The child sat on the wall by the gate, huffing his reluctance to comply, and gave a petulant grunt in response. The mother forced a smile, imagining she must've been exactly the same at that age, but knowing full well that that was all manner of bullshit.

The house had all the trappings of a middle-class family: garden tended to more for the neighbours than themselves; a silver Volvo 4x4 parked up on the drive – vacuumed, washed and waxed; curtains tied back, hanging neatly with straight, micro-managed creases.

The curtains began to close in response to the darkening skies, leaving the front garden at the mercy of the insipid street lights to illuminate its synthetic splendour.

The kid kicked his heels against the wall, watching as an

off-white van with no markings pulled into the space across the way, parking in front of the Turners' house at number 28.

The driver – a man, mid-thirties – seemed to be searching out an address, glancing at a slip of paper in his hand, then looking about the street, his face underlit by the ethereal glow of the dashboard lighting.

The man spied the boy on the wall, and watched him with a strange flicker of recognition in his face.

The boy half expected the side window to lower, and the man to lean out and ask for directions, but the window remained shut, and the man just watched as he sat, and kicked…

The boy stared back at the new arrival. 'What are you fucking looking at?' he muttered under his breath without moving his lips, talking the way his father did when he wasn't aware of the boy's proximity. 'Fucking weirdo!' he slurred, like the tough, streetwise kid he wished he was, fuelled by his growing unease at being observed.

He rose from his perch, the levels of self-awareness becoming too hot to bear, and began walking towards Simon Bryce's house at the end of the road.

He heard the van's engine start up again, and pull out, and he had to fight an impulse to quicken his walk. He started swinging a nonchalant arm in response to his growing discomfort.

'Excuse me, is this Deacon Road?' a voice called from the passenger window of the van. 'I'm looking for number 25.'

The kid heard a slight Irish twang colouring the man's voice; it seemed somehow familiar, a voice he'd heard before, but he couldn't quite place it.

He stopped and swung an arm towards the neighbouring house. 'It's that one,' he said, 'the one next door.'

'Ahh, tanks,' the man said, 'it's hard to see the numbers when it's dusk like this.'

The van pulled in and parked, the metallic rasp of the handbrake cutting through the silence.

The driver hopped out, slid the side door open, and began fumbling through untidy stacks of cardboard boxes.

The kid continued walking towards Simon Bryce's house, listening to the clamour behind growing distant.

The street suddenly went quiet, the air pregnant, deathly silent save for the gritty sounds of fast-approaching footsteps.
'This is for the animals, you fat, fucking pig!' a voice seethed.

The man rushed up behind the child, placed the business end of a captive bolt pistol against the back of his skull, and before the boy could react, pulled the trigger.

The air shocked to the thud of high-carbon steel smashing through bone, and the kid dropped to the ground like a wet towel.

The man jogged back, tossed the pistol in through the open door and pulled a folded bag from his back pocket. He snapped it open and pulled it over the boy's head to catch the fluids.

He spun a nervous look about the street as he looped a zip-tie around the child's neck and pulled it tight; he was still alone.

He knew that the risk he was taking in such a built-up part of town was huge, but the voice had told him it would be okay, and that 'He' would make sure the coast was clear. He was, after all, doing the Lord's work.

He hoisted the body onto his shoulder and strode to the open door, flinging the boy onto the boxes with a resolute shrug.

He quietly pulled the door closed, taking a pump-action spray bottle from the jamb as he did, and gently nudged it shut with his hip.

The man began pumping the contents of the bottle over the spatters of blood and a puddle of cranial fluid on the pavement, the stench of bleach burning his nose. Then he turned, jumped back into the driver's seat, and sped away…

*

Kill number four was in the bag. He was getting good at this, guided by the voice of retribution – his mentor.

He'd completed the final painting earlier that evening, and he now had work to do. Another creation. Another 'piece'. Another message to present to the waiting world, and this one would really make them sit up and take notice.

FIFTEEN

EWELINA

DI GUTTERIDGE RECLINED in his antique, mahogany sleigh-bed, the taste of the bolognese he'd made earlier still rich on his tongue. He was holding off brushing his teeth to leave the flavour of the red wine lingering in his mouth for as long as possible. The only alcoholic intake he allowed himself these days – after the drink and coke problems of three years back – was in cooking, and the fact was, the alcohol boiled off, leaving just the rich tang of the Merlot behind. But that was enough to satisfy the ex-addict pangs that would, in all likelihood, remain with him forever.

He had the case file open on his lap, and the reading glasses he'd only really needed in the last year and a half perched on the tip of his nose. The weight of them made him feel old, imagining he must look the way his uncle Ross did whenever he had watched him as a child mending clocks. But he'd been glancing at the file off and on all evening, and realised he wasn't seeing it anymore.

He squared the sheets, folded the file shut, and tossed it

onto the bedside table. He removed the specs, pinching the bridge of his nose. The day had been long, and he was tired.

His head flopped back against the headboard, leaving him staring through the ceiling. It looked as blank and featureless as his social life.

He rolled a look to the bedside clock – 23:06. He stretched out an arm and took up his phone, woke it, and scrolled through to Ewelina's last text – '*I'm out with a friend tonight, but I can see you after, if you'd like?*'

His reply was simple – '*Please.*'

Gutteridge wondered if she really was with a friend, or if she was with 'a friend'.

He didn't want to think about it. He knew she was a long way from being one of the 'Barton Street' prostitutes – she was far too classy and attractive for that and didn't have a drug addiction to feed by doing tricks. But she was definitely something that many in society – the ill-informed and judgmental – deemed similar enough to baulk at.

She was an escort, plain and simple, and she'd claimed – during the police interview where Gutteridge first encountered her – that she didn't extend her services to anything carnal. But Gutteridge had doubted her words, putting himself in the exact same circumstance in his cognitive-empath, role-playing mind, and came to the conclusion that if *he* himself was working one of the 'jobs', and the woman he was escorting was attractive enough, and wanted something 'extra', then he would, in all likelihood, expand what 'services' were available to protected sex for a little extra money.

Would that be any different to a one-night stand? he wondered, something he'd indulged in plenty over the years. He figured not.

He closed the message, opened his picture files, activated the drop-down menu at the top left of the screen, and tapped 'Hidden'.

One image flashed up. It was of him and Ewelina, although she tended to Anglicise her name to 'Eve'.

It was the only picture he had of her anywhere. A photo taken of the both of them by a passer-by during a sweetly memorable day at the castle in Warwick.

Gutteridge had had the camera function open on his phone to take a photo of the northern tower – the castellations and octagonal-form turret tickling his interest in architecture, when the woman of a passing couple, both looking to be well into their eighties, asked if he'd like her to take the photo for him so he could be in it too, as – in her world-wise words – 'You two look so sweet together...'

Gutteridge smiled at the memory, opening his fingers against the screen to zoom in on Eve's face. She didn't look embarrassed to be next to him, and on the contrary, the gleam in her sparkling grey eyes suggested otherwise.

He remembered how she'd wrapped her arms around his, leaning her body against him, and smiled for the camera. All actions seemingly laced with a discernible sense of fondness.

That was the first time he'd been physically or emotionally aware that she was actually *with* him. Until then, she'd just been this striking entity sharing his day: walking the grounds; sitting opposite at a table eating lunch; partaking of afternoon tea; breathing in the same summer air and exchanging coy smiles, but always with an invisible wall of separation that somehow made the experience unreal.

But the touch had finally made her flesh, a physical affirmation of the wafts of scent that the summer breeze had been carrying from her delicate neck to his grateful nose throughout the day.

He remembered how he could feel the rise and fall of her flat, toned stomach breathing against his elbow, and how she'd lowered her head fondly onto his shoulder as the old woman walked towards them to hand back his phone, with a motherly smile warming her heavily lined eyes, and a genuinely meant comment tripping off her tongue about how 'in love' they looked.

Eve had given his arm a gentle squeeze at the old woman's suggestion of the word 'love', and he'd never truly been able to work out if that action had meaning, or not.

He was also aware that – in all probability – she had only been spending time with him as a form of thank you for helping her out with a situation, when one of her 'clients' had been a bit too overzealous with his champagne consumption and ended up letting his lust for her undeniable beauty get the better of him.

Gutteridge had warned the man off, slapping him with an official caution, and Eve had asked if she could buy him a drink to thank him for his assistance as his shift was coming to an end.

He'd known it was unwise to accept, but the *man* behind the DI frontage had pushed through and said yes, in all probability motivated by the exact same lustful desires that had caused the drunk to embarrass himself, and Gutteridge had to work hard not to make the same errors and keep it professional. The irony wasn't lost on him.

They'd met several times since that first drink, including the weekend trip to Warwick and nights spent at his cottage, and in Gutteridge's estimation, the debt must certainly have been paid. So, he had to assume she continued seeing him because she wanted to, and because she liked him? But either way, for now, it was their private little arrangement. She was discreet, and he was happy to continue with it, as long as it worked, although he did find himself craving her company with increasing regularity. That bothered him, as in the long term, this surely couldn't go anywhere – a detective on the Gloucester Constabulary and a paid escort.

Gutteridge checked his messages; there was nothing new waiting, so he closed the screen and dropped the phone back onto the side table next to the clock.

He swung his legs clear of the duvet and, with concerted effort, rose to his feet.

He'd had Keaton drop him off at the gym straight after work, and his legs felt decidedly gelatinous. He always tended to hit the weights whenever a meeting with Eve was on the cards. She fuelled his urge to get back in shape – the only thing in his life that did, except, maybe, DS Keaton?

He gave his thighs a runner's stretch, and made his way into the bathroom…

*

Gutteridge climbed back in bed, the taste of Merlot and basil now replaced by mint.

He turned off one of the side lights, but left the other one on, its low-wattage bulb painting the walls and ceiling with a warm and inviting apricot glow.

He rolled onto his side and curled into a semi-foetal position, the memories of Warwick at the forefront of his mind: the squeeze of his arm; the head on his shoulder; the calm softness in her manner. He smiled, and allowed his consciousness to drift, and his eyes to close…

*

The metallic slam of a door outside by the road woke him, followed by the coarse, whistling rasp of a diesel engine as a car pulled away, leaving silence in its wake.

The apologetic scraping of masonry by the back door ended the silence, followed by the bright, metallic ringing of delicate, lithe fingers fumbling in the dark for a key.

The oak-panelled door amplified the judder of the key in the lock; it turned, and the creak of the hinges announced a new arrival.

Gutteridge resisted turning a look towards the sound, and instead, shuffled to the farthest side of the king-sized bed to leave the warmed side free.

He could hear soft footsteps in the living room downstairs, the click of a key being placed on the coffee table, and the brush of a coat being removed and draped over the back of the sofa.

He'd made a fire earlier to chase back the chill that the evening had brought along with it, and he considered rising to welcome the guest. But that wasn't their usual routine, so he remained as he was, facing the wall, listening to the movements of his muse and the woody *tick-tack* of knife-point heels on the stairs.

The latch to the oak-plank bedroom door *clacked* open; it swung in, and stilettoed footsteps stepped apologetically into the room behind him.

'Hi,' Gutteridge whispered, without moving an inch.

'Hey,' a voice responded. Soft, sweet, with an Eastern European edge softening the vowel.

Gutteridge lay listening to the clatter of shoes, and the *brush* of fine cloth gliding over unblemished skin as the undressing routine began.

He wanted to turn and watch the unveiling of the long, perfect limbs, but he felt that would be treating her like he was just another of her jobs, and he liked to think that what they had together was something different, something *more*, even if there was a chance that that wasn't the case.

He had his hopes and dreams – like anyone else – and the girl disrobing behind him definitely resided at the core of his most ardent fantasies, and he didn't want to do anything that might sully, or cheapen, whatever *this* was.

'Did you have a nice night?' Gutteridge asked, more as a social pleasantry than anything, dreading the answers that may peel from her perfect lips.

'Yes, thank you. I was out with Magi. She's been having boyfriend troubles, so I took her out to Wagamama for a meal and a chat. The food's good there, we should go sometime,' she suggested.

Gutteridge relaxed into a smile. Nothing to *wish it were different* tonight. Her James-Bond villainess accent excited him. 'Okay,' he agreed, 'we could certainly do that. That would be nice.'

The sounds of disrobing ceased, replaced by a pregnant silence… 'So, aren't you going to ask me about my day?' she said, her words hinting at something specific.

The question seemed strange and out of place. Gutteridge reran their previous conversations in hope of pinpointing what she may have been alluding to.

'Your day? Em… okay. How was your day?'

She drew a breath in readiness. 'Good,' she exhaled, with a carefree air woven into her voice. 'At first, of course, I'll be starting at the bottom, sitting beside one of the established graphic designers to learn the ropes – all these companies have specific ways they like things done, so you need to learn them. Then they say they'll give me a chance to take the lead on some smaller projects, whilst being shadowed of course, to see how I handle myself. But the people are nice, and I seem to fit in.'

Gutteridge shuffled around to face her, his crimping brow broadcasting his confusion. She was standing over by the chest of drawers, wearing one of the clean, plaid cotton shirts that had been hanging on the back of the chair, her long, naked legs extending from beneath the low-hanging hemline. She looked cute, adorable, but still every inch the 'goddess' she was. 'Graphic designers? What are you talking about, graphic designers?'

She loosed a smile and a coy shrug like an excited child. 'I started this week – my new job,' she announced. 'Well, there's no point studying fine art and graphic design if I'm not going to pursue a career in it, now, is there?'

Gutteridge's confusion slow-morphed into happy surprise. 'Are you being serious?'

She smiled and nodded her delight.

'But… I thought? Aren't you…?'

She tilted an understanding head and shook it. 'No… no I'm not. I only took escort work to help pay for my tuition. That's *not* who I am, not really.'

For the first time ever since he'd known her, she looked self-aware, and strangely vulnerable.

Gutteridge had only ever really seen her as the self-assured, celestial being she was, and this was all new to him.

She turned humble. 'I… I come from a poor background. My family in Poland don't really have money, so… you do what you have to do to get what you want, to be who you want to be.' Her eyes seemed to dampen.

Gutteridge extended a compassionate hand, a *you-don't-need-to-explain-yourself-to-me* expression warming his eyes. 'I'm pleased for you, Eve. Seriously. Really pleased.'

She winced a smile, paused, then shrugged the shirt off the sylphlike sweep of her shoulders. It slipped from her arms and fell to the floor, revealing her exaggerated perfection. 'Do you want me?' she asked, looking midway between self-confident, and pleading her uncertainty.

Gutteridge didn't know what connotation was hidden within the words of the question, and he didn't want to break the moment by asking.

Eve stood before him, 5' 11" of perfect body shod in a blood-red bodice that matched her lips, gloss-black, tousled hair tumbling around the angelic sweep of her face. A prize in any culture, and in any situation, and the only answer Gutteridge could muster, was 'Yes'.

He would worry about the reality of what she may have been asking later, much later. Right now, he wanted her, and she looked every bit as irresistible as she was.

She approached the bed, prompted by an invitational drawing back of the duvet. She slipped beneath the pillowy warmth, climbed aboard, and lowered her lips onto his.

The sweet taste of her breath, and the sticky gloss coating on her lips drew Gutteridge's mind from the case, exactly what he needed to distract him from his week. He inhaled her, clutching her tiny waist in the gentle cup of his muscular hands.

He reached down, pulling her panties aside, and slid his gratitude inside what she claimed willing to give… They exhaled as one…

'F-Fuck me,' she whispered into his ear, her voice unsteadied by the surge of epinephrine, 'I w-w-want you…'

SIXTEEN

GUTTERIDGE'S RINGTONE SEEMED DEAFENING in the post-storm calmness of the night that had been. Ewelina lay on her side, long-limbed and naked, legs and arms intertwined with Gutteridge's like tendrils of the wild rose she was.

Gutteridge stretched to take up his phone from the bedside table, trying not to wake Eve, who was managing to sleep through the commotion.

He woke the phone and strained his eyes at the screen. It was Keaton. He swiped to answer.

'Erm… Gutteridge,' he said, in a half whisper. Glancing at the time – 10:52.

'Oh. Sorry, sir. Are you not alone?'

He grinned. 'This isn't a fishing expedition, what do you want?'

'Sorry to be bothering you on a Saturday, but I knew you'd want to know what happened last night. I'm outside in my car.'

Gutteridge sat up and swapped the phone to his other ear. 'You're outside? What's happened?'

'Have a guess.'

'Another painting?'

'Correct. And you won't believe where.'

'Why? Where? Tell me.'

Keaton huffed a smirk, almost in admiration for the gall of the perpetrator. 'The bold son of a bitch has plastered it all over the wall of the Crown Court building, above the entrance, directly facing the police station.'

Gutteridge paused from the conversation for a beat… 'You're fucking joking. Tell me you're joking.'

''Fraid not. It's all over the news.'

Ewelina stirred from her slumber, not instantly recognising where she was. She saw Gutteridge sitting up holding the phone. The expression on his face spoke volumes. 'Is everything okay?' she asked.

He quickly covered the mouthpiece, and politely shushed her with his finger.

'Sorry!' she mimed, clapping a hand to her open mouth.

Gutteridge felt instant shame for treating her like a dirty secret. 'It's okay,' he smiled, 'it's just work.' He placed a gentle touch to her naked hip, to indicate everything was fine, and turned to carry on the conversation. 'You still there?'

'Yes, sir… you do have a thing for Eastern Europeans, don't you?'

'Careful.'

'Sorry…'

He huffed a laugh. 'It's okay, I'll be down in twenty… *Slag!*'

'*Knob-head!*' she responded. 'See you soon.'

Gutteridge swiped the phone off and sat in reflection.

Eve was now sitting upright, looking appalled and uncomfortable. 'I'm so sorry, I didn't think,' she pleaded. Her English was impeccable, and if it wasn't for the accent, you'd never know she hadn't been born here.

Gutteridge shook a smile. 'It's fine, sweetheart. You have nothing to apologise for. Okay? I have to go, I'm in the middle of an important case.' He baulked internally at his use of the word 'sweetheart', imagining he must've sounded like his father.

Eve shuffled to the edge of the bed. 'I'll get dressed as fast as I can and be out of your way.'

Gutteridge shushed her for the second time, but on this occasion, it was meant to be calming. He halted her progress with a soft hand on her shoulder, and gently pulled her back into bed. '*You*, lovely girl, don't need to go anywhere. You can stay here and sleep. Have breakfast, take your time, no rush. Okay? I'm just sorry I can't stay to be with you.'

She looked up into his face. She thought him especially handsome in the flat morning light filtering through the curtains, a shadow of stubble coarsening his jawline.

There were twelve years dividing them, but it wasn't obvious enough to bother her. He was in good shape and dressed young. He was kind and attentive – at least to her – and had a life she wished she could be part of, not just the sporadic moments they occasionally shared together – as nice as they were. They just gave her a view into a life she wished she could be at the core of. It was her only real regret in taking up escort work to bridge the gaping hole in her life options. But the fact of the matter was, he was a detective, and she knew it wouldn't look good, and she could weep at the fact.

Gutteridge stroked her face, twisting a smile into her searching grey eyes. He felt like quitting his job just so he could stay – a move that would also clear the road to being able to turn their trysts into the relationship he so wanted. But right now, there were children missing, and the sickening thought of yet another painting aided his rising.

He tucked her into the duvet, delivered a kiss to the dome of her forehead, and made for the shower…

SEVENTEEN

FATHER DYLAN closed the door to the vestry and walked through the blue-lit archway into the nave of St Peter's Church.

The mid-morning sun streamed through the large circular window on the southern end of the building, casting vibrant, gemstone colours and gothic shadows along the aisle to the altar, as if God himself was guiding the priest to the stage of his life's calling.

He stepped onto the path of light, and genuflected his respect, more out of routine than belief. He'd been noticing the anger of the world around him of late, and truly wondered if the god described in the book that he'd assigned his life to – a true god, a compassionate god – would really allow that world to be, without word or intervention, be it fire-and-brimstone retribution, or plain, simple guidance. His faith faltered, and not for the first time.

He rose from his respectful bow, and walked the path of light to the altar, his heavy robes whipping at his legs as if punishing him for questioning his beliefs.

He had Mass tomorrow, a wedding the day after, and a Christening midweek, and had noticed layers of dust during evening service that the new cleaner had missed, or possibly wasn't thorough enough to be bothered with, but either way, it was a look that was far from godly.

He drew the cloth and surface cleaner he'd brought with him from the large pockets of his robes and began to swipe the marble clear of evidence of neglect. 'Next to godliness,' he muttered into the reverberating solitude, his voice echoing around the pillars.

There was a ligneous bang from the doors at the farthest end of the hall that lapped the room, and the priest's eyes rose in time to see a figure dart into the confessional booth. He only caught a fleeting glimpse, but he was certain it was a man.

He held his stare for a while, but the figure failed to re-emerge.

He huffed a sigh, placed the cloth and bottle down on the marble slab, and made his way through the corridor of pews towards the entrance doorway.

The priest stepped tentatively up to the booth and stooped a respectful head. 'Erm. We're having a day of confession next Saturday, if you could maybe wait until then, I am quite busy today with preparations for Mass…?'

There was no reply. He could hear the creaking of the seat inside the cabinet, but no other sounds came forth from the panelled door.

He sagged, then forced his spirits to lift to something more in keeping with his apparent eminence. 'Okay,' he said, 'I can hear you now, if it's something that can't wait.'

The priest entered through the dark-stained confessee door, sat and latched it.

He shuffled to get comfortable, keeping his eyes respectfully averted from the woven wicker screen set at face level – his only protection from the admissions of wrongdoing that he had to endure as part of his 'work'.

He sat silently, and waited, expecting the usual opener – *Forgive me father, for I have sinned* – but nothing came forth.

'Do you seek forgiveness, my child?' he asked.

The shadow sat in silence. The priest could hear him thinking about his question. 'I don't know? I don't think so,' came the reply.

'But— you've sinned? Do you have a sin you wish to confess?'

Again, a pause… 'I'm not sure.'

The priest's brow flickered. He could hear the remnants of an Irish accent. 'You must know if you've sinned, my child. *Have* you defied the will of God?'

The shadow shifted in the seat, and leaned forwards to bring his face closer to the mesh. 'If the god that defines what is to be considered a sin, then asks you commit that sin, is it still to be considered a sin?'

The priest pondered the question, then realised he hadn't really understood it. Or maybe he had, but it was so strange a question that it had failed to register in his mind. 'Erm? What exactly do you mean? Can you explain yourself more for me? I'll try and help in any way I can, but I must understand the motivation for the guidance you seek.' The priest was getting disquieting vibes from beyond the mesh, his instincts fine-tuned from years of listening.

'I guess what I'm asking is this: I *hear* the voice of God, and I serve him – the same way *you* must. But, sometimes, the voice sounds so much like my father's, that I wonder if I'm wrong to presume that it *is* God?'

The priest rocked back from the words drifting through the wicker. *What the hell?* he thought. 'Can you perhaps tell me what it is you've done? What it is this *voice* has encouraged you to do? I must assume that whatever it is, in your heart, must be considered a sin, otherwise you wouldn't have felt compelled to come and talk with me?'

The shadow sat silently, save for the rhythmical breaths of

someone deep in thought. 'But how would I know?'

'Well, do you think God would encourage you to commit a sin?'

'Yes.'

'You *do?*'

'*Yes*, I *do*... Did God not instruct Noah to build a boat for those lucky enough to be chosen, so that he may drown unexpectant hordes of the innocent and ill-prepared? Would you not consider Noah's selfish adherence to his instructions, and his decision not to warn others of the impending massacre, a sin?'

The priest considered his waning faith. It was times like these, when, deep inside, he agreed whole-heartedly with the arguments being presented, that he struggled to be the voice of reason. But he had to staunchly adhere to the go-to response that, for him, simply didn't cut it anymore – *The Lord works in mysterious ways.*

'It sounds to me like you've made up your *own* mind on this. Do you wish me to try to convince you otherwise? Is that the guidance you seek?' He wasn't sure that, if the answer came back as 'yes', he was adequately equipped to do so.

'I– I just thought, you're a servant of God, right? So, I wondered, if I brought him forwards, allowed him to travel to my mouth, you could talk to him, and tell me if it *is* God who guides me, or if it is – as I sometimes suspect – my father?' The shadow shifted in his seat, then settled again, voice lowering to a whisper. 'Thing is, the voice was there before, when my father was still alive. So, it *can't* be him, can't have *been* him, can it? How could it have been my father's voice inside of me, before I'd even killed him?'

The priest straightened in his seat... *Did he just say that? Did he just confess to murder?* he questioned. *Or did I mishear it?*

The shadow – just a flimsy partition away – sounded

psychotic, and the priest felt ill-equipped to deal with the situation he found himself facing.

The priest pushed through his inflating anxiety, doubts and fast-growing insecurity. 'When you say, "bring him forwards", wh-what do you mean?' The priest broke his code and turned a furtive look towards the shadow through the corner of his eye... The silhouette through the gauze wasn't moving, and the profile looked – in the blade of light spilling through a crack in the door – to be that of someone relatively young.

'He lives inside of me. Sometimes on my shoulder, sometimes in my ears, or in my mouth... Right now, he's behind my eyes, but I have them tightly shut so he can't hear us,' the shadow whispered, 'but I could let him pass to my tongue, *if* you wanted to speak to him?'

The priest recoiled from the mesh window. His unease soared; he didn't know what to do or say. Never in any of the teachings at theological college did anyone explain to him how to handle a psychotic nutcase sitting just two feet away, and he instinctively knew the need to tread carefully.

He breathed deeply and took a stab at it. 'I– I don't know your name,' he said, his voice shaking, 'or anything about you, but I can't help wondering if, if maybe, the best thing for you to do, would be to see a doctor, o-o-or maybe, a psychiatrist?'

The shadow's head lifted, then shrank back from the mesh panel and melted into the darkness beyond. The wood began to creak to the tune of the stranger rocking in his seat, his breathing becoming heavy and laboured. The rocking turned agitated, the hiss of the breathing vocal and laced with swelling fury... Then it ceased, and all went quiet...

'Who da fuck do you think you aare?' a voice asked, but not the same voice, a very different voice. This voice was much deeper, unmistakably Irish, and laced with aggression.

The priest flinched at the perceived change. He'd seen no one leave the booth, or enter, so who the *hell* was this?

'I-I-I don't understand? Who is this I'm talking to?'

'You don't need to know who I am. What you *do* need to know is that if you do anything to harm moi boy, I'll come for you, and find you, and I'll slit yer feckin' throat. Do you hear me, you self-righteous cunt?' the shadow said, sitting motionless, cycling seething breaths.

'I didn't… mean…'

'I know what yer meant. I know your kind, thinking you know it aaall, when in fact, you know feck-all of the real world you presume to command. Sat alone in your ivory tower, masturbatin' to the thoughts of boys in white robes, because you're not man enough to defy the teaching of the stilted religion you blindly follow and learn what it is to please a woman the way a real man would, and can. Because moi boy's a good boy, see. He's doing the Lord's work, the *real* Lord's work, not this laughably diluted, sanctimonious bullshit you deliver to the world like shit from an arsehole, and I won't have some superior, self-roiteous wanker loik you, suggesting moi boy needs to see no shrink, do you feckin' hear me?'

The priest sat shaking.

'Oi said, *do* you feckin' hear me!'

The sounds of grinding teeth cut through the threat-drenched air. 'Yes! Yes! I– I hear you…'

The shadow sat motionless for a beat that felt like an hour, then stood, and hung in the sound of the priest's stifled sobs. 'And if you try to follow him, *or* me, the next time your congregation sees you, you'll be a feckin' head in a box! Hear the words Oi speak and dare to tell me I don't mean it…!'

The door of the booth crept open, and the shadow left.

The priest's eyes flitted between the mesh window and his own door, his shaking hands holding the clasp for all he was worth, waiting for the door to fling open, and the hurting to begin… but nothing…

The main doors to the hall creaked open, then slammed shut, the crash echoing throughout the nave and the bell tower. The shadow was gone, and the priest was alone once more.

He slid to the floor of the confessional and folded himself around his knees. He wept for his life and his humbled dignity, and all he could think about was, where was his precious God when he needed him…?

EIGHTEEN

AN HOUR AND THREE CHANGES of radio station later, and Gutteridge emerged from his front door, and trotted from his cottage to Keaton's waiting Renault Megane.

Gutteridge had exited the bathroom clad in a towel, only to find Eve stretched out on the bed, arms above her head, her long, toned torso lying open like a submissive gift, and he couldn't resist taking her just one more time, ending the night in the way it had begun.

He popped the passenger door and dropped inside, looking a little undone but strangely elated. He fiddled with his tie, squaring the hurriedly wound Windsor knot.

Keaton smirked; she could smell the feminine scent drifting off her partner: Lancôme Trésor, if she wasn't mistaken – classy.

'Morning,' Gutteridge said, 'sorry about that. The shower was playing up.'

Keaton fought not to smirk and pulled out, darting a final look towards the cottage as she swung a U-turn in the road to double back towards Gloucester.

She saw a female figure in the bedroom window watching them leave, wearing a shirt six sizes too large for her. She was tall and beautiful, with tumbles of jet-black hair cascading around her face, and Keaton felt an unexpected pang of jealousy that surprised her.

'You're a terrible liar when you're flustered,' she said, leaning in to sniff his neck. 'Mmmm. She smells amazing! I could go for that myself.'

Gutteridge turned his shoulders to face her.

'And before you try to deny it, I just saw her… she's stunning.' Keaton allowed herself a cheeky smile as she negotiated the roads. 'You see, like I said, "a dark horse".'

Gutteridge resigned a sigh.

'I don't know why you're having to be so secretive about it. You're allowed a relationship, you know, it's not illegal.'

Gutteridge considered her words. 'I know. But it might not be ethical, or even possible,' he explained, finally opening up.

Keaton's expression turned to concern. 'Why?'

Gutteridge pondered his possible answers, and the prudence of giving one. He loosed a sigh. 'Because, some professions just don't mix.'

Keaton darted him a baffled look, before her face brightened to something akin to shock. 'She's not a hooker? Is she?'

'Noooo, she's not a hooker.' He thought about what he'd said, deciding if it was true or not. 'She's *not* a hooker, and the thing she *is*, or *was*, she no longer does.'

Keaton couldn't hide her intrigue. 'What *did* she do?'

Gutteridge didn't answer, looking lost in his thoughts.

'For fuck's sake, Pat. How long do we have to be partnered together before you realise that I have your back? You're a rank above me, yeah, but I'm still your friend. So, what is she? What's so problematic?' she insisted. 'I'm sure I recognise her, have I encountered her before?'

Gutteridge sagged… 'You might have done. She works at a graphic design company, at least she does *now*, but before that, she worked as an escort to make ends meet, to help pay her way while she was studying.'

Keaton slow-turned a *what-the-fuck* look across at him. 'Is that all? I thought you were going to tell me she was a hired assassin with an overzealous trigger-finger. I know in your old-fashioned mind you probably think she was just one step away from being a whore, but this is a transaction-based world we live in now. People sell themselves: their image; their recommendations; their *influence*; and sometimes, just sometimes, businessmen want to pay to have someone beautiful on their arm for an evening. It takes the hassle out of a social occasion.'

Gutteridge spun a look to consider Keaton's ear. 'Do you really think that?'

'*Yes*, I *do*,' she insisted, her eyes remaining locked on the road unravelling ahead.

'But she's been in the station. How would *that* look to the others?'

'Why…? What for? Providing tricks?'

'Noooo, nothing like that. In fact, the opposite.' He took and released a despairing breath. 'One of her clients got a bit drunk and started not accepting "no" as an answer.'

'And was he good-looking, this guy?'

'What?'

'This guy. Was he good-looking?'

Gutteridge had to take a moment to cast his mind back. 'Um? I guess so?'

'Well, there you are then. A good-looking guy who hired her for the evening wanted more, and she turned him down. Not exactly the actions of a prostitute now, are they? Unless she's shit at it.'

Gutteridge went quiet, staring into the footwell.

'A penny for them?' Keaton said.

Gutteridge broke from his trance. 'I think she wants more.'

'More? You mean a relationship?'

'I think so.'

'And you?'

He nodded like a berated child. 'I think I do. She makes me happy, and she makes me give a shit.'

Keaton had never seen him like this before. He looked vulnerable, lost, human. Far removed from the SIO front she was more used to dealing with. 'So. Go for it. What's stopping you?'

He turned to look towards her. 'You think? You *actually* think that could work, without ridicule?'

'If this unfairly beautiful, gorgeous-looking lucky bitch of an angel makes you happy, then *yes*,' Keaton said, her voice laced with a pinch of mild sarcasm. 'And besides, who gives a shit what others think? It's our own happiness that counts. One chance at life, mate. Live it!'

Gutteridge allowed a smile to tickle the corners of his mouth. Once again, he'd fed off Keaton's relatively youthful optimism, and was thankful for it. 'Well, we'll see… and thanks.'

He broke from the conversation and swapped metaphorical hats. 'So, what do we have?'

Keaton passed him her phone; it was already open on a picture she'd taken of her television's screen at home. 'I spoke to Bryant earlier, when I first saw *that*,' she said, pointing to the image on the phone. 'I told him I was planning to contact you next. That's the reason you haven't been called by anyone else, just me.'

Gutteridge swiped around the picture; it looked to be a frame from a regional news channel, breaking a story about a new Tick-Tock. It was the same as the previous two, but the image was far too grainy to see if there were any changes to this particular version.

'I can't believe this tosser's plastered it up the side of the court building. Is he taunting us?'

'Maybe,' she replied, lifting a shrug to salute her cluelessness, 'but chances are, he doesn't even know we're onto him. There's been nothing in the papers to suggest we are, right?'

'Right.'

'Still, I can't work this one out,' she added. 'We don't really have enough info on him yet to even try to work out what his motivations might be.'

'I know,' Gutteridge agreed, 'it's fucking frustrating.' He took his phone from his jacket pocket and flipped the case open. A slip of paper fluttered onto his lap. He frowned, and picked it up, turning it in his fingers. It was a receipt, from Wagamama. It had writing on it in red biro – *Thanks for last night, you're a lovely man. Am I allowed to be fond of you? Good luck with the case. E. X*

His heart lurched in his chest. It had lurched before with his dealings with Eve, but this was a different lurch, a new lurch, less lust, more hope for something greater than he'd previously thought possible.

With a furtive glance sideways, he slipped the note carefully into his inside pocket. He would put it in the drawer with the others, along with the tights she'd left behind on her first stay over; the scarf that still had her scent woven through it that he would often sleep with; and the piece of folded tissue with the deep mauve lipstick print emblazoned upon it that he'd found perched on top the bathroom's waste basket.

He scrolled to Bryant's number and punched it. It rang...

Bryant answered. 'Hi Pat. Where are you now?'

'I'm in the car with DS Keaton. We're on our way over. Are you there, at the station?'

'I'm afraid not. I'm in the bloody Lake District this weekend, typical! We booked it months ago, and I couldn't let her down again, she'd divorce me!'

Gutteridge laughed. 'Don't worry, we've got this.'

'I only found out myself because Keaton called,' Bryant said. 'It was on the fucking news before any of the night shift had even noticed. I mean, Christ almighty! How unobservant can you be!' He sighed and laughed ironically. 'Observant girl that one, you're lucky to have her on your hip.'

'Yep. Very,' Gutteridge agreed, smiling across at Keaton, who was trying to listen in over the whine of the engine.

Bryant continued, 'Also, I just had word that forensics and the fine-art team have finished their report on the section of wall at Knutsford. Apparently, it makes for very interesting reading.'

'In what way?'

'I don't actually know. McWilliams tried to explain it to me, but the line was terrible, and I struggle to decipher his bloody Glaswegian accent at the best of times. Could you take a look when you're at the station, let me know what they've found?'

'Of course, sir. Not a problem.'

'I've got to go out now and buy stuff for a bloody impromptu barbecue this afternoon, I'll talk to you later.'

'My heart bleeds,' Gutteridge laughed.

'Talk soon, and thanks for this.'

'No problem, sir. Try and have fun.'

Gutteridge dropped the phone from his ear. The lights ahead turned red, and Keaton pulled up on the line. 'Anything new?' she asked.

Gutteridge was staring out of the side window at the car next to them. The man driving turned and caught his eye. *That could be him,* he thought, *right there, an arm's length away, and we wouldn't even know it.* It occurred to him that they knew nothing, and he had a creeping suspicion that time was running out in some awful way. The clock was ticking, and they needed results, but results followed leads, and they had very few of them.

'Nothing on the new painting *yet*,' he said, turning his attention back into the car. 'The report from fine art and forensics has apparently landed though. It'll be interesting to see what they've come up with.'

'There must be something of relevance if there's talk of the report. Usually, if no one's mentioned it, it's because it contains nothing worth reading.'

The lights changed to green. The station was just ahead on the left, with the court building opposite. 'Don't know, but you're right. Apparently, it makes interesting reading. I hope that means there is something of use. Oh *hell!*' Gutteridge slurred.

There were at least three film crews and a good handful of reporters milling about in front of the Crown Court building. A ladder – manned by a uniformed officer – had been propped up against the galley entrance and secured with a rope.

Gutteridge could see Gustav Hoegen from the CSI team attempting to study the mural with discretion enough to not raise the suspicions of the broiling press pack that there might be something more serious occurring.

'Okay,' Gutteridge said, turning in his seat to face Keaton, 'we have to be clever about this, play it down. Act as if we're just involved because it's classed as vandalism, and that we have to make a report as a matter of course. But try to look matter of fact about it if you can, be light-hearted, okay? No serious or concerned looks. Remember, we're being watched by eyes attuned to be suspicious.'

'Okay, Chief.'

Keaton pulled into her designated space outside the station and shut the engine off.

Gutteridge spun looks out of all the windows but couldn't see any of his team around. 'Right, can you go in first and locate a copy of this report from forensics and fine art? I'll pop up and see if Hoegen's found anything useful. I'll meet you out by the court building. Oh, and put it in a plain folder or envelope, we don't want the cameras snapping the cover page and blowing up the image.'

'Okay. Consider it done.' They alighted the car, and Keaton made her way inside…

*

Gutteridge sprang up the rungs of the ladder, attempting to look nonchalant for the cluster of watching press below. He'd done much climbing in his late twenties, and had all but conquered the vertigo that had plagued him as a child.

He hopped off the top of the ladder just as Hoegen turned to greet his arrival. 'Pat,' said Hoegen, with a nod.

Gutteridge returned the nod. 'Anything?'

Hoegen drew in a breath, standing to step back and clear the view. 'Pretty much the same as the others, except *this* again,' he said, discreetly indicating the end of the conveyor in the painting with his powdering brush.

The hanging child was now first in line for the cull, its neck pinched perilously between the blades, just one tug on its shackled feet away from being decapitated.

'What do you think it means?' asked Hoegen, in his soft Dutch accent.

Gutteridge read the words scrawled beneath in the same deep red, sanguine paint – *AN EYE FOR AN EYE. A KILL FOR A CULL!* 'I have an idea, but I daren't vocalise it for fear of making it real.'

'I didn't have you down as superstitious.'

'Nor did I, until all this began. I just know something bigger is coming, and that scares me shitless!'

Gutteridge turned from the wall to glance at the press, then back to Hoegen. 'So, did you find anything of use?'

Hoegen shook a regretful head. 'No… no prints; no fibres, hairs, fluids; fuck-all. The only thing I *did* find, was this.' He stooped to pick up a clear evidence bag from his case and handed it to Gutteridge.

Gutteridge spun his back to the watching hacks, and raised it to eye level, turning it in his fingers. 'What is it? I can't see anything?'

'Look harder,' Hoegen said, stepping in to point his pinky at the bag. 'There.'

There was a small torn-off piece of clingfilm in the bag, barely visible sandwiched in the middle of the like-minded polythene.

'Couldn't that have come from anywhere?' Gutteridge asked. 'Someone's sandwich wrapper, for instance?'

'It's possible, but that wouldn't explain how it was stuck to the paint. I suppose it could have blown up here while the paint was still drying, but it's quite elevated, and I've been watching the way the litter around here tends to blow about. It doesn't seem to drift up this far, and there was very little of the litter you'd expect to find on a flat roof like this when I first came up: no crisp packets; sweet wrappers; newspaper pages, none of what you would usually expect to see, so it seems unlikely. Besides, the few bits that were up here were covered in months, or years, of grime. *This*,' he said – lifting the evidence bag into the core of the conversation, 'is clean.'

'I see your point. Well, if you do find anything else, let me know straight away.'

'Will do.'

The bright, metallic creak of weight-loaded aluminium caught their ears, and they turned to see Keaton nervously arriving at the top of the ladder, a report clamped awkwardly beneath her arm.

'Here, let me,' Gutteridge said, rushing forwards like a gallant knight to help.

She strained her armpit towards him, and he leaned in to relieve her of the impeding document.

He offered a hand, and she climbed the last few rungs, her cheeks flushing crimson.

She stepped onto the roof and gulped back an exhilarated breath. 'The press were trying to hassle me as to why we're so interested in this particular piece,' she said, flicking her curiosity towards the new artwork, and holding the look, studying it for differences to the last one. 'A couple of them seemed to recognise you and wondered why someone so senior would be involved. I just told them it's because it's on an official, municipal building, and they seemed to swallow it.'

'Okay. Good,' Gutteridge whispered, keeping his lips static like a nightclub vent, aware that all three of them might be being recorded, and that the footage could be run past lip readers.

'Have a quick look yourself while you're up here,' he said, 'then me and you'll clear the roof and regroup in the incident room. Let's take a look at what we have so far.'

Gutteridge's phone buzzed in his pocket. He drew it out and swiped to answer it. 'Gutteridge.'

He listened, and nodded, Keaton and Hoegen watching his changing expressions, all seemingly centred around a theme of concern.

'*Fuck!*' Gutteridge spat under his breath, turning a shoulder and covering the mouthpiece. 'All right… okay. Thanks for letting me know. Forward me the report. Oh, and good work.'

He rang off, hovered for a beat, then turned back to the interested parties looking on, eyeing the press below with caution.

Again, he ventriloquised his speech. 'We have another missing kid, a boy, thirteen, last night, from right outside his fucking home.'

'No! No way? Shit!' Keaton spat, trying to stop the despair that was gnawing at her sinking heart from showing in her face.

'Yep… this cunt's getting bolder. But what's he trying to achieve? There seems to be a reason why he's doing this. Some hidden meaning, other than just jerking off over the remains – although he might still be doing that? But somehow, I don't think he is.'

'We don't even have a body yet,' Keaton reminded the group, to Gutteridge's growing frustration. 'Are we even sure that they're dead?' It was a fair question, and one worth asking.

'Well, we don't know, but Carl seems to think it likely. He estimated that the amount of blood used in each painting must be in the region of four to six pints. That's virtually all of the blood in a child, without actually running it through a mangle.' His own verbal imagery briefly sickened him. He swallowed it back. 'I think it's safe to assume they're dead, but that's obviously not official.'

Hoegen turned from the huddle to finish his examination. Gutteridge leaned in to address Keaton, his tone clandestine. 'Call the team in, I don't care what they're doing. We can't afford another day without our minds fully on this. I need to know where we are with it all before I can call the next shots.'

Keaton turned her eyes to the new artwork. The feeling in her gut was anything but optimistic. 'It's a countdown, isn't it?'

Gutteridge looked to the report in his hand; he'd already seen something of interest in the pages as he'd flicked through it. 'With what I've just seen in here,' he said, raising the report between them, 'I'd say, almost definitely…'

*

The team, minus Bryant, and Banks – who was 120 miles away at a wedding in Macclesfield – sat in a semicircle around Gutteridge, who was perched on the edge of his desk.

They were all in normal clothing, called in mid-flow of their everyday lives, and looked bizarrely casual in light of what it was normal to see in such a serious-minded environment.

Each member of the team had gathered together the fruits of their investigating labours, and were flicking through their files, readying themselves to present their findings – *if* they actually had anything of value worth presenting. They were about to find out.

Gutteridge opened the report from art and forensics. 'There're copies of this being passed around. Look at it. Take it in. It's important.'

Gutteridge turned to the part he deemed most interesting. 'Now, the section that I think is most relevant is on page 16.' The team riffled to the appropriate page.

'The Art-and-Antiquities Crime Unit have the ability to use X-ray radiography and infrared reflectography on paintings, usually used to examine the brushstrokes beneath what's directly visible, to see the progression of the finished piece, and establish if the work looks to have been done by a master, or if it's a forgery. But the problem is, you need to bounce the radiation off a plate, and you can't do that with a brick wall, it's far too thick.'

Gutteridge woke his computer, moused to a freshly downloaded file, and opened it.

'So, they 3D-scanned the surface into an image file, then amplified the undulations in the textures to see if there was anything visible beneath the surface worth seeing. They weren't really expecting to find anything; it was done more so they could say they had. But they *did* find something, and it's interesting.'

Gutteridge spun his computer screen around towards the crescent of faces, the light illuminating the fascination in their eyes.

'So... is that other writing, hidden beneath the *main* writing?' asked Stanton.

'Correct,' said Gutteridge, tapping the mouse to advance to the next image. The writing had been highlighted.

Stanton leaned in closer to read it out loud for the group. The writing was scrawled and angry. Her voice – soft and searching – didn't fit the words.

'Art is my gift, my voice, my chalkboard at hinting at the will of the God who commands me. I am his Son, his servant, and the ill winds of your ignorance are blowing with anger towards you. Stop the killing, stop the murder, stop the supping of the flesh of the innocents, or you will learn of the power of sorrow, and of loss, and the keening in a way that will stain the cloth of your very souls, and you will know of the pain you have forced me to feel by your greed, never to forget. An eye for an eye. A tooth for a tooth. A life, for an undeserving life. Bow down, for *He* is coming, the clock is ticking, and time, alas, is running out.'

Gutteridge allowed the resulting silence to hang for a while, until it was broken by a coarse Glaswegian accent expressing the same thoughts they all harboured. 'He sounds like a fucking nutter!'

Gutteridge looked across at Keaton with her degree in psychology. 'Some may argue it's more complicated than that?'

Keaton sank back into her seat. 'It is, but I'm happy to let that diagnosis stand... You're right, he sounds nuts.'

'What do we think it means?' asked Parker.

Gutteridge sighted his use of the word 'we' – Parker often being the last to present anything of use – but let it go. He shrugged. 'How can we know, until he shows us, and then it'll be too late. But one thing I *am* certain of, is that whatever it is he's talking about, it's going to be something different to the graffiti we've already seen. Something *more*. Something *bigger!*

'Like what?' Koperek asked.

'I don't know. I really don't know. But something.'

Gutteridge rocked back to break from the moment and looked to Parker. 'Okay. CCTV. Anything?'

Parker drew in a frustrated breath. 'Nothing yet. He walks to his sites, and he seems to be aware of where a majority of the cameras are. The ones he *hasn't* been aware of tend to be owned by shops and stores, and they're invariably low cost and of little use. Just pixilated blurs really. But I'm not done yet. I'm looking for corresponding vehicles in the immediate and not-so-immediate areas, to see if there are any repeat sightings.'

'Okay, good. Stay on it.' He turned. 'Koperek? Any other MP cases corresponding to this Tick-Tock's efforts?'

'No. Nothing. Not as yet. I'm drawing a blank. But I think that must mean the missing children that we *are* aware of, are probably – and let's hope this is the case – all that are missing. Occam's razor.'

'Well, let's all hope for that,' Gutteridge muttered, almost to himself. 'McWilliams. The web, anything?'

'Aye, plenty of talk about this nutter's work, but no leads as to who he might be. But I'll keep looking.'

'Corbould?'

'No. Nothing we don't already know, except maybe, the handwriting.' He consulted his notes. 'They say, whoever wrote these was right-handed; mid-level educated, probably comprehensive, or similar; definitely artistic by the quality of his paintings, but this bit's weird. They say the handwriting they've analysed has been done by different hands? Two, to be exact.'

But we know he works alone, right?' Gutteridge asked, turning back to Parker.

Parker nodded. 'Only one person visible on the CCTV footage.'

Corbould shrugged. 'That's just what Bob Radley says, and he ain't shit. I'm just passing it on.'

'Okay,' Gutteridge said, 'let's keep that in mind.'

McWilliams looked pensive. 'You know, that writing that the scan found. There was a word in there that doesn't seem to fit...'

'Which one?' Gutteridge asked.

'"Keening", it's Irish, means "lamenting", "wailing". You don't think our guy might be Gaelic?'

'That's good,' Gutteridge said. He turned to the rest of the room. 'Does anyone else here know of that word?' No one answered. 'Fuck. Okay. Irish...'

He finally turned his drifting attention to Stanton. Physically, she was short, but looked taller because of her slender proportions, and until Keaton had joined the squad a few years back, she was the one who got all of the unwanted male attention. 'Who have you and Banks managed to re-interview so far? Find anything?'

She shuffled through her papers. 'Thomas Leinster, missing from Friday, 10th April. He and a friend had been to McDonald's with the friend's parents. We interviewed the parents, but they make very unlikely suspects. Thomas, the friend – Kyle Wragg – together with another boy – James Gommersall – left to play after they'd returned, walking to the Longlevens Recreation Ground. At *some* point, they split up, and no one seems to know precisely where. He never made it home. But the Wragg boy *did* say something about thinking that he saw a white-ish van hanging around that looked suspicious, but we know no more than that.'

Gutteridge spun towards Parker. 'White, or off-white van. See if we can pull up any footage of anything like that corresponding with the times of abduction?'

'On it, Chief.'

Gutteridge swung back to Stanton. 'Sally Tweets?'

Stanton closed her eyes and breathed. She had a daughter of comparable age to the Tweets girl. 'Sally Tweets, aged twelve, went missing from the road she usually played on – Colin Road, near to her old primary school. She'd been in town earlier in the day with her mother to buy supplies for high school; do some clothes shopping; books; magazines; the usual sort of thing. They had lunch at KFC, then went home straight after. Again, she went out with friends to play, never came back. We've yet to interview the child she was with, but we're on that next.'

'Okay. Good. Keep me informed. Anyone else?'

'We're interviewing the parents of the new missing child – Jayden Peek – now they've had some time to calm down.'

Gutteridge considered if he'd prefer to interview them personally, but decided against it, at least for now. Stanton and Banks had the questions that needed asking already to hand, so the interview would probably flow better with them at that particular helm.

'Okay, team. Good work so far, but we need to keep it moving. I know there's not much to work with yet, but let's keep seeking those avenues. If we're lucky, we'll find one that leads straight to him.'

Gutteridge shuffled his thoughts… 'Stanton, Banks, carry on as you are. Corbould, drop on with McWilliams and help search the web for clues to who this nutter is.'

McWilliams and Corbould exchanged a look and nodded. 'Will do.'

'Koperek. Expand your search to see if any similar murals have appeared anywhere else in the country, in fact, the whole of Britain, including Ireland, you never know.'

She nodded.

'Parker. You continue searching CCTV, and look for

a white, or a near-white van. See if a repeat appearance corresponds to any of the disappearances.'

Another nod. 'Boss.'

'Me and Keaton will continue to free float to wherever the evidence leads, in hope of digging up something. If any of you finds *anything*, however insignificant, don't delay, call me…'

Gutteridge stood and stretched the stiffness away from perching on an unforgiving desktop. 'Go home, try to enjoy your time off, because I'm going to be putting in a request for weekend work, and I don't foresee a problem with them accepting it.'

The room mumbled its understanding.

'Thank you for coming in. Have a good day.'

The huddle disbanded. Gutteridge turned back to face them. 'But keep your minds on the case, let it percolate in the back of your thoughts, and I'll see you all on Monday.'

Gutteridge wandered from the huddle and turned pensive. Something that had been said during the meeting was playing on his mind, but he wanted to keep it to himself, at least for now.

NINETEEN

GUTTERIDGE'S SUNDAY should have been perfect – or as close to perfect as was possible with a new child abduction case kicking at the back of his conscience.

He'd returned home on the Saturday to find a shepherd's pie Eve had prepared for him sitting in readiness atop a freshly cleaned kitchen countertop, with heating instructions written on a pad, punctuated by a skilfully rendered heart, an 'Eve', and a kiss. It just needed sliding into the oven, et voila, dinner.

He'd called her to see if she fancied sharing it, and she'd said yes. He'd picked her up; they'd eaten together; they'd shared a movie. *Speed* – the 1994 classic. Then she'd stayed the night for the second time in succession, the first time that had ever happened, and the night had passed as sensuously and delightfully erotically as the previous one.

Sunday, then, had all the makings of an idyllic day, but an early morning phone call drove a spike through his whole weekend, and what should have been a dream began slowly morphing into a nightmare. He'd been forced to leave Eve for the second time, collecting DS Keaton on his way through Gloucester.

His Saab 9-3 sped through the back roads towards Stroud. Nothing said, nothing offered, no voices, just silence cutting through the air of disbelief and impending sense of dread.

Gutteridge's instincts had proven right, but he wouldn't have minded being wrong, just this once.

Keaton made a move to cut through the awkwardness. 'Do we know which one it is? Or is it a new one?'

Gutteridge shook his head and swallowed. 'No, we don't know that yet… but they think it's a boy.'

Keaton frowned. '*Think* it's a boy?'

Gutteridge flashed regretful brows. 'Apparently, it's hard to tell. The genitals have been removed, and the body is heavily mutilated.'

The silence returned…

Attempt number two… 'I'm not that au fait with Stroud, where is this bridge?'

'It's a viaduct. Runs over the River Frome and the adjoining canal that runs parallel to it. It's pretty secluded, and perfect for whatever you would call this… this… *mindless* fucking act!'

The silence returned and remained for the rest of the journey.

*

Gutteridge parked in the nearby Waitrose car park. They made their way down to the towpath that wound through the surrounding trees and woodland, and set off along the uniformed-officer-lined pathway to the horror awaiting their arrival.

'Carl from pathology is already there,' Gutteridge explained, 'but he's waiting for us to arrive and walk the scene before he gets fully into it.'

'Okay.'

'And Bryant's on his way back, he should arrive later today.'

Again: 'Okay.'

Keaton felt out of her depth, and Gutteridge could hear it in her voice. 'Are you okay?'

She swallowed back the feeling of unreality and nodded unconvincingly.

'It's just another case. Treat it no differently than you would any other. If you just remember that, you'll be fine.' He wanted to reach out and comfort her with an affectionate touch, but decided it could be taken as patronising. So he settled for more advice. 'Walk the scene, become the perpetrator. Try to question his motivations, and live his actions. Look, see, and gather the evidence, the way you normally would… In that way, it's really no different to any other case; you just have to try to look past the horror and see what's there, and you'll do just fine.'

Another unconvincing nod, but this time, partnered to an appreciative smile.

Glimpses of the crime scene began to flash sporadically through the low-hanging branches as they traipsed along the footpath, serenaded by inappropriately joy-filled birdsong and the fresh scent of morning dew.

The watching eyes of the ribbon of uniformed officers mournfully saddened the nearer they got to the tents and hastily hung tarpaulins that transpired to impede the view of the press and the public.

The red-brick arches loomed high above their upward gazes, not as tall or imposing as some viaducts Gutteridge had visited during moments of downtime, but still, undeniably impressive, and suitably overwhelming.

Two of the arches had been filled in with brick, with what looked like windows and a doorway left clear, and Gutteridge made a mental note to look up what the history of that addition may have been. He then felt guilt for being a tourist with the body of a child just metres away, and he turned his mind back to the tents ahead.

They flashed their IDs to the interested officer guarding the cordon, who stepped aside in time to reveal Carl emerging through a parting in the tarps, wearing a full suit, mask, overshoes and gloves.

He drew the hood from his head and whipped the mask off his face. He looked white and ashen, his demeanour that of someone unwell. 'Pat. Jane,' he said with a nod, his voice strangely unsteady.'

'Are you all right?' Gutteridge asked, the concern for his long-time friend showing in his voice.

Carl shook his head and darted a look back towards the tent. 'No. No I'm not.'

Gutteridge twisted a look towards him. 'Surely, someone like you must have seen everything?'

'I have, but I've never seen anything like this!'

Keaton's dreading eyes locked onto the hanging white sheets, and the insanity they apparently obscured.

Carl stepped back and dragged a bag full of PPE towards the new arrivals. 'I'm afraid I must insist on full suits; overshoes; masks; hoods; hairnets; and double gloves.'

'Of course, old friend,' Gutteridge agreed.

'And prepare yourselves,' Carl said, darting a concerned look towards Keaton. 'Are you *sure* you need to do this?' he asked, singling out the one detective he knew to be virgin to this level of crime scene.

Keaton felt her hackles rise, but sensed the lack of patronisation emanating from him. 'I'll be fine.'

'Do you have kids?' he asked.

Keaton's brow flinched. 'No, not yet?'

Gutteridge stepped in on her behalf. 'She'll be okay, she's strong.'

'She needs to be,' Carl added, 'this isn't run of the mill.' He considered her stern facade… 'Okay.'

The pair of them began suiting up. Nothing existed at all except the swelling thud of their heartbeats in their inner ears, and the white sheet doorway obscuring the glaring hiccup to everyday normality.

Suited, masked and gloved, they both approached the white tarpaulins… Gutteridge pulled his mask down briefly. 'Let's try to tread carefully, so as not to ruin any possible footprint evidence. Whatever we see, let's try to put ourselves in *his* mind, see if we can't link somehow to his thought processes.'

Keaton nodded, but her eyes remained locked on the sheets.

Gutteridge replaced his mask, stepped up first, parted the curtain, and slid through inside…

The sheet whipped open again, and Gutteridge stumbled back through the opening. 'Fuck me! Oh fucking Jesus!'

Keaton peered at him. 'What is it?'

Gutteridge took a moment to regather himself, shaking his head, then turned moistening eyes to face her. 'I don't think you should do this. It's too much.'

Keaton recoiled unsteadily from his words, then resolved to step in again.

The look in Gutteridge's eyes frightened her, nearly forcing her into submitting to his recommendation. But as a fighter who'd always tackled the world head on, she fought the inclination to quit. *Fuck it*, she thought; she was going to do this.

'No. I'll be fine. I need to see this.'

But Gutteridge wasn't so sure *he* could, and in some convoluted way, he was glad of Keaton's defiance; it meant he wouldn't be going back in alone.

He took a moment, then nodded, and stepped back to the doorway. Attempt number two…

Keaton followed close behind, using Gutteridge's broad shoulders as a shield as they made their way inside, like a clutched cushion when watching a horror film.

They shuffled into the tented area with deliberate motions. Keaton could sense reluctance through Gutteridge's back.

She took a breath, and stepped aside to see…

The sight that met her appalled eyes hit her like a punch to the gut… Her pupils shrank to nothing in the pools of her shaking blue irises. Blood rushed from her head, and she nearly blacked out, but she managed to catch herself, slumping forwards and gulping massive lungfuls of air into her pounding chest in an attempt to remain conscious.

'*Shit!* Are you okay?' Gutteridge asked, turning to place a gentle hand against the arch of her heaving spine.

She nodded – a lie. 'I'll be fine. Oh my God in heaven, Pat!'

The body of a boy had been suspended on multiple strands of tying wire, hanging like an art installation in the core of one of the sub-archways between the main pillars of the viaduct.

The victim's stomach and chest had been sliced up the middle and opened up like the carcass of a spatchcocked chicken.

Intestines lay coiled on the ground beneath him. His head had been removed and suspended with more tying wire in the core of the clamshell chest cavity, looking out from the shadow of his hollowed-out body towards the new arrivals, one eye open, the other half closed and sinking to the right.

The hands, arms and feet had been bound behind the body with string, forcing the ribcage open, giving the 'sculpture' a look of a book opened enough to rupture the bindings.

Keaton's face crumpled, and she began to weep. An involuntary hand clapped across her folded abdomen, signalling her desire, one day, to have children. But this, *this*, threatened to taint that dream.

Gutteridge turned his attention from the horror to Keaton, bent double and clutching her gut, swallowing back her impulse to vomit. '*Go!*' he said. 'Go out outside for a minute. Gather yourself together. Come to terms with it, and *then* come back in. But *only* if you feel you can.' He smiled to try and console her. All she could see was the fattening of his cheeks above the hem of his mask, but she appreciated the gesture.

'Okay. I'm sorry. I'm so sorry,' she muttered, slipping back outside, passing Carl as he made his way back in.

'Fucking hell, old friend,' Gutteridge slurred, 'this is a whole new level of sick!'

'Yep. I know… I tried to warn you… Come on, tell me what you see with that big brain of yours, take your mind off it.'

The atmosphere in the hastily erected tent had an aroma like a butcher's shop. The meat, although fresh, emitted a sweet, coppery tang that clung to teeth.

The stench of viscera polluting the air they were being forced to breathe transpired to remind Gutteridge that, under it all, beneath the pomp and the finery; the egos; the illusion of personal importance; the pretence; they were all just meat.

Gutteridge tore his eyes away from the mutilated corpse, and began assessing the scene… The words 'A TOOTH FOR A BEAK' had been poured onto the ground ahead of the body in what looked to be blood. There were a myriad of insects accumulating around the words and the coils of intestines: beetles; flies; worms, but no larvae, not yet.

He stepped in and climbed the stepladder that had been set up to examine the fixtures that the wires were suspended from… large, dome-headed screws wound into rawlplugs, each with a length of wire wrapped and twisted around the heads. Twelve in total, but there were at least another six dotted around that had been prepared, but unused.

Gutteridge stepped up a rung to look closer. The screws had light coatings of rust where the driver-bit had compromised the nickel coatings.

'How long has this been here? Are we certain it was put up last night?' Gutteridge asked.

Carl nodded. 'Yes. The woman who discovered it walks her dog this way every morning. She seemed pretty sure it wasn't here yesterday. Why?'

Because there's rust on these screws. They've been here a while, much longer that this,' he said, indicating the body. 'He must have been here before to set this up, placing the fixings in readiness. If that doesn't point to premeditation, then I don't know what does.'

He climbed back down again and considered the text. 'An eye for a beak,' he read out loud.

'He certainly sees himself as a warrior for the animal cause,' Carl suggested.

The child's stomach was sitting atop the coil of guts like a glacé cherry on a cake. Gutteridge lifted his chin towards it. 'Can you check the contents?'

'I always do.'

'I know that, but could you pay *particular* attention to what he's eaten, and where it might have come from. I want specifics.'

'What's your hunch? What exactly am I looking for?'

Gutteridge shrugged his insecurity at the value of his theory. 'Fast food: burgers; nuggets; fries; anything like that really.'

The brush of rubberised fabric drew them from their conversation. 'You think that's how he's picking them?' said a humbled voice. It was Keaton, making her way back in, still looking frayed and undone, but decidedly stauncher and more together than a minute earlier – however forced that front may have been.

Gutteridge took a sideways step to mask the body. 'You okay?'

'I'm fine. I'll be fine.'

Gutteridge wrapped his arm around her shoulder and gave it a squeeze. 'I was the same the first time I saw anything close to this bad. And trust me, it was nowhere near as bad as this is.' A lie, but said to appease Keaton's shame.

An image of Gutteridge's ex-wife flashed his thoughts. Of her dead, lifeless eyes watching him arriving home. He blinked it away.

Keaton stepped in. 'Can I see?'

Gutteridge thought about suggesting otherwise, but he could see her actively steeling herself.

'Okay. But only if you're sure.' He stepped aside for her like a curtain unveiling a sideshow freak. She moved with conviction towards the blip to the sanity of the world.

Carl had the case files open in his double-gloved hands, looking at the pictures. 'I think this is Jayden Peek, at least, I'm pretty sure the *head* is, but I have to be certain that the body is too, and not the remains of one of the other two kids. The two that we know of, that is.'

Gutteridge drifted away into one of his thoughts, his mind recalling a relevant quote… '*He* that is down, need fear no fall,' he murmured.

'Pat?' asked Carl.

Gutteridge broke from his musing. A dismissive shake of the head. 'Nothing. Just a hymn. By John Bunyan. I thought it relevant.'

Keaton levelled a firm gaze, absorbing the extent of the

outrage suspended before her, fronting her considerable disgust. Nothing felt real. 'We have to catch this wanker!' she said. 'And fast!'

TWENTY

A MAN – ATTEMPTING TO LOOK OFFICIAL – stepped up to the doorway of the 'Gan Feoil Tea Rooms', located midway down Gloucester's Westgate, a short walk from what was once considered the city's main high street, before 'The Quays' took the title of the main shopping and dining focal point. He was carrying an over-square case and wearing a light-grey suit that cut a balance between comfortable and formal.

He checked his watch – 15:36. He'd purposefully picked a time when business was likely to be slow on a Tuesday. He leaned on the polished brass handle, and entered the door…

The space inside smelled fresh and inviting, the aroma of herbs and spices not usual to a standard kitchen cupboard flavouring the air. The place looked deserted.

The cafe was decked out in rustic style, with mismatched tables and chairs that gave the whole space a feel that took him back to the farmhouse he grew up in.

Expertly crafted frescos on the wall gave the room a Mediterranean, almost Tuscan feel, and the visitor felt he could very well eat at a place like this, which, after some of the sights he'd been forced to face during his working day, was indeed rare.

The man could hear voices emanating from what he assumed was the kitchen area. He quietly closed the door behind him, and approached the counter…

The man tried listening to the conversation drifting from the kitchen, but the lovingly polished Italian coffee machine seemed to be cycling through some pre-programmed cleaning routine that made eavesdropping virtually impossible.

The machine finished its cycle with a click and a gurgle, and the voices resolved through the resulting silence.

'I do what you tell me, I do. Have I not always done so? But… why does it feel so wrong?'

'Does it feel wrong, my Son?' another voice asked. Softer. Wiser. Older.

There was a pause. 'I can't lie, yes. Yes, it does.'

'Yours is not to question my will, yours is to do my bidding, so *we*, together, can correct the world and what it has become. This wasn't in my plans, and is, in truth, wholly against my wishes. I must, therefore, communicate to my children through your actions. Do you understand?'

'I do, but—'

'Shhhhh. Quiet, my child,' said the wise voice. 'The world has become a place that no longer comprehends the importance of words, it only comprehends actions. *These* are my actions, and they will listen, and hear, and sink to my waiting feet, begging for mercy on bended knees for the things they have done to the world I was kind enough to gift them.'

The man suddenly coloured, uncomfortable about listening in, and coughed to draw attention to his presence.

The kitchen fell silent, and a few beats later, the door opened, and a man – looking to be in his thirties – stepped tentatively through to take up his place behind the counter.

He looked surprised to see the man there.

'Kieran O'Leary?' the man asked.

'Erm... yes? Do you require a table?' O'Leary took a menu from the stack and rounded the counter to escort the man to a seat. He stopped, and turned, looking confused. 'How do know my name? Do I know you?'

The man loosed a laugh. 'No-ho,' he smiled. 'My name's Mr Hood, I'm from the Food Standards Agency. We're in the area doing spot checks on eateries. It's nothing to be worried about, we just take a quick look around to see if your food preparation routines are sound and up to standard, and I have to say, without yet seeing your food prep area, it looks to me like you run a very clean and tidy operation here,' he said, looking about the place in an exaggerated manner. 'So, you work here with one other?'

O'Leary stepped back behind the protection of the counter. 'No, just me?'

'But... I thought I heard you speaking...?'

O'Leary's brow furrowed.

The man decided to let it go. 'It doesn't matter.' He took out a clipboard from his bag and slipped a pen from beneath the clamp. 'So, you work here alone...' he said rhetorically, noting it down. 'Do you *ever* get help in? Weekends maybe?'

O'Leary shook his head. 'No. No, never.'

The man's eyes squinted towards the denial, his eyes flicking a look towards the kitchen door. 'Okay. Makes life simpler for me, *and* you,' he grinned.

The man took up his case from between his feet and made to round the counter.

O'Leary stepped across to block him. 'What? Where are you going?'

The man stuttered, taken aback at being impeded, but he'd had it happen before, plenty of times. 'It's nothing to worry about, Mr O'Leary. I just need to give the food prep area a quick once-over, to check it's up to scratch. That's all. I *am* legally allowed to enter a food preparation establishment to do so, but I'm *sure* we don't need to get all official about this, now, do we?' He delivered another empty smile for effect, then gently, but authoritatively, shouldered past O'Leary's reluctance.

He rolled through the doors into the kitchen, making quick notes that the front of house seemed clean and orderly.

The door swung shut behind him, and he was surprised to see no one else there.

He'd assumed O'Leary was lying, and that was what had fuelled his reluctance to let him pass. But he sighted the fire exit door in the far corner ahead of him, and figured that whoever it was had gone, or snuck out to hide behind the bins, but either way, it was the end of the day – his last inspection – and he was willing to squint a bit for an easy life.

'Well, it all seems clean and tidy in here.' Another note on the clipboard. 'Where do you store your meat products?'

Again, O'Leary responded with a confused look. 'Erm. I don't have meat products. This is a vegetarian cafe.'

'Oh!' the man said, spinning a look in the direction of the shop front. 'I didn't realise. I don't think it indicates that anywhere in the signage, unless I missed it?'

'Just the name?' O'Leary said, a hint of mild sarcasm woven into his voice.

The man consulted his notes. 'Gan Feoil Tea Rooms?'

'Gan Feoil is Irish, it means, "no meat".'

'Ahhhh. You learn something new, eh? I would suggest adding a warning– a *sign* I mean, letting people know. Most people around here don't speak Gaelic.'

'It's not Gaelic, it's Irish.'

'Well, still,' the man added.

He wandered through the kitchen, past neatly stacked racks of vegetables, made another note, then spied a large refrigerator. 'So what's in here then? Butter, cheeses?' He stepped in, to the dismay of O'Leary who flinched an arm out towards the appliance.

The man popped the locking handle, and swung the door open…

He sank back from the appliance with a kind of wilting faint, his legs giving way beneath him like a newborn deer, and stumbled to the floor.

There was a body of a young girl – a child – looking like she was aged in single figures, bundled into the corner of the refrigerator, her open eyes staring wide and colourless, her throat cut.

Her skin was pallid and pasty-white, the cotton dress she wore stained red-umber like a bib. Her scattered legs were buckled beneath her, looking like a discarded doll.

Her long, fair hair had been twisted into a crude, makeshift rope, and tied to the racking above to keep her from sliding down.

'*Jesus Christ!*' the man howled. 'What is this? What have you done! What's happening, here? Oh *God*!'

He tried shuffling back from the dead-eyed stare watching him through the sinking curtains of chilled mist, but his progress was halted by a pair of legs blocking his escape.

He turned terrified eyes towards the ceiling… O'Leary stood over him, his face strangely lacking in emotion in the halo of the sterile glow of the strip lights bleeding through his auburn hair. 'What a shame yer had ta foind dat,' O'Leary said, his voice now slurring broad Irish. 'Ah can't very well be lettin' you leave. Dat would give moi boy problems, an ah can't let dat happen. Wrong place, wrong time.'

O'Leary produced a foot-long, glinting chef's knife from somewhere behind his back, raised it lazily and swung it with conviction like a falling pendulum into the man's chest, pinning the hand he attempted to defend himself with to his kicking heart.

The man simpered, slid to the ground, and began to struggle: struggled to escape; struggled to draw breath; struggled to comprehend why the course of his day had deviated so badly.

Slick films of crimson plasma pumped from around the blade past the back of his hand, his life emptying onto the tiled floor around him like an expanding mat of death, staining his worn, grey suit cherry black.

'Sorry, mate,' O'Leary said through his deadpan face, 'you just got in the way, that's aaall. Loik I said, wrong place, wrong time. No haard feelings.'

TWENTY-ONE

'YOU OKAY, NOW?' Gutteridge asked.

Keaton sat in the passenger seat looking humbled by the whole experience. The predominately wooded scenery flashed past her side window, trees and hedgerows stuttering in and out of view like a linear zoetrope.

The sun made a rare appearance in a sky that was otherwise empty, save for the chem-trail-blazing planes that criss-crossed the cyan backdrop to the beauty of nature, its nuclear brilliance burning through the fanning clusters of leaves that spring had brought forth.

But in her now permanently damaged mind, she couldn't see any of it as relevant, or important, at least not important enough to give a shit.

'It doesn't feel real,' she said, mewing the words like a child forced to face loss for the first time.

'Brings it home, doesn't it?' Gutteridge said.

'Yes… it does.'

'You'll be all right. Give it time.'

Gutteridge had dropped Ewelina off at her flat before collecting Keaton, and he checked his phone for follow-up messages, but there were none.

He wondered if she might be upset, and who would blame her if she was? But she'd seemed genuinely understanding about yet another interruption to two stumbling attempts at normal life. But surely, it must have upset her, mustn't it? *Why coppers marry coppers*, Gutteridge thought.

'Everything all right?' Keaton asked.

'Hm? Oh. Yeah,' he said, forcing a smile. 'I was just contemplating calling Bryant and giving him an update.'

He scrolled to Bryant's number, and called it…

The phone rang twice before it was answered. 'Bryant.'

Gutteridge could hear the faint rush of wind and the monophonic drone of tyres through the earpiece. 'It's Gutteridge.'

'Hey, Pat. So how did it go?'

'Horrific. We think it's the Peek boy, but Carl wants to make certain that the body is his too, just in case it belongs to one of the others who are missing.'

'What do you mean?'

'The *head* belongs to Peek, we're pretty sure of that, and we assume the body and the entrails do too. But we need to do checks of course, just to be absolutely certain.'

The phone hung silent. 'So, they're not– *Jeeesus!*'

'Yeah… it's… it's grim,' Gutteridge empathised.

'Where are you now?' Bryant asked.

'We've left. Hoegen arrived just as we were finishing our sweep of the scene. He, Carl, and the SOCOs are going to do their thing, process the entire area. They don't need us stamping around destroying the evidence any more than uniform already have. It'll take a few days to be thorough though. The coroner's truck was stood by too, ready to take the remains, but I have a feeling he's going to be stood around for a good while yet; Carl seemed determined he won't miss a thing. They're going to get the body down and begin the autopsy ASAP, not that they'll be needing a scalpel!'

Disquiet on the phone again. 'We can't keep it from the press any longer. Not now. Not with this,' Bryant said.

Gutteridge shook a head Bryant couldn't see. 'Nope. Kerry Marston from the *Echo* was just arriving as we left. We managed to dodge her, but I assume the internet channels will begin firing on all cylinders, and it won't be long before the nationals are speeding over here – if they're not already.'

'You're probably right. Are you okay?' Bryant asked.

'Yeah, I'm fine. *We're* fine. Keaton was a bit shook up at first, but she's good now. It's fair to say *neither* of us have seen anything quite this sick before.' He delivered a smile across to Keaton. The second time he'd presented that lie.

'I'll be back myself in a few hours,' Bryant explained, 'but I doubt there's much to be done until tomorrow?'

'Nope, not till tomorrow, give Carl the room he needs. You should have stayed up there, enjoy the Lakes for one more day.'

'Nahhh,' Bryant responded, dismissively. 'Lianne's mother was getting on my tits. Glad to get away if I'm honest. Li's coming back with them at the end of next week. Peace, quiet, and a nice glass of Talisker single malt, that's what I'll be doing with the rest of my day, before the shit-show begins in earnest tomorrow.'

Gutteridge huffed a smile. 'Sounds good. Well, enjoy your afternoon of freedom. I'll fill you in tomorrow, and interview the woman who discovered the body, see if she might be in need of counselling. She seemed pretty shook up. Oh, and I've also warned the rest of team that this might be the last weekend they get to spend with their families for a while, *assuming* the budget gets agreed, that is.'

'It's agreed!' Bryant insisted, nearly cutting him off.

'Right. Okay,' Gutteridge responded, acknowledging the importance woven into the instant response. 'I'll get Jane home, and I'll see you tomorrow.'

'Okay. Bye.'

'Bye, sir.' Gutteridge dropped the phone from his ear and swiped it off. Keaton looked unsettled. 'You all right?' Gutteridge asked.

She sighed... 'I'm just not sure I can be alone right now? Not with the images of that... that... *child* floating around my brain...'

'I know. Well, I could drop you off somewhere else if you'd like? A friend's maybe?'

She drew in a despairing breath and loosed it. 'I don't really have any of them, at least none that don't have swarms of sprogs charging around their legs like roaches, and I'd struggle to handle that more than the loneliness.'

'Hm, you're probably right there,' he said, craning a look out of the side window and indicating to join the roundabout that led to Quedgeley... 'Well. You could come over to mine, if you like? I'm not sure I could stand too much of my own company, either.'

Keaton turned her pretty blue eyes his way and looked strangely coy. 'Erm. Okay,' she shrugged, a smile licking at her cerise lips, 'but only if you don't mind.'

He smirked. 'Of course I mind, you're a massive inconvenience. But let's do it anyway...'

*

Jane Keaton had never before been inside Gutteridge's cottage, she'd only ever seen it from the outside, and as they approached the eggshell-blue panelled door, she wondered if the decor inside would match the chocolate box exterior.

Rambling roses – just coming into bloom – embellished the olde-worlde facade, creating contradictory highlights of blood red and the purest of whites that peppered the cotstone exterior. A far cry from the modern semi where she lived, and she found herself harbouring the faintest of pangs of jealousy.

'It's a lovely place, Pat.'

He turned an appreciative smile back to the compliment as he fumbled for his keys. 'Thank you. The bloody place takes up most of my spare time, but it's worth it – I guess. A place like this can sometimes be more of a hobby than a home, a bit like owning a classic car, I suppose.' He turned his attention back to the windows watching their approach, reassessing his own forgotten appreciation for his efforts through Keaton's exploratory gazes. The place did look good: quaint and idyllic, a look that wouldn't appear out of place in a Walt Disney movie.

Gutteridge slipped the key in the lock, opened the door and stepped aside, swinging an invitational arm to Keaton to pass inside. She smiled up at him as she accepted the offer.

She still seemed to be displaying a back-foot demeanour after nearly blacking out at the crime scene. It had embarrassed her, and she'd found the whole experience humbling, making her feel more like a newbie than the time-served detective she was.

But Gutteridge's almost fatherly understanding had put her at ease, another trait to add to the ever-growing list of things she found attractive about the man, right beneath – his cottage.

She stepped into a small, narrow hallway lined with tech-fabric jackets and boots caked in mud. Gutteridge – it seemed – was an avid gardener, and far more outdoorsy than his suits would have suggested. Something – to her mind – that wasn't instantly apparent.

Gutteridge's eyes and ears were scanning for sights or sounds of Ewelina's presence. He *had* taken her home, but she was proving to be quite the spontaneous one, and it wasn't outside the bounds of possibility to think that she might have decided to take a taxi back to surprise him. But after a few moments' listening, he could hear nothing.

There were three doors leading off the hallway: the one ahead was open, and Keaton could see a kitchen that cut a surprisingly stylish balance between old-world charm and cutting-edge design – another surprise to flesh out the man.

The door to her immediate left led into a living room, and the one that bisected them was closed; she assumed it led to a cupboard, or a small downstairs cloakroom.

The air smelled strangely fragrant, herbs mixed with spices indicative of a delicatessen, and a smoky, woody atmosphere that comes from a home with an open fireplace. She considered she would very much like to live here.

'Come on through,' he said, slipping off his coat and hanging it with the others. He motioned to take her jacket, and she complied with a temperate smile, and it joined his coat on a shared hook. But she kept her bag with her and carried it through into the living room.

Two large and inviting Chesterfields sat at right angles to each other, with one directly facing the cavernous log fireplace, perfectly placed for group discussions.

The walls were painted a warm shade of cream, with pictures hanging at jaunty levels around the perimeter of the room, but none of them appeared to be photographs or captured memories, just unrelated works of art sharing a common wall space, tasteful and indicative of a collector with an eye, but failing to paint the picture of a man with a social life.

She felt belated embarrassment for her comments about not being an art lover, however light-heartedly they may have been delivered.

'Would you like some tea, or coffee? Or maybe something a bit stronger?'

It surprised Keaton to hear that there was alcohol in the house, knowing of the problems – according to the privately relayed words of others – she'd been instrumental in helping to solve. But she'd had a hell of a day, and the words 'something stronger, please' sat poised on her shapely lips. She delivered them, curious to see if Gutteridge would join her.

She lowered her frame politely onto the couch directly facing the fireplace and twisted to watch Gutteridge leave through an adjoining door into the kitchen. He took a half-empty bottle of Pino from the door of the fridge, a glass from the rack, and after giving the kettle an exploratory shake to check it was full, slapped it on and grabbed a mug from the cupboard.

She released her held breath and allowed a smile of considerable relief to play at the corners of her mouth.

*

Gutteridge carried the glass of Pino and a piping-hot mug of Earl Grey back into the room, and delivered the wine to a welcoming hand. 'Cheers,' he said.

'Cheers, Pat.'

He sat beside her, twisted into the corner of the buttoned leather. He took up a remote from the coffee table and pointed it at the stereo on the wall.

The CD player whirred into life, and seconds later, tastefully melodic classical music drifted from the speakers, a full complement of operatic singers taking turns to please the listeners' ears with exemplary vocal skills, reciting words Keaton felt she recognised from somewhere in her past.

'What's this?' she asked, genuinely interested in the answer, the music tugging at her soul.

'Vaughn Williams. A serenade to music.'

'It's lovely.'

'Isn't it? I only really like classical that's emotive, not the standard plinkety-plonk stuff that means nothing. Just the pieces that carry your mind away to thoughts less ventured.'

Keaton stared back at the unexpectedly poetic response. Did she actually know anything about the man she spent a majority of her waking life with?

'What?' Gutteridge asked, clocking the look.

She held the stare. Purposefully. Playfully. 'Nothing,' she said. 'It's just, people can surprise you.'

Gutteridge – now lying back in the encapsulating embrace of the cushions – rolled a look her way. 'Pleasantly?' he asked.

'Oh yeah. Very much so.'

It was now Gutteridge's turn to hold the look… He considered how attractive Keaton was, when the distractions of work weren't present to stifle his appreciation.

Her crystalline-blue eyes burned through him. Was there a look in there, somewhere, he'd not seen before?

Gutteridge's fixed gaze suddenly made Keaton's self-awareness boil. His facial features were strong, masculine, different to the slightly preened and effeminate types she'd been inexplicably seeking of late. 'A man', to put it plainly, and as lingering and potentially uncomfortable as the look he held felt, she resisted turning away.

'Would you like to sit in the garden?' he suggested. 'It's nice out now. Be a shame to waste it.'

'Yeah. Why not…'

They stood, and he led the way.

As Keaton passed a speaker, words in the music caught her ear – '*Sit, Jessica. Look how the floor of heaven is thick inlaid with patines of bright gold. There's not the smallest orb which thou behold'st, but in his motion like an angel sings, still choiring to the young-eyed cherubins.*'

'*The Merchant of Venice*!' she blurted, with an unrestrained level of triumph, as she followed Gutteridge through the patio doors into the garden. 'We did it at school.'

'Well done,' Gutteridge said. 'Act five, I believe, but don't quote me on that.'

The garden was even more of a surprise to Keaton than the house. A meandering pathway winding through clematis-woven arches and scattered pockets of seating. Raised beds and borders strewn with every abundant floral colour imaginable, somehow looking orderly but random, an air of naturalness to its contrived placement. Skilfully executed and supremely calming.

The perfumed scents hit her nose, wafted by the thermal breezes, finally clearing the meat-locker stench that had been hanging with her since leaving the crime scene.

'I've got a brook,' Gutteridge announced, sounding oddly boastful, dropping down a steep, treelined path towards the babbling sounds of running water. Keaton followed, glass of wine in tow.

'It comes up to here if it rains hard, but it's never reached the house, touch wood,' he said, indicating a place on the embankment he'd marked with a metal peg, and then extending an arm to rap his knuckles on a nearby tree trunk.

'It's lovely,' Keaton said, her voice distant, distracted. To her, this was as idyllic as it gets.

Gutteridge led her back up the steep bank by her hand to a table and chairs set on a flagstone landing. 'Jane,' he offered, drawing a seat out for her to sit.

She rounded the table, sat, and thanked him.

He rarely ever called her Jane, and it felt strangely romantic to hear him form the word with his mouth. His strong, defined mouth.

He sat opposite, took a sip of his tea, and placed the mug down on the ornate wrought-iron table sitting between them.

The sun was catching her eyes. They looked almost turquoise in this light. The resulting shadows defined her soft but vivid jawline and the recurve of her cheekbones, and Gutteridge, for the life of him, couldn't fathom this woman being single.

He shifted in his seat and considered her. 'What's wrong with you?' he asked.

Keaton frowned at the question, but sensed it woven with light-hearted intention. 'What do you mean?'

Another shift in the seat. 'I mean, what is it that's so wrong with *you*, that you can't find a man? Because whatever it is, from where I'm sitting, it certainly isn't obvious.'

She huffed a snigger. 'I'm guessing there's a compliment hidden somewhere in that question?'

'Of course,' he confirmed, 'I mean, let's face it, you're one of the most beautiful women I know, and you're funny too. Nice; kind; considerate; lovely to look at, so what's the deal?'

His warm words briefly took her breath, something that didn't escape his notice. '*Jesus*, Pat. Knock it off. Are you *trying* to make me fall for you?' she said, forcing a comical tone into her words to hide the fact that she meant it.

'Sorry,' he said, 'that's not my intention. I guess I just care.'

Keaton could finally see what the beauty with the tumbling black locks she'd seen watching from the bedroom window must see in Gutteridge, and she found herself hankering for the same, however out of bounds the possibility of *that* particular bad idea may have been.

'Would you like to stay for dinner?' he asked. 'I've got everything to make a panang with sticky rice? Or I could knock up a bolognese if you'd prefer something like that?'

She smiled inside and out. *Of course!* she thought. *He's an accomplished cook as well! Of course he is.* 'I do love a Thai,' she said, 'but I wouldn't want to be a burden.'

He laughed that off. 'You're not a burden, it'd be a pleasure to have your company.'

She'd never seen him this relaxed before, but there was a barely perceptible spark of excitement illuminating his chestnut eyes that she found herself hoping had meaning…

'Okay,' she agreed. 'But only if you're sure. That would be lovely…'

*

Keaton sat at a tastefully laid dinner table, and leaned forwards to savour the jasmine undertones drifting from the dish of rice placed before her.

The wine was having the desired calming effect on her shredded nerves, and the events of the day had taken on a surreal air that had transpired to push them away from a reality she wished to deny.

Gutteridge returned to the table brandishing another basin. The rich smell of the panang filled the cottage. He placed it down and smiled at Keaton's appreciative gazes as she watched him serve.

'Smells amazing,' she said, as he scooped a serving spoon into each dish.

'Let's hope it tastes it, eh?' he grinned.

He thought about lighting a candle, but decided it could send the wrong messages, or more accurately, send messages that threatened to show too much of the subconscious desires that he was having to fight to hide.

He took to the seat facing Keaton, and paddled a hand to invite her to make a start…

Keaton allowed herself to relax into the evening, removing her waistcoat and unbuttoning her blouse just shy of her small but pert cleavage, not an action made with any real intention in mind, but the change, although subtle, had an undoubted effect on the only man in the room.

'So, what's this girl's name, again?' Keaton asked, passing the question off as small talk as she spooned rice onto her plate.

'Girl...?' Gutteridge asked. 'Oh... you mean Eve?'

'Eve. That's it. Nice name. She's very beautiful,' Keaton added.

Gutteridge froze a look through the rising curtains of steam lifting from the food, directed at Keaton's questionable intentions at bringing Eve into the conversation. He attempted to read the room. 'She is... *as* are you.'

Keaton stopped spooning. 'I am?'

A pause... 'Yes. Well, you know you are.'

'Relevance?' she asked.

A shrug. A shake of the head. 'I don't know? I can't... I guess... I just thought you should know.'

The room fell still and silent, save for the spitting of the logs in the fireplace. 'Are you trying to make me fall for you, again?' Keaton asked, in the same, playful undertone as before.

At that moment – to Gutteridge – Keaton looked as attractive as any woman he had ever laid eyes on, and his ability to resist – such that it was – was crumbling. *But would that be wise?* he thought. *But do I even care?* The answer – in the darkening light of a world where a child can't play without fear of being murdered – was *no*.

'If I *was* trying to seduce you, is it working?' he asked.

Keaton felt her stomach roll and her skin tingle. 'It might be.'

'Just *might*?'

Keaton was still holding the serving spoon, poised motionless like a mannequin above the untouched bowl of panang sauce.

Gutteridge sat back out of the conversation. 'I can't do this. *We* can't do this, it wouldn't be wise.'

Keaton lifted an almost imperceptible shrug. 'What? Potentially complicating our lives in a way that we might end up regretting?'

'Yes. Is that *seriously* what we'd want to do?'

Another telepathic shrug. 'Probably not.' She followed suit, and sat back from the core of the conversation, shifting a tilted look his way. 'Have you ever thought of me in… in *that* way before?'

He lowered his fork onto his plate. 'Of course I have. It would be impossible not to. I mean, you're not only lovely to be with, you look amazing, and we spend a third of our lives together, and *that* is exactly why it would be a terrible idea.'

She smiled regretfully. 'I guess you're right. You're always right. Still, I care for you, and I want you to know that.'

'I know you do, and I you. And although I'm right, and I *am* right,' he added, 'believe me, I truly wish I wasn't, and *that* is what's dangerous.' Gutteridge smiled, and rose from his seat, dropping his scrunched napkin onto his chair.

He rounded the table to Keaton's side, lifted the bottle of Pino from the cooler, and topped up Keaton's glass.

Keaton stretched up and delivered a gentle peck to the side of his cheek. Gutteridge turned to the show of affection as she sat again. 'Thank you for tonight,' she said, her voice soft, 'it's helped a lot.'

He flinched the subtlest of smiles, his eyes lost in thought. 'It has been nice, seeing you out of work. We should do it again.'

Keaton's lower lids licked at the coronas of her electric-blue irises in contemplation. 'I'm not so sure we should.'

Gutteridge's brows darkened, then brightened again. He laughed. 'Perhaps you're right… Come on. Tuck in. Eat before it gets cold.'

TWENTY-TWO

GUTTERIDGE LAY AWAKE for much of the night before finally drifting off to sleep, head resting on his folded arm.

He woke with his hand lying lightly across Jane Keaton's ribcage, the ball of his thumb resting against her diaphragm. He could hear and feel her breathing, and found it comforting, if a little perverted. She'd barely stirred, sleeping on her back the whole time, which Gutteridge remembered reading in some psychology journal indicated someone at peace with themselves.

He'd offered her the spare room for the night, which she'd accepted, but in the confusion of chit-chat and reminiscences about childhood memories and past relationships, they'd ended up sleeping in the same bed – his – and it had taken every ounce of willpower to not let things go further. But sleep is all they'd shared, apart from, maybe, relief?

Keaton stirred and woke with a stretch.

Gutteridge slid his voyeuristic hand politely from her body. She reached across and took it, and placed it back on her stomach. 'I don't mind,' she said, smiling at him through morning eyes. 'It's nice to be held. I miss it.'

Gutteridge stuttered in the moment, loins stirring to the feeling of her flexing ribcage. 'I know, but—'

'Hey,' she cut in, 'I'd probably be offended if you didn't want to hold me.'

He blinked and smiled appreciatively towards the welcome display of social realism, rare in such a modern world. 'Okay.'

She had on his Depeche Mode T-shirt. It hung like a nightgown from her sylphlike frame. She looked adorable.

'What time is it?' she asked.

'Early yet, about 5:30, I think?' He lifted his head from the pillow to glance at the clock. '5:36,' he said, correcting his estimation.

'I slept like the veritable log,' she said.

'That'll be the wine…' he suggested. 'You had half a bottle.' It was now his time to stretch. 'Would you like a cup of tea to help clear it?'

She smiled at the offer. 'That would be lovely. If you're sure.'

He turned to shuffle from the bed. 'Hey,' she said, stopping him mid-flow.

He turned back, resting on his elbow. 'What?'

She peered into his eyes, looking from one to the other, then lifted a kiss to his lips. Her mouth felt soft, warm, pillowy, and he thought his head was going to explode. 'Thank you,' she said. 'Yesterday was a real struggle for me, you really helped.'

He mirrored her gratitude. 'Glad I could be of assistance…'

*

Gutteridge pulled in to drop Keaton off at her house. She was to dart inside to quickly change and reapply her make-up, not wishing to arrive at the station in Gutteridge's car, and do the walk of shame in the clothes she'd had on the day before, make-up patched up only from what she happened to have in her bag.

The station itself was a vocal conduit highly adept at passing gossip, a whispering superconductor, and she didn't want to do anything that might risk fuelling it.

'I'll see you there,' Gutteridge said, stooping a glance through the open door. Keaton bowed a smile, nodded, and pushed the door shut quietly with her hip to avoid waking the road's certified curtain-twitchers.

Gutteridge watched her saunter to her front door, shapely hips swinging to the rhythm of her femininity, thoughts of what it would have been like to 'let things go too far' at the forefront of his mind.

She turned a pensive, blue-eyed smile back at him from the front door, turned the key, and made her way inside…

*

The station was humming to the news of the discovered body, pockets of gossip fizzing to the excitement of having a real-life serial killer at large in their district.

For many, it was their first involvement with any such case, a far cry from the random stabbings, hit-and-run cases, or assisting in insurance-fraud claims. *This* is what it was about. *This* is what attracted most to 'the job' in the first place, and it was actually happening, now, to their confusing mixture of dismay and excitement.

A briefing had been called for 9:00, and all relevant officers assembled in the incident room, their faces expectant but anxious, and in some cases, strangely elated.

Keaton drifted into the room like smoke and inconspicuously took a seat close to the front.

Gutteridge – standing at the head of the room watching the troops assemble – caught her eye. She took a quick look about to check for prying eyes, then sent a knowing smile his way. He responded with just a blink as all eyes were on him, with Bryant hovering close behind.

A large screen had been set up behind Gutteridge, a file of images from the Jayden Peek crime scene sitting at the ready on a laptop.

The hum of the room succumbed the weight of Gutteridge's gaze. Animated talk of the case, or the weekend exploits of the younger members of the team, petered off until silence remained.

'Thank you,' Gutteridge said. 'Now, we know why we're all here. The first body surfaced yesterday morning, Sunday May 3rd. Myself and DS Keaton attended the site, along with Carl McNamara, Gustav Hoegen, and a team from CSI. Uniform secured the location, which is the viaduct at Stroud, just a short distance from the A419. I know some of you know it, if not, look it up on a map.'

He took a moment to consult his sheets. 'The body was discovered by a Mrs Janet Dando, at approximately 07:20 hours, the call being made from her mobile to emergency services and logged at 07:27. We have a transcript of that entire conversation. It might be worth everyone having a read of it.'

Gutteridge noticed the screensaver on the laptop flash up, and swiped to remove it.

He continued. 'The forensic team will carry on processing the scene today, then uniform will step in to help sweep the entire area: footprints; items of clothing; anything that may have been dropped – the usual.' He turned his attention to his phone and swiped to an open browser window set to Met Office weather. 'Rain is forecast for later today, about 15:00 to 16:00. So time is of the essence. I'll be sending a few of you over after this to assist forensics, help gather what we can before it's all washed away, and maybe peg tarps over certain areas of interest to try to preserve them.'

He turned morose. 'Now, we have pictures from the scene,' he said, indicating the screen behind with his pen. 'If anyone here has had a heavy weekend, or doesn't feel up to it for any reason, step out now, or avert your eyes, because, to put it mildly, these images are fucking grim! In my twenty-odd years on the job, *I* have never seen anything like this!'

No one stood. No one turned away. A room of interests fuelled by morbid curiosity looked on with pregnant fascination. Gutteridge would have been disappointed if anyone had stood to leave, so was pleased.

He turned his attention to the laptop, and with an unsteady breath, opened the file...

The whole room rocked back from the screen in unison, a lilting groan of shock warming the air.

A voice from the back of the room hissed the word '*cunt!*' Koperek released a fluttering groan like she'd taken a kick to the stomach, and all onlookers squirmed in their seats.

Gutteridge turned a brief look over his shoulder to the horrific reminder of the events of the previous day, then with a swallow, turned away again. 'As you can see, the body has been heavily mutilated.' He tapped the slide show function on the laptop, and the images began to shuffle through the portfolio of a deranged mind. 'Carl has confirmed that all body parts at the location came from Jayden Peek, including his...' He paused to swallow back the stomach acid that was climbing his throat. '...his genitals, which had been removed. They were found in his mouth, which had been sewn shut!'

Keaton felt light-headed again. She wasn't usually this squeamish, but *this* was a kid. *This* was a child, for heaven's sake, and that fact alone put a whole new spin on it. She realised her hand was clasped across her womb again, and quickly removed it.

Gutteridge paused the slide show on one of the images and indicated an area of the screen using a ruler as a makeshift pointer. 'There's a hole in the back of the skull, almost certainly the cause of death, and originally thought to have been made by something like a pickaxe, as the hole is thought too large to have been made by the usual size of bullet, and there's no apparent exit wound that you would expect to find with such a large-calibre weapon. But according to the preliminary examinations, the presence of some form of localised GSR fanning from the entry wound would seem to indicate the possible use of a device called a captive bolt gun, which is an instrument used in the humane killing of cattle.' He allowed himself an ironic *huff* at the word 'humane'. 'But until we have the full report on our desks, all we can do at this point is pour conjecture on the possible causes of such a wound. So have a good look at the images. No theories of what may or may not have caused such a wound would be considered too ludicrous to contemplate at this point, so don't be shy at coming forwards.'

Keaton raised her hand. Gutteridge nodded. 'Jane?'

The use of 'Jane' instead of 'Keaton' in front of the team made her pause briefly, and it didn't go unnoticed. Bryant's brow furrowed.

'Erm, yeah. I was thinking, I know McWilliams has been scanning the web for Tick-Tock-related leads, with art predominantly the key component of the search. But it might be worth refocusing the search more down the line of animal rights, you know, extreme content: carne-haters; die-hard vegans or vegetarians; that sort of thing?'

Gutteridge dropped eyes to ponder the suggestion. 'Not a bad idea. Ian, could you get onto that? I know you've probably got square eyes from all of this, but...'

'Aye. That wunna be a problem, there might be something in it. I've pretty much come up with a blank with the Tick-Tock thing, so a new direction might not be a bad idea.'

'Okay. Good,' Gutteridge said. 'Anyone else?'

Parker stood tentatively. 'I found a few clips of what seems to be the same make and model of van patrolling the areas where the children were reported missing. It does look to be white, or white-*ish* in colour, like the Wragg boy said he saw. There's no markings or sign-writing apparent in the footage, it looks plain. It invariably seems to be dark during the times when it's patrolling, so the footage is grainy, and there's no way of making out a number plate, but it looks like the make and model is a Vauxhall Vivaro.'

'Okay. That's a start. Can you do a search of all regional owners of white or off-white Vivaros, say in a ten-mile radius of Gloucester to start with, and begin ticking them off.'

'I've already started. DVLA are assisting, compiling a list as we speak.'

'Good,' Gutteridge said, 'very good. Also, the fact that this guy seems to be stalking his victims at night – assuming this van is his – might simply be because he's intelligent enough to work under the cover of darkness, but it might also be because he has a job to go to, so let's compile a full log of the times and locations of all these sightings. Something to refer to later if we ever get a suspect in custody.'

'Yes, sir,' Parker said, taking to his seat again.

'So, what have we got so far?' Gutteridge asked the room rhetorically. 'Our perp is a male, probably young, or relatively young – you'd have to be pretty fit and strong to carry a dead weight like that up a ladder and string it up. He might be Irish, or of Irish descent. Maybe he works on a farm, or has access *to* a farm, or possibly even a slaughterhouse, to use or steal this captive bolt gun thing. Actually, contact all known farms and slaughterhouses in the area, see if there have been any burglaries. Specifically, see if anyone is missing one of these gun things. Also, it might be worth touching base with all of the art colleges and fine-art unis, see if any of them have had a student they remember being particularly unstable, or extreme in their views.'

'I'll take that,' said Koperek.

The door on Gutteridge's left shoulder crept apologetically open, and Tamara – DCI Bryant's PA – stepped tentatively inside the room and indicated to Bryant she needed a word. Her look was sullen.

Bryant ducked into the corridor and pulled the door partially closed. The words echoing through the gap seemed monophonic and serious.

Bryant's head dropped. He sagged visibly. The whole room watched, deathly silent save for the hum of the muttered conversation.

He placed a touch to Tamara's shoulder, nodded, and turned back into the room. The look on his face spoke volumes; whatever it was, was bad.

He levelled a look at Gutteridge's waiting eyes and shook a pessimistic head.

'What is it?' Gutteridge asked.

Bryant stood static in the doorway, breathing long breaths, his map defused with a look of dejection and disbelief... 'Another body, Forest of Dean, near Cinderford.'

'What?' Gutteridge hissed.

'A body. Someone's found another body!'

'Another one, already! A child?'

'No, an adult this time. A man. Naked. Crucified. It has to be our guy?'

The whole room took a break from reality, mouths hanging wide.

'*Crucified?* How? To what?'

'A tree.'

'*Fuck!* This is getting out of hand,' Gutteridge slurred.

Bryant nodded. 'The press are going to have a fucking field

day! Apparently, there's a throng already gathering at the main doors downstairs.'

'We should make a statement,' Gutteridge said. 'Do you want to do it, or should I?'

Bryant forced an insipid smile. 'I can do that, you get over to Cinderford, that's far more important. I'll come over and take a look when I'm done.'

Gutteridge nodded. 'Yes, sir...'

The briefest of thoughts of the stiffest of drinks and a fat, finely chopped, nose-stinging line of coke flashed into Gutteridge's thoughts; he pushed it away again. 'Okay! Peters, Koperek, McWilliams, you crack on. The rest of you, get yourselves over to Stroud to help in the sweep. And if you encounter any press, please, for Christ's sake, say nothing.'

Another thought snuck in through the back door of his mind, of Eve, of her eyes, of her toned, hard body like pliable granite writhing beneath his, and the sweet taste of her breath off her ruby-red lips. He allowed that thought to linger, fuelled by guilt. He needed to call her...

TWENTY-THREE

THE NAKED BODY OF A MAN HUNG in grotesquely demeaning posture from a tree, arms out wide like the Angel of the North, wrists nailed to branches spreading from the main trunk like a crucifix. The perpetrator had obviously spent time choosing a tree that suitably resembled the biblical abomination, and he'd chosen well.

Hemp rope looped a friction-scalded neck, forcing a blackened tongue from the mouth like a tarred tennis ball. The rope had been tied off to higher branches, and Gutteridge had to assume that was how the body had been hoisted the full eight feet that it was from the ground, looking out over a circular clearing in the woods, lording over the world it had left behind.

The word 'MARTYR' had been carved down the elongating body, legs stained purple from the pooling of the blood.

The feet, too, had been nailed unceremoniously to the tree, and Gutteridge had passed at least two puddles of vomit on the approach to the scene.

'Do we know who he is, yet?' Gutteridge asked Carl McNamara, who was approaching to intercept his and Keaton's arrival. He unmasked and stretched his mouth wide to enjoy the fresh air.

'No… no ID, or clothes, or cars left unaccounted for in the immediate area. But I don't think anyone has actually begun checking the missing persons log, not as yet anyway, but let's be honest, it's hard to even know what this guy looks like until we get him down, his face is so distorted from the pressure of the ligature.'

Keaton's gaze was glued to the grotesque monstrosity polluting the purity of the surrounding woodland. 'So, that must mean he was brought here, and not someone who was here already, then killed; unless someone who happened upon him did this, then took his car? But how would the killer have got here himself?' she said, her mind working overtime, and speaking her musings allowed. 'No,' she said, 'he *must* have been brought here. It's a body dump. An elaborate one, but a body dump all the same.'

Gutteridge considered the carved 'MARTYR' again. 'This feels like the same guy, but why kill an adult, now? Why the change in MO?'

'I think the word "Martyr" might have some relevance here,' suggested Carl.

Keaton piped in. 'Maybe this guy was involved in this mess in some way, an accomplice perhaps? And maybe our perp had to off him for some reason, and that's why he's been tagged as a martyr? A martyr to the cause, maybe?'

'Fuck knows,' Gutteridge griped, 'but that would kind of fit. But until we know who he is, we're just guessing.'

'Hey!' a voice shouted, with an air of triumph, excited and softly Dutch. 'Look!'

It was Hoegen, looking animated from atop his ladder. He began climbing down holding something. 'Get an evidence bag,' he said.

He reached the bottom rung and stepped around another CSI who was taking casts of imprints in the soil.

Carl stepped to his case, pulled out a fresh tamper-evident bag, checked it for tears, and opened it up. He presented it to Hoegen.

'What is it?' Gutteridge asked, leaning in cautiously to look, alive to the fact that he wasn't yet masked, gloved or suited.

'It's another torn-off piece of that clingfilm, the same as I found stuck to the mural above the courthouse. It was snagged on the stub of a broken branch up there,' he said, indicating a point high in the tree. 'I photographed where. It looks and feels the same as the other. I did some research. Household clingfilm tends to be around 10mu, *this*, is closer to 20. It's a more industrial grade. At first, I thought maybe a pallet wrap? But, no, it feels too flimsy for that. But it might be for industrial food use?'

Carl's mind drifted off to another place entirely. He turned his eyes to the tree, and the body nailed indignantly to it. 'I had a case once, before I moved to the Gloucester Division. A prolific burglar we could never find evidence on was finally caught in the act, and when they brought him in, he was entirely wrapped head to toe in clingfilm,' he said, lifting his chin to the evidence bag. 'That's how he was preventing leaving evidence behind. I wonder if our guy's doing the same sort of thing? Because I'll level with you, it's fucking unusual, and deeply frustrating for me not to find anything of use at a crime scene, especially ones as "wet" as these are.'

'I know it is,' Gutteridge said, 'and no one's thinking anything of it, and if he *is* wrapping himself like you said, that would account for it, right?'

'Right.'

'Well, that, in my book, is evidence, old friend.'

Carl smiled his appreciation for Gutteridge's attempt at delivering consoling words.

'Oh!' Carl suddenly remembered, like someone had jabbed him with a fork. 'I found a knife wound to his chest, and a defensive wound to his right hand, and they look like they might marry up to the same blow, if you assume the arm was held high and folded at the elbow,' he explained, demonstrating with his own arm. 'They're hard to see because of the coagulated blood around the nail, and the carvings to the chest, but it looks – on first inspection – to have been done with a chef's style knife, or at least something very similar.'

'...*and* it was upside down when it went in,' added Hoegen. 'The cutting edge at the top. Very unusual.'

Carl took up the baton again. 'Our victim may have been lying down, with our perp at his head end when the blade went in? I reckon the piercing through the hand was a defensive wound, and it sliced through his palm before entering his body, effectively pinning the hands to his chest. I'll check the angle of insertion when I'm back at the mortuary, but it seems to fit, but either way, it must have been done with considerable force.'

The word 'slice' caused a muscular spasm to tug at Gutteridge's groin.

'The pooling,' Hoegen said, directing the words to Carl.

Carl reanimated again. 'Ah. Yes. There's slight lividity around the area of the back and the buttocks,' he said, indicating where on Hoegen, who'd turned his back on Carl to assist in the explanation, 'but mostly in the legs, as you can see. It would suggest to me that the body was lying on the ground, or propped up, seated in a corner somewhere for a short time before it was moved here and strung up for the world to see. That would almost certainly indicate that he was killed prior to this outrage,' he said, flicking a finger towards the body. 'But whatever that length of time was, it wasn't very long, or the pooling to the back would have been more pronounced. I'd say the victim was killed sometime in the last twelve or twenty-four hours.'

Keaton wandered from the group, leaving them to their theorising, drawn forwards by a desire to face her revulsion of the crucified corpse. The uniformed officers encircling the patch of open ground watched.

She forced herself to come to terms with the true horror of the scene; she had to, this was all new to her, and it threatened to end her career *if* she couldn't learn to deal with it.

Her stomach churned, flipped and folded as her gaze addressed the corpse. Wandering eyes fronting sights alien to a majority of the population, except those deemed privileged enough to witness such unthinkable horror.

Should that feel special? she wondered, because right now, gazing up at the blackened tongue protruding from the blue lips; the deep, carved humiliation; the elongated neck; the blood-red eyes ballooning from the pressure of the rope they hung from, it certainly didn't feel it.

But she hadn't fainted; she hadn't swooned; and she'd held the impulse to vomit deep in the core of her flexing larynx. Slowly, and methodically, she came to terms with the sight before her.

A lesson learned – detachment. Cold, stonewalling detachment. And that – in the scheme of all that was happening around her – at least made that small but crucial part of her happy.

Gutteridge's phone hummed in his pocket. He took it out to see who it was. It was Bryant. He answered it. 'Go ahead, sir.'

'I'm on my way over, is it him?'

'We think so, it has to be related, even if not directly. We think this might simply be someone who got in the way of his plans, but at this point, that's just theory.'

'I'll accept your judgment on that. The press are getting frisky on this, clamouring for info. It's already on the national news channels. Listen, we need to get the Dando woman in for interview, can you do that this afternoon?'

'Dando? Is she the one that found the body of the Peek kid?'

'Yes.'

Gutteridge consulted his Tag Heuer – it had just gone midday. 'Anytime from three o'clock onwards?' Gutteridge suggested.

'Call Tamara, see if she can set that up. Oh! And we've had a slightly bizarre call from a Father Dylan. He's the priest, or the rector, or whatever these people are referred to,' he said, slightly dismissively, 'at the St Peter's Church in town. He says he wants to speak to someone in charge of the case. I don't know why, but it sounded like he thought that what he had to say was important. I think that should be you, you're more versed in the facts of the case than I am. Maybe you could go and see him after you've interviewed the Dando woman?'

'Of course, sir. Sounds like a plan, I'll pencil it in.'

He dropped the phone from his ear and looked about for Keaton. She was still standing in the clearing staring at the body like it was a drive-in movie cinema screen, and the film that it was reflecting back at her was inherently intriguing.

He walked up behind her, placing a gentle hand on her shoulder. She jumped slightly at the unexpected pressure and broke from her stare. 'Sorry, sir.'

'Getting used to it yet?' he asked.

'I… I am… it's funny, and a bit disquieting, but you *can* build a wall, can't you?'

'You can, and you have to, else we couldn't possibly do the job for any length of time without…' He petered off.

'… without turning to drink and drugs?' Keaton suggested, finishing his sentence, looking back at him over her shoulder, her body still fronting the corpse, eyes full of knowing.

He huffed a smile in response. 'Indeed.'

'I'm glad you beat it, sir,' she said, 'you're too good to end up washed out.'

He smiled. 'Listen, can you walk this with Carl and Hoegen? I have to go and interview the Dando woman.'

She flushed, insecure. Gutteridge noticed. 'You've got this, Jane. You're an excellent detective, so push aside those doubts. Walk the scene, try and channel our perp: his movements; his motivations; his *perversions*. See what he sees. Feel what he feels; and write it all down. Okay?'

Keaton drew in and exhaled a full lungful of breath. 'Okay,' she agreed, 'it'll be good for me.'

'That's a girl,' he smiled, realising too late how patronising that must have sounded. 'I'll see you back at the station. Actually, call me when you're done here, I'm seeing a Father Dylan after the Dando woman, he might have something of interest regarding the case, so if you're done by then, we can go together. I'll pick you up.'

She spun on her heels, armed with her new-found acceptance of the unthinkable terrors the human psyche was truly capable of, and began walking the scene…

TWENTY-FOUR

DS KEATON DROPPED into the bolstered leather sports seat of the black Saab, thanking Gutteridge for leaning across and popping the door for her.

'Thanks for coming to pick me up,' she said, 'it's a long way for you to have come.' She settled in and belted up. 'How was she?' she asked.

'The Dando woman? She was fine. Cried some, but that's understandable, given the circumstances.'

'Scarred for life?'

Gutteridge lifted his shoulders. 'Probably. But time should go some way to healing that. At least that's the hope.'

'Anything of use come out of it? Anything we can work with?'

Gutteridge pulled his belt out, and clipped in. 'Not really. Just an explanation of how she happened upon the body.'

'I can't imagine how that felt,' Keaton said, peering out of the side window. 'It was bad enough seeing it when I knew what was coming. But imagine being out walking your dog, then turning a corner to find, *that!*'

Gutteridge flashed his brows in agreement. 'Actually, no, I *can't* imagine it. Oh! There was one thing. I think she might have seen our guy?'

'Really? You're shitting me. When?'

'About three weeks before she found the body, which actually, would tally up with my tests.'

Keaton's brows crimped closer. 'Tests?'

'Yeah. Remember the screws had a dusting of rust where the nickel coatings had scuffed off? Well, I scuffed some similar screws in the same way back at home and left them undercover in a leafy part of my garden, a similar environment to the viaduct arches, and already there's a light coating of rust, and if you compare them to how rusted the viaduct screws were, it looks like an extra two weeks in those same kind of atmospheric conditions will create comparable results. It certainly takes a lot longer than just one night.'

'Did she give a description?'

Gutteridge see-sawed his head. 'Yes, and no. He had on a hoody, and was up steps, drilling holes in the arch with a yellow battery drill. A DeWalt, I assume, but they're too popular and widespread a brand for that to be of any real use to us. He had on gloves, too, and it was late, about nine, or nine-thirty at night, according to her, so it was dark.'

'Didn't she think it was weird, some random guy drilling holes in the bridge?'

'Viaduct, and yes. But apparently, he said he was from a firm of civil engineers, and he was installing sensors to measure possible movement in the structure. He claimed it was his last job of the day, and he had to get it done, so she thought nothing more of it. Oh, and get this, she said he had a slight Irish accent.'

'Fuck! So, McWilliams was right. It *must* have been him.'

'She's lucky,' Gutteridge said, 'he could have decided to kill her there and then, just for seeing him.'

'Maybe. But that would have seriously fucked with his plans for the grand unveiling of his latest piece,' Keaton said with a flamboyant waft of the hand.

Gutteridge signalled and turned right onto the A40 towards Gloucester.

'Any idea of age?'

'She reckoned mid-thirties. And something else she said was curious: she told me when he moved, it sounded like he had pockets full of empty crisp packets.'

'What does that mean?'

'I don't know. But apparently, he rustled.'

Keaton frowned again. She'd done a lot of that of late. Then she recalled what Carl McNamara had said earlier. 'It couldn't have been the clingfilm thing, could it?'

Gutteridge clicked his fingers in mid-air and slapped the wheel. 'That's it! That's fucking it! Clingfilm.'

'*Damn* it! If only she'd have called it in. So fucking near,' Keaton mourned. 'He was *right there*!'

'I know, but we'll get him. At least we have confirmation of some of our hunches. He's Irish, slim, thirties. He plans ahead. He's intelligent, too.'

'How do you figure that?'

'To instantly come up with the lie about civil engineering and sensors, they're not the words of an idiot.'

'Guess you're right. Okay, so what's the deal with this priest?'

'He's called Father Dylan, but I don't actually know what he wants. He called the station and asked to talk to me, or more accurately, talk to whoever is in charge of the case. He says he has information. I guess regarding the murders? Other than that, I have no clue...'

*

Gutteridge swung open the heavy oak doors and stepped respectfully into the vestibule of St Peter's Church. Keaton followed...

He felt an urge – despite not being in any way religious – to bow his head. Years of indoctrination as a child, he assumed. But he fought the urge, and overcompensated by walking tall.

'What are you doing?' Keaton asked.

Gutteridge darted her a look. 'What do you mean?'

'You look like you have a rod up your back, or you forgot to remove the hanger from your shirt this morning?'

He tried to disguise the resulting corrective slouch within the movements of two steps forwards and a twist of the body. 'Don't know what you're talking about,' he said, unconvincingly.

She giggled. 'Whatever. *Sir*.'

He smiled with his back to her. He could definitely fall in love with this one. *If* he allowed himself to.

Father Dylan exited the vestry door, prompted by the sounds of echoing footsteps, and approached the visitors with muted enthusiasm. He extended a hand to shake.

'Father Dylan?' Gutteridge asked, paddling his hand in response. The priest nodded, taking the hand and shaking it with all the expected limpness of a man of the cloth.

'Thank you for coming,' the priest said, in a solemn voice he'd trained to be soft and unassuming. 'I was in two minds whether to speak to you, or not.'

Gutteridge cocked an eye. 'Why's that? Are you breaking a confidence by contacting us?'

The priest was visibly wrestling with his conscience. 'Yes, I– I think I am.'

'And what made you feel the urge to do that?'

'Because, the confidence I'm thinking of breaking, I believe has something to do with the recent murders that are in the news at the moment.'

Keaton and Gutteridge exchanged a look. 'Do you know who he is?' Keaton asked.

'No, but I think he might have been here.'

'When? And what for?' Gutteridge asked.

The priest consulted with his conscience again. 'I believe a man who came in here to talk in the confessional *may* have been the killer.'

'Why aren't you sure?' Keaton piped in. 'Did he not say he'd done it?'

The priest shook his head. 'No, and this was before the murders were even in the news. But after I found out about the killings and the missing children, it occurred to me that this man might have been involved.'

Gutteridge was growing slightly impatient at the slow-dripped cryptic feeding of information. 'But *what* did he actually say that made you think that?'

Keaton darted a calming look to Gutteridge; he saw it, and with a nod, took a breath. 'In your own time, Father, but can you try to tell us what it was he actually said that raised your suspicions?'

The priest took to a seat in one of the pews and tried to settle into the discomfort of breaking a sacred trust. 'This is what I'm struggling with, it's not so much *what* he said – although that is relevant – it's more *how* he said it. He sounded extremely unstable, and this didn't occur to me until after he'd left, but he, I believe the word is..."manifested"? Yes, manifested. He manifested more than one personality. And he also claimed to have killed his father?'

Gutteridge settled into a pew two in front of the priest's and twisted back to face him. 'Tell me, this man, did he have an Irish accent by any chance?'

The priest's face washed with a look of uncomfortable recognition. 'Yes. Yes, he did. But only very mild, *until*, that is, he became what I realised later must have been his father, and then it was very broad Irish, similar to my uncle who lived in Ardmore.'

'He *became* his father?' Keaton interjected.

'Yes. Well. I believe so. The "father" voice kept referring to "my boy" in relation to the *other* voice, the one I *believe* was actually his.'

Gutteridge shifted uncomfortably in his seat. 'Sorry. Are you saying this person – whoever they are – was switching personalities?'

'Yes, and that's not all. He claimed to have done things that would obviously be considered sins, but at the behest of a voice that he claimed to be that of God himself!'

'And what were these sins?'

'He didn't actually say, we never got that far. He…' The priest paused and began to shake. He swallowed. 'He – the father manifestation – threatened to cut my throat, and said that if I got involved, he would…'

Gutteridge stooped a compassionate look towards the priest. 'Go on, Father. It's okay.'

The priest took a breath. 'He said, if I got involved, the next time anyone sees me, I'll be a head in a box.'

Gutteridge straightened in his seat at the comment. Keaton, who was taking notes on the sidelines, winced visibly.

'You're doing great, Father,' Gutteridge said, caressing his words, 'and I hope you realise you've done the right thing by contacting us about this.'

The priest lifted watery eyes to Gutteridge's kindness. 'Is it him?' he asked. 'Was it the man who did these despicable things?'

Gutteridge's eyes flashed regretful. 'Yes. I think it probably was.'

The priest began to quake. 'We're taught to forgive, and to love. But how can I love a man like that? Would someone explain that to me?' A tear broke rank and meandered down his cheek.

Gutteridge reached into his inside pocket and drew out a card. 'Father. Here's my number.' He handed the card over. 'If you encounter this man again, call me.'

The priest took the card, and a tissue from his cassock, and wiped his eyes dry. He looked at the calling card with a kind of childlike diffidence. He looked pathetic and humble. Keaton wanted to hug the man, but policy and convention forbade it.

Gutteridge stood from the pew. 'Oh,' he said, turning back. 'Did you get a look at him?'

The priest shook his head, his eyes to the ground. 'No, no I didn't. At least, not a proper look. But his silhouette looked young. Late twenties or thirties.'

'And did any of these manifestations give a name?'

Again, a shake of the head, the memory of the encounter sending slow, ice-cold fingers dragging down his spine.

'The only name mentioned, was "God", and *He* had no part in anything this man has done, I can assure you of that.'

It was peculiar to the priest, almost amusing, the juxtaposition he found himself in. Thoughts that the one guiding light in his devout life had not been there to protect him in his time of need, balanced against an iron-clad desire to *believe* through fear of his encounter with evil, instilling in him a push-pull indecision where 'believe' was winning, but only just. A mockery of sorts, he considered, similar to those diagnosed as terminally ill developing a desire and a will to find 'Him', their supposed creator, who had inexplicably chosen to take them slowly, with pain and indignity, and well before their clock spring has wound down.

Gutteridge extended a compassionate touch to the man's shoulder. 'Thank you, sir. You've been a great help. We may need to take an official statement at some point, but that can wait till another day. Okay?'

The priest forced an insipid smile. 'Are you going to stop him?'

Gutteridge thought about the question for a brief moment, then decided to lie, but only in his levels of certainty. 'Yes. Yes, we are…'

TWENTY-FIVE

SPATTERING RAIN speckled off the windscreen of the cream Vauxhall Vivaro. O'Leary's back hunched over the wheel, leaning into the urgent sweep of the wiper blades, pleased that he had managed to complete his latest 'work', his latest 'piece', his latest 'message' to an ignorant world that needed prodding to make them listen, before the skies had opened and the heavens descended.

He'd been doubting the words of the voice in his head, the voice of his mentor, but now, after tonight, it was all beginning to make some sense, even if not perfect. He felt he'd turned a corner, but was he really sure?

'Did I do good?' he asked.

'You did, my Son,' came the response from the voice of wisdom. Deep, low, resonating off the tin and the hard plastics of the utilitarian interior.

O'Leary fell silent again. 'What is it, my child?' asked the voice. 'I sense a reluctance inside of your mind.'

O'Leary shook his head so slightly it threatened to be imperceptible. His eyes dropped to his lap. 'Why so young?' he asked. 'Why a child?'

'You feel a child can be absolved from blame, simply because they are perceived as innocents?'

'No. I mean, yes... I– I don't know?'

'A child wears the stains of their parents' misguidance, what better way to punish that wanton corruption of purity than to take from their bosoms the gift they chose to besmirch?'

'But, is that not unfair?' O'Leary asked.

'What *is* fair?' asked the voice. 'Is it fair to murder an animal, simply because the mouth that grins wide when it slays the beast craves the taste of the flesh whose life it denied? Is the temptation of that flesh not to be considered the same as the apple from the tree of knowledge?'

'I know, but—'

'Did my Son – my own flesh and blood, not die on the cross to absolve the sins of those who stood, and watched, and let it happen?'

'You're right. I know you're right, and it *is* an honour for me to be chosen, believe me. But... it's just sometimes, as wrong as I know it is to feel it, I find myself, enjoying the killing—'

'Shhhh... Quiet, my child... To take the young is to send the strongest message we can, and in gifting their souls to heaven so near to the seeding of their corrupted lives is to end, early, a senseless reign of tyranny and killing, a lifetime's worth of supping on the meats of the creatures they chose to disrespect.'

O'Leary considered the words of 'The One' and allowed himself to find solace in their questionable logic.

He turned the bleached-bone coloured van into a gravelled driveway. The wet pebbles looked like a million flayed skulls carpeting the floor of hell in the hot, halogen glow of the sweeping headlights.

He crunched along the path of sinners, approaching a red-brick building that had once been a working farmhouse, a lot like his childhood home, but that was now no longer alive to the calls of animals waiting their inescapable fates.

He parked in the avenue of ghosts, and the engine fell silent.

O'Leary sat absorbing the calm, welcome after the storm of the week that had been.

'Will I be considered a saint?' he asked the empty cabin.

'You already are, in my eyes, and that is all that matters, and all that *should* matter. But rest assured, my child, the world will speak of your deeds for centuries to come, long after you have left this world and you are rightfully sat on my right hand.'

O'Leary gifted himself a smile he hoped God wouldn't sense. He took up his phone and a wafer-thin carrier bag loaded with takeaway from his favourite Chinese and exited the van.

He ducked through the rain, fumbled his key into the lock of the front door and rushed inside.

The interior was a tasteful mix of pine, Victoriana and minimalistic Shaker that gave the place a country-cottage feel Nancy Lancaster herself would have found pleasing.

Tiffany-style shades and industrial lighting illuminated the high ceilings, walls lined with objects of interest from lives been and gone: jelly moulds; tapestries; barometers; pre- and post-war signage of products both still, or no longer, in production.

Red floor tiles and stained-glass panels accented the space, with strategically placed rugs to soften the echoes of voices and the treads of passing footsteps.

He shook his coat dry, hung it on one of the coiling limbs of a steamed bamboo coat rack, and made his way into the kitchen to secure cutlery.

He heard a noise, a soft clank of metal on crockery. He rounded the frame of the door to see a face turn to front him from the butler sink. 'Heyyyy, love,' the face said, fondness and gratitude in her voice and eyes. 'I didn't hear you come in.

Ahhh, thanks for doing this. I really wasn't in the mood for cooking tonight,' she said.

The female – petite but long; with vivid green eyes full of life shining from within a frame of curling brown hair; light skin that avoided the sun; clad in a Kate Bush 'Hounds for Love' T-shirt and loose-fitting sweats – approached to relieve O'Leary of his delivery and greet him. She raised a kiss to his hungry lips on balletic toes.

'Mmmmm… I've really missed you today,' she smooched, wrapping her free arm around his neck. 'I hate when you have to work late,' she whispered into his ear, as if they weren't alone.

She dropped onto her heels again and smiled into his eyes, a sexual telepathy of things to come, but later. Much later.

She turned, carrying the bag back to her preparations. 'I have plates warming in the oven,' she said. 'I'll put this out. Why don't you go through and take a load off? I'll bring it in to you.'

O'Leary hadn't yet muttered so much as a single word, but that was so often the way. He wondered what Sophie – the girl he'd met not a month after first arriving on British soil – got out of their relationship. But she'd been with him for fourteen years now, seeming to find attraction in his unassuming nature, a stark contrast to the cocksure, alpha-male types she used to encounter on a regular basis before she relocated from London. She appeared to find comfort in the knowledge that O'Leary existed and was there for her. But O'Leary felt he should at least make an effort to feed the cauldron.

'I– I had to work late to prepare more stock,' he offered in way of explanation of his late arrival, but without being prompted, 'quiches; flans; more walnut cake, that sort of thing.' The words sounded ridiculous as they rolled off his tongue, especially in the scheme of all he'd actually been doing of late in his secret, parallel life.

Sophie paused from her wrangling, stood from the breathy whir of the open oven door, and turned a look back at him with bright, but matter-of-fact eyes. 'I know,' she smiled, with a dip in her voice. But the smile seemed forced, as if delivered to pacify an insecurity she was painfully aware needed management.

She erupted back into whatever it was she was doing. And O'Leary made his way into the living room…

*

A miniature golden-haired poodle lay curled up on the far end of the chintz camelback couch. It woke as O'Leary's shadow passed across it. It stretched, stood, and padded over to greet him.

The animal turned subdued as it sniffed at the coppery tang flavouring his skin, a tang that was ingrained over time, even seemingly through the nitrile gloves and the clingfilm barrier he'd taken such meticulous efforts to adorn.

O'Leary's hand recoiled from the eager nose. He didn't want to witness the longing in the eyes of the animal for the taste of meat. That would threaten to turn his love for the creature into contempt for what he knew it truly was.

'Sit yourself down,' came an instruction entering through the door behind him. He complied, carefully shovelling the dog along to make space.

Sophie passed him a tray. 'Careful, the plate's hot,' she said, twisting a twee, theatrical smile over her coyly shrugging shoulder as she left to collect her own.

The smell of the sweet-and-sour tofu drifted into his nose, a stark contrast to the stench of refrigerated decay that had gut-punched him earlier while installing his latest 'piece'.

Sophie rounded the arm of the couch and sat to join him. 'Don't wait for me,' she chirped, but he did, and he always would. Manners: his mother's abiding gift to him, before she passed away and the path of his life deviated so negatively. It was the one thing that had made following the instructions of the god who'd chosen him as the vehicle of his message so hard to implement. But his mentor *was* the supreme being, and he'd had to learn.

O'Leary allowed the lord and master to pass into his mouth so he could share in the food. He wondered if a god, *the* god, really needed to eat, or if he simply enjoyed the taste.

'Ohhhh, *fuck!* I hate this!' Sophie said, tilting a compassionate look towards the muted television set that O'Leary hadn't even realised was on.

'What?' he asked.

'Another murder! Sick bastard!'

O'Leary watched as the latest news of his killing spree unfolded on the screen... A Rolodex of the most innocent, carefree and happy headshots of the missing or murdered flashed one after the other, then a single of the 'martyr' who'd happened upon his store and the body in the fridge. Brief texture shots of the viaduct crime scene followed, then it cut to a man, suited in grey, addressing the cameras from some hastily arranged press gathering. The caption below read – 'DCI Bryant, Gloucestershire Constabulary'.

'Turn it up,' Sophie urged, a fork load of chow mein hovering at the ready by her distracted mouth.

O'Leary reluctantly complied and took up the remote from the arm of the sofa. The orange bar climbed the side of the screen just in time to hear DCI Bryant hand over to the SIO, whatever that was?

The lens swung left and found DI Gutteridge's face, taking a moment to pull focus. His serious eyes loomed large on the screen, brows suitably wilting. The caption changed to – 'Senior Investigating Officer – DI Gutteridge'.

'I can't tell you too much at this point, without threatening to compromise the case,' Gutteridge said, pressing a personal point home to the ignorant hacks looking on, 'but we have a number of leads we are currently investigating that we *hope* will lead to the identification, and ultimately the arrest, of the person responsible for these crimes. We *don't* want the public to live in fear, however, we do ask that you remain vigilant, and for the time being, at least, we urge families to restrict play for their children and loved ones to homes and back gardens, and to avoid secluded or outdoor spaces.' Gutteridge's face turned to a mixture of concern and regret. 'These *are* horrific crimes, and we are treating this with the utmost urgency. We *will* catch this man,' he assured the lens, 'and he *will* be brought to justice.' He broke from his speech with a sweeping look about the interested throng that returned to the main lens. 'If anyone watching this feels they have information pertaining to the case, even if they fear that information irrelevant, we urge them to come forwards and help bring this to an early conclusion. Thank you for your time.'

The story petered out to the sounds of press clamouring to present persistent questions to backs that had already turned to leave.

O'Leary pressed the mute button again, but Sophie's eyes remained glued to the screen. 'I was talking to Julie, earlier,' she said, 'she knows someone who works for the police. *She* told me that the boy they found had been sliced up the middle, and opened up like a flower, all of his insides scooped out and left on the ground beneath him!'

O'Leary's hand slid involuntarily beneath the tray to his crotch at the thought of the mutilated boy, and of the passion in his creation, before a leaden veil of unease lowered like a Venetian blind around his brittle certainty that what he was doing was somehow justified.

Could God have this wrong? he questioned. *And would God really be there to protect me in my hour of need? After all, he'd left Christ to die on the cross, hadn't he? And that was his own child, his own 'flesh and blood'.*

His mind flipped its processes. *But if this is all so very wrong, as the press and society would seem to be implying, then why am I beginning to enjoy it? Am I wrong to enjoy it?* he wondered. *This work that is so essential to our cause, charged by none other than the creator of all things, himself?*

Eat, he thought, *distract your mind.* He would quiz his god again tomorrow. But was that really soon enough?

Things seemed to be running away from him, threatening to get out of hand with a barrelling sense of inevitability.

It put him in mind of the go-cart he'd built as a child from parts of an abandoned pram found at the disused copper mine in Cork. Crudely constructed from small offcuts of plywood found lying around one of the outbuildings, and 4" x 2" batons nailed in cruciform. Simple beam steering for feet to control the rider's destiny, and a loop of bailing cord added for good measure.

He'd towed it to the top of the steepest lane near the farm. Not as steep as Cork's Patrick's Hill, maybe, but close enough for it to be impossible not to feel fear for its intimidating incline, regularly attracting thrill-seeking locals with sleds and fertiliser bags for miles around during winter's heavier snowfalls.

He'd sat, calmed his fears, lifted his feet clear of 'the black' and hung on…

It was the heaping feeling of exponential acceleration as he thundered down the hill that had burned into him like a branding iron. As the wheels gathered speed, his self-awareness spiked. He'd never before been more alive to his own mortality, outside of the fear and humiliation of his father's beatings, that is.

His panicking mind scrabbled through a Rolodex of abort-options that peeled away from possibility with each mile-per-hour he and his flimsy creation thundered away from what his fear was able to handle.

As the tarmac's unforgiving surface flashed past his naked elbows, the denier of his clothing – in the fog of his fear-frozen self-awareness – seemed to dissolve away to something resembling tissue paper as he barrelled down the hill.

The buckthorn hedgerow that eventually arrested his descent left him with scars no longer discernible from those left by his father's aggressive displays of 'affection'. But the memory of his snowballing inability to control his own fragile destiny stuck with him, cemented by the pain of the slashing buckthorns, and now, once again, that feeling resurfaced…

O'Leary realised his subconscious thoughts had remained lingering on 'the boy', and he'd been massaging his groin without even realising it, and suddenly felt the filth and feculence of his impurity soaking his warping intentions.

His hand recoiled from his erect penis, nearly knocking his tray to the floor.

'What's happened!' Sophie asked.

'Erm. Nothing…' he stuttered, catching the tray. 'I thought there was a spider.'

Sophie loosed a fond but mocking laugh. 'Gay lord!' she quipped, with a matey barge of the shoulder.

O'Leary's eyes snapped towards the slur. 'What…? I'm not gay. Why would you say I'm gay?'

Sophie frowned. She looked perplexed. She broke from it with a huff and a smirk. 'I know you're not gay. I just *called* you gay, because you're acting gay,' she grinned, then turned her attention to his tray of food. 'You'd better get that eaten,' she suggested, lifting her chin towards his plate, 'before you knock it everywhere because you encountered an earwig. Then the dog'll get it, and you'll be hungry, and the dog'll get fat, and I'll be hacked off because I'll have a fat dog and have to cook you something else.'

O'Leary dropped a look at his food, and then across to the dog – who was patiently waiting for leftovers.

'Eeshh! What have you done?' Sophie said, sucking in air through her teeth.

O'Leary turned back to her. 'What?'

'You've got blood on your finger – did you cut yourself?'

She took his right hand in hers, rotating it to inspect his forefinger. There was a crimson film of coagulated blood coating the digit like a rubiginous sock.

O'Leary watched with bewildered eyes as Sophie hunted for the source, but to no avail…

'I can't see a cut?' she said. 'Where the hell's it come from?'

'I don't know,' he said, feigning confusion, but he knew very well where. His finger, or perhaps the blade of his knife, must have broken through the skin of the nitrile glove while he'd been slicing up the body of the girl he'd had stashed in the refrigerator, and he'd been far too engrossed in his 'work' to even notice. His mind snapped to one thought and one thought alone: *Fingerprints!*

Fuck! he thought, tugging his hand politely from Sophie's grasp. 'It's nothing, it's probably just beetroot.'

'Beetroot stains bright red; that's not red,' she said.

'I said, it's *nothing*,' he snapped.

She leaned away from the spores of annoyance drifting off him. 'Are you all right?' she asked. 'Is there something wrong? You seem – I don't know – tense?'

He took a breath and settled into the silence of his own thoughts… Sophie watched.

'My father used to call me gay,' he said, 'you know, poofter; faggot; queer.'

Sophie frowned. 'He was joking, though, right?'

O'Leary shook a regretful head. 'No. No he wasn't. He wanted me to be more the way he was. You know, hard; tough; manly.'

'What does that even mean?' she asked – mocking the word. '*Manly?*'

He sneered in agreement. 'Unless you met my father, you wouldn't understand.'

She smiled compassionately with a tilt of the head. 'I could try, if you'd let me? And anyway, yes I would, I've seen the scars. You explained them to me the first time we got drunk together, remember?' She huffed a smirk to lift the tension in the air. 'Actually, you probably wouldn't, you were plastered.'

Coyly, he laughed… 'I've still got the headache.'

She smiled, fondly, then allowed the smile to melt away. 'I love you, Kieran,' she said with conviction.

He levelled his eyes with a fond and temperate gaze looking back at him. 'Do you?'

'Yes… I do…'

His eyes fell away to his lap again. 'But… what if I'd done things? Things you might not like. Things you might not understand.'

Sophie craned her neck to try and draw his eyes up again. 'Like what?' she asked.

He shrugged like a scolded child. 'Like… things. Bad things. Things that—'

No! Stop! snapped the voice of wisdom, from deep within his mind. *She's not ready yet. She won't understand. She's not one of us.*

'She might?' O'Leary said.

Sophie straightened in her seat. 'She might? She might what? Who are you talking about?'

O'Leary looked confused again. 'What?'

Sophie shook her head, conveying her confusion. '*You* said, "she might". Who might? And might what?'

O'Leary didn't respond, he just looked lost.

Sophie sagged. 'Your father really screwed you up, didn't he?'

O'Leary forced God down into his stomach again, far away from the conversation. 'Yes. Yes, he did.' His face turned pensive, reflective, thought-filled. 'It's funny though. I sometimes feel him with me, like he's here for me, more than he ever was when he was alive, you know, before I...'

Sophie watched and waited for the end of the sentence, then realised it probably wasn't coming. She rubbed his shoulder affectionately. 'Maybe he is. Maybe he's trying to make amends for the wrongs of the past. I'm sure there was good in him, somewhere.'

O'Leary smiled and shrugged. 'Perhaps.'

Sophie broke from the moment. 'Come on, eat your food, then we can go to bed, it's getting late. And maybe there's something I can do to take your mind off things,' she said, her whole face burning with playful mischief...

TWENTY-SIX

O'LEARY HELD HIS GOD FAST in the core of his gut, hoping the mentor would sleep.

He emptied his pockets onto the bedside table and slipped off his jeans. He was slim-built, but a lack of body fat gifted him an athletic look that Sophie found attractive.

She watched him disrobe from beneath the white linen duvet, her hand cupping her groin, rubbing, massaging. She felt the warm swelling filling her hand, and she slid a finger inside. She was already wet, it slipped in easily. She hooked the finger deep and her eyes rolled.

O'Leary pulled the covers back and joined her. He watched, fascinated, mesmerised by the witnessing of self-satisfaction.

Sophie's body was petite; toned; her breasts small but firm. She was still warmed through from the exertion of cleaning the plates and wiping up, and her limbs and joints felt oiled.

O'Leary reclined on his elbow and continued to watch, his enraptured fingers stroking the full length of the medial ridge of her flexing midsection. She groaned with pleasure at the feel of his fingers upon her. She opened her eyes and rolled a look his way. 'Do you want to take me?' she asked, already seeing the answer in his eyes.

She laid him down with an insistent hand against his shoulder, and climbed aboard his athletic nakedness. He was already erect.

She rose high on her knees, adjusting her position until she felt him pressing firmly against her perineum, then rolled her hips back, and sat.

Breath left her body as he glided inside her. She took a moment to regather herself, then dropped an undone look into his scrutinising eyes.

Her flushing face peered into his soul, framed by a valance of tumbling, chocolate-brown hair. The wet tips stroked his cheeks as she began to rock, and rise, and fall, and fuck.

Her mouth swung wide like a tripping heroin addict, eyes softly shutting, feeling it, taking it.

O'Leary watched her stomach roll like a belly dancer's midriff, eyes hypnotised by the rhythmical motion like midnight waves licking at a beach. His hand reached once more for the feeling of skin on muscle, feeling it pulse, feeling it stretch, feeling it contract. He hardened at the sight and drove himself in deeper. She simpered. He grinned.

He watched his toying fingers as they brushed the valleys partitioning each and every perfectly formed muscle group as they rolled and flexed above him.

The fingers straightened, touched and aligned, morphing into a blade of skin, bone and fingernail.

The brushing motions became linear, more cutting than caressing. He allowed his lids to close, and in the corrupted distortion of his mind's eye, his hand became a blade, pressing into her firm, writhing body and he sliced, and cut, and dissected…

O'Leary felt the rush of his warping fantasies through his pulsating groin, but he wasn't yet ready for it to end.

His hand softened again and took Sophie by her tiny, hourglass waist, lifting her clear of his erection.

She was rolled onto her back with slight surprise in her eyes, and he straddled her, forcing her knees apart with insistent legs. His eyes had the devil in them; it excited her.

He sat back on his calves, forcing her even wider with an aggressive spread of his knees. His knifed hand returned to her prone body, watched by his satanic gaze, and once more, began feeding his corrupted fantasies, applying long, dragging strokes down the full length of her body, his nails leaving white tracks in the pink of her stimulated skin.

She arched her back in response, reading his wants with curious accuracy.

His teeth began to grind, his face a grimace, and he guided himself inside her again.

He lowered onto her delicate frame and began to push, and stroke, and rut, becoming more animal with each passing second that he took her for his own.

Sophie's lids fluttered with every stabbing violation. She allowed her eyes to open a slither so she could witness the rapture on his face, soft-focused by the blur of her long, interlocking lashes.

O'Leary looked strangely handsome in the glow of the sterile white light illuminating his sweat-jewelled face. His features looking strong and chiselled in the glare of the localised light.

Sophie's eyes slowly closed, puckered, then flashed wide, confusion buckling her brow. 'What the f-f-fuck?' she stammered, her voice unsteadied by floods of dopamine.

She bent her eyes to the side to find the source of the sterile light and saw the illuminated screen of O'Leary's phone through the corner of her eyes next to her pillow facing him. 'You'd better not be watching porn!' she threatened, erupting from the haze of her pleasure, reaching over to grab the device.

O'Leary lunged from his folded arms, making an attempt to grab it first, but in his haste, knocked it from her grasp.

The phone slid from the mattress, clattering onto the polished, hardwood floor, and spun beneath the bed.

Sophie pushed him off with an arrogant elbow and scrambled onto her stomach, reaching for the device, her hand feeling beneath the bed until her fingers hit something flat and hard. She fumbled it into her grasp and lifted it clear of the dust bunnies and cobwebs. O'Leary made another grab for the phone, but she slapped the hand away.

The screen had gone to sleep. She stroked it awake again, and looked…

Her emerald eyes widened, shook, and hardened. A hesitant hand moved to cover her mouth, comprehension of what she was seeing taking a moment to hit home.

Sophie's jittering pupils shrunk away to dots in an attempt to block the horror of what was emblazoned on the screen just inches from her face.

'What is this?' she hissed, as she scrolled through the album of aberrations.

She began to shiver, then shake, her breath stuttering. She tore her disbelieving eyes away from the phone long enough to front O'Leary. 'What in all that's holy is this?' she said, turning the phone towards him. She began to weep. 'How did you get these?'

O'Leary looked panicked and guilty, but strangely unashamed.

A flurry of confused thoughts began to jostle for order in Sophie's mind, delivering a clarity she'd rather have denied. His changing moods; his hermetic manner; the days he'd worked late, and how she now realised they coincided with the dates the children were reported missing.

She started to sob, then cry, as though she already knew the repugnant answers to the question 'How did you get these?'

Her tear-glistened face crumpled to the realisation that she was naked, alone, and defenceless in bed with a total stranger.

She looked to the phone again and the surreal image upon it… a photo of the headless body of a child, sliced along its entire length and suspended by wires, its face peering from within the shadows of its spatchcocked body, shocking her stampeding mind into submission.

O'Leary sat like a cornered bird at the foot of the bed on folded knees, panicked eyes flitting from face to phone, extending tentative, involuntary reaches for forgiveness and understanding. 'You don't understand, you *can't* understand,' he said. 'It's God's work, God's will, he's in me, Sophie. I have to do this!'

She shrunk against the headboard, trying to meld with it, frantically attempting to create distance between herself and O'Leary's insanity. 'It's you! Oh dear God, it's you! You're the one. Y-Y-You killed these children!'

O'Leary looked lost, condemned, almost pathetic. How could this man she'd known for fourteen years be the monster the world had been seeking?

She turned to the phone again, stuttering fingers fumbling desperately at the screen for further evidence of her inability to judge character. Feeling the cold denial like crippling indigestion. But she needed to know, to know the truth, however repugnant.

New pictures appeared behind her unsteadied fingers, of a girl, young, cut into neat cubes on a tabletop, her severed head sitting to one side and looking strangely calm, almost alive. She recognised her from pictures on the news: it was the Tweets girl!

She went limp, buckling under the force of the awe and the trauma. What would, or could, she do?

She turned her attention back to O'Leary who was now kneeling bolt upright, face eerily calm, passively threatening eyes peering at her from beneath squinting, torpid lids. 'Dat's a shame dat is,' he said, his voice slurring thick Irish like he'd been drinking. 'I've been meanin' ter meet ye, moi boy seems to loik you, and I thought you'd be good fer him, and then, you had to go and foind dat. So now, Oi caan't be lettin' yer leave, now, can I?'

Sophie recoiled from the stranger's words, looking back at O'Leary's inquisitive gaze. She didn't recognise anything of the man behind the eyes, and she knew she'd have to make a run for it, naked or not.

She started to shudder. 'I loved you,' she sobbed into the dim-lit room, her chattering jaw drowning in tears. 'W-Whyyyyyy…?'

O'Leary slow-lifted a shrug to a tilted head, a dismissive blink, he was almost smiling. But which one was it? Kieran, or Conor? The answer came and hit her hard. 'Only moi boy can answer dat one, but since you won't be seein' him again, I suppose it doesn't really matter, now, does it?'

'Oh, *pleeease,* I– I don't understand,' she sobbed, 'I… I don't know…' She suddenly switched to flight mode and hurled the phone to the farthest side of the room.

O'Leary's head snapped right in time to see it clatter off a chest of drawers.

Sophie sprang from the bed, clambered to her feet, and stumbled towards the door.

She was out and on the landing before O'Leary could react, dashing for the staircase, her terror-weakened legs barely able to hold her weight.

Tears fogging her vision, she fled, naked, thumping down the steps towards the front door. She missed a footing and careened down the final four treads on her heels, her ankle folding beneath her like a deflated tyre, and she sank to the floor with unexpected elegance, clutching her foot.

With a grimace, she slumped her back against the wall just in time to see O'Leary arriving at the top of the rise, arms spanning the handrails, striding towards her two steps at a time, his face livid and unrecognisable.

She screamed and with a heave, she took to her feet again, limping for the door, ignoring the blinding pain firing through her leg like a skewer through marrow.

She saw her car keys hanging from the hook on the wall, but there was no possible way she could retrieve them and get to the door before O'Leary was on her.

Her hand reached for the lock to the soundtrack of urgent, thudding footsteps. She grabbed the latch, twisted it, and wrenched the door towards her with all she was worth.

She swung a look behind her as she ran for the sliver of night sky peeking through the gap. O'Leary was at the bottom step now and lunging in her direction. She let out a desperate wail, tugging the door shut as she hobbled through the opening and made a run for it.

She sprinted as fast as her twisted leg would allow, screaming into the frigid night air. She could feel the kick of her vocal cords in her throat, her screams filling her head.

The door behind her crashed open. 'Where da fuck do you think you're goin'?' O'Leary growled into the night air.

Sophie's bare feet stung as they slapped along the pebbled driveway. She could see the road, and the meandering glow of approaching headlights warming the tarmac.

Fast, crunching footsteps behind fuelled another scream, the intervals sounding shorter, faster. He, *it*, was gaining on her.

The hiss of tyres on the wet road ahead grew louder; she sprinted for the widening fan of light ahead, arms pumping. The feeling of cold air on parts of her body usually clad in cloth felt surreal and cripplingly vulnerable, but she didn't care; she wanted to live.

The hiss of the tyres was now just metres away, the light ahead intensifying, announcing the car's imminent arrival.

Sophie screamed with all she had, lungs stinging to the shredding harmonic of her desire to escape a fate that had been orchestrated purely by accident.

Her hysterical screams filled the midnight sky and the rain-soaked foliage of the surrounding trees, looming large in the murk like badger baiters observing a kill.

She was just ten feet from the road now, when a blunt, biting, percussive fist connected with the base of her skull, and the scream became a guttural grunt. She faltered and fell, skidding to a semi-conscious halt on her chin and her chest.

The salty, mineral flavours of the gravel mixed with the metallic tang of blood, filling her mouth as she watched the car fizz past, the tail lights – reflecting off the wet road – dimming along with the sound of the engine, the sound of hope – as if it had ever existed – and in the blink of a desperate eye, it was gone.

All went quiet, save for the throb of a heartbeat in her lacerated chest.

A hand took her hair, gathered it into a bundle and dragged her head around towards the door. Her body curled like a serpent, still stunned by the blow, arms dragging limply by her sides.

She could feel the rip of perimeter hairs tearing from her scalp as O'Leary dragged her towards the house again; she blacked out momentarily at the pain, then woke again to find him stood over her, water cascading off his fringe onto her face. She could see his genitals high above her, and tried raising a desperate kick, but the exertion sent a stabbing pain slicing along her spine and over the back of her skull, and the leg fell limp again.

'You've got fight, A'll give yer dat,' O'Leary said, a wicked grin on his face.

She continued to drift in and out of consciousness, O'Leary's face closer to her own with every evanescent waking moment, until it was just a foot away from hers, and he had his hands tightly wrapped around her throat.

Relentless thumbs dug hard into her windpipe, and she felt her head swelling to the pressure, forcing her tongue from her mouth as she coughed vomit into O'Leary's gurning face.

She panicked, fear leaking onto the gravel from her supine body and mixing with the rain as she attempted to struggle free, but the weight sat upon her was just too overwhelming, and all she could do was claw desperately at the hard, granite expression looming over her.

O'Leary's livid lip curled as he squeezed harder. She felt a crack deep in her neck, her windpipe fracturing to the relentless pressure.

She wilted, washing oddly calm, resigned to her fate, desperately praying for him to wring her whole throat, cutting off her carotid artery so that she may at least pass out from a lack of blood to the brain, and save her the fear and humiliation of dying – knowledge left over from her training as a nurse.

But the violence remained focused on her trachea, and she began to drown in her own mucus, eyes reddened, bulging, watching the face at the end of the unyielding arms glower with impure enjoyment as she began to slip under…

Sparking flecks of colour washed O'Leary's face away into the fingers of darkness encroaching on the periphery of her final, fading view of the world, and with a last, violent, choking squeeze, she was gone…

TWENTY-SEVEN

TERRENCE MANLY LAY listening to the resonant beep of his alarm clock, its relentless, nagging tone clashing in his inner ear. He wondered if the uncomfortable harmonic billowing around his head was the onset of some form of tinnitus – not that he actually knew what that was – or if maybe he had an ear infection? He would try and make an appointment with his GP later in the day, after he'd completed his morning chores.

His interest in the sound subsided, and he reached out to slap the alarm quiet again. The LCD screen displayed 3:55am, burning through the murk like a beacon to his unwillingness to rise. He sighed, and his head slumped back onto the soft embrace of the pillow.

It had been far easier to rally himself when his wife was still alive. She would rise with him as a show of solidarity for the ungodly hours he had to keep as a dairy farmer, making him tea and a slice of toast, heavy with Marmite and delivered with a bleary-eyed kiss to fuel his morning. But without that, without *her*, it was hard, and only seemed to be getting harder.

He lay pondering the ceiling… Perhaps he needed another wife, another 'Angela'? Not that anyone could truly fill her shoes, he thought – more out of respect for her death than anything real-world, because in reality, of course they could.

What they'd had together wasn't particularly special or in any way extraordinary, just satisfyingly comfortable and convenient. He'd treated her well, and she'd appreciated it, and if it wasn't for the cancer cutting her down so young, they would have been happy to remain that way.

His thoughts turned to Phillipa Trent. She'd shown interest in Manly from the very moment his wife had finally succumbed to that terrible disease. It had felt inappropriately soon at the time, but as time had passed, those thoughts had subsided, and he now felt able to feel alive to how attractive and buoyant Phillipa Trent truly was without the feelings of guilt that, before, had built a wall around his affections.

But would she really be suitable for a life like this? he had to wonder. She *did* come from a farming family, so it's not like she was unaware of the hours. The 24-7-365 lifestyle.

He yawned and stretched his limbs awake. No doubt he'd see her down the White Lion on Thursday, maybe he'd ask her on a date? 'A date,' he said out loud, mocking the concept. A forty-two-year-old man forced into contemplating a date.

He allowed his eyes to close to the thought of her. She *was* beautiful, perhaps not in a Cindy Crawford, Ariana Grande way, but in a real-world setting, yes, very. And fun too – that was important.

His hand moved to his crotch at the thought of her full, round lips and come-hither eyes, and the way she would lift an affectionate touch to his shoulder whenever he made her laugh; what more evidence did he need?

'Nope!' he said, withdrawing the sinful hand from the warmth of his pyjama bottoms. 'The *other* girls need you,' he said, stretching again.

He rocked his legs to sit up, and stood from the bed to check the weather, see which of his clothes he would be needing for the day that lay ahead: wet-weather nylons; dry-weather warm; or dry-weather light…?

He was hoping for dry-weather light, and after a quick peek through the curtains, smiled…

*

Manly stepped from the door of the farmhouse, clad in jeans and a cable-knit sweater. He had on a T-shirt underneath for when the early morning chill eventually lifted, and stooped for a sip from a steaming mug of tea. His other hand cradled a slice of toast coated in a marbled slick of Marmite and butter.

He turned and carefully hooked his pinky around the door handle, trying not to spill the tea, pulling it shut to keep the heat in and the insects out.

He made his way across the yard and stopped midway. It was quiet. Too quiet?

The field where half the herd currently resided was the one directly adjacent to the milking sheds, and the 'girls' would nearly always be standing by the gate awaiting his arrival, or at least close by. But today, their booming calls were distant and sounded complaining.

'So, why's that a thing?' he mumbled, looking about the yard for a valid reason, but failing in his efforts to find one.

He quickly gulped a few exaggerated swallows of the tea and tipped the rest away, setting the mug down on a wall. He folded the toast and wolfed it in just three mouthfuls, wiping his fingers on his jeans as he made his way to investigate.

He crossed the field towards the herd who were gathered at the farthest end looking uneasy, their heads turned towards him, watching his approach. The horizon behind burned vivid orange. They looked as if they were on fire.

'Come on,' he clapped, trying to effect movement. 'Don't you lot want emptying this morning? A full service and MOT?' he offered.

The cows shifted uneasily, turning looks to each other for reassurance and solidarity.

Manly rounded the herd and clapped low, the sharp slap of skin on skin kickstarting their reluctance to comply.

A few more claps and a couple of jaunty slaps on some of the more reluctant rumps later, and Manly finally effected compliance.

He escorted the herd to the gate and swung it open, but the cows stopped shy of the posts and stood watching him with puppy-dog gazes.

'What the fuck is wrong with you lot today? *Get* in!' he snapped, swinging a politely invitational but insistent arm towards the adjoining courtyard. Once again, the cows all turned uncomfortable looks to each other, then one by one, began filtering through.

'*Thank* you,' Manly said, sarcasm and relief flavouring his words. He frowned, and with a shake of the head, laughed it off.

Manly lolloped across to the milking sheds, yawning his misting breath into the frigid air, but couldn't hear the coconut-husk sounds of hoof-on-cobble that usually serenaded his journey.

He stopped and turned to observe the sea of pleading faces shrinking away from the shadows of the sheds, watching him from the gate. 'What *is* going on? What the hell is wrong with them this morning?' he asked. He stretched his neck long to do a quick head count, to see if there were any missing… ninety-six in this group, ninety-eight in the top field. He counted ninety-seven; he must have counted one of them twice, but they were definitely all present and correct.

Manly shrugged it off, and turned to fire up the equipment; he felt sure the herd would follow as soon as the sound of the pumps began, eager to unload their heavy burdens.

Something had obviously spooked them. Maybe that feral dog Bill Tomlinson had been talking about down the pub two nights ago?

Manly stretched over one of the holding pen fences and slapped the switches for the lights. They flickered on one at a time, warming the straw-covered floor in popping pools of fluorescent radiation.

Manly twisted a curious look back at the huddle of cows as he made his way along the central corridor that dissected the rows of milking bays. He laughed at their new behaviour, finding mirth in their clandestine weirdness.

His progress was halted by something blocking his route. He stopped, and turned, swiping instinctively at whatever was hanging across his path, stumbling back from the obstacle.

The surprise melted from his face, and his skin turned ashen, his expression now mimicking the cows' . Manly fumbled back, aghast at the new addition to his farm, woven defiantly across the path of his daily routine.

A net of tying line criss-crossed the bars of the milking pens, spanning the corridor like a spider's web, but instead of insect carcasses, this web was laden with neatly partitioned sections of body, hanging grimly like an exploded diagram of human anatomy.

It was a child – Manly could tell that much – and at once, he knew it was the work of the Spatchcock Killer, a name penned by the *Daily Mail* that had stuck, and that was now used by all of the major news outlets.

The sight was so at odds with reality, it created a feeling of distance and detachment, and it didn't instantly hit home exactly what it was he'd discovered.

There was surprisingly little blood beneath the 'installation'. The child's head was suspended on the left, looking out into the milking pens. The rest of the body had been cubed, the severed legs and arms dangling beneath like the pendulums of some ghoulish clock.

There were what looked to be pieces of paper pinned to each and every individual body part, and on closer inspection, Manly could just make out they were segments of a butcher's beef-cuts poster, the child's mutilated body contrived to mimic the macabre diagram.

The realisation of what he was alone in the shed with finally hit home, and Manly bowed a stomach load of bile onto his feet, staggering back from the abhoration, leaving a trail of his revulsion in his wake.

He spat his mouth clear of the acidic taste, wiping it clean on his wrist. 'Oh shit! Oh fuck!' he mumbled. 'W– Why would—' More vomit splashed the floor.

His head shook frantically, affirming his denial. He'd been around death plenty, all farmers had, but not like this. This seemed cruelly needless and unnecessarily demeaning.

He turned and ran from the shed, the observant herd lumbering back from his urgent sprint as he made for the house and the phone within, the understanding voice of sanity hopefully just one swift call away.

He knew, deep down, this moment would damage him for life – that was a given – and all thoughts of Phillipa Trent and his own happiness dissolved in the stinging light of this new event in his life, but he desperately wanted to minimise just how much by involving the sobering voice of authority as soon as was humanly possible.

He took his phone from the charger and prodded the '9' key three times. It started ringing.

His thoughts turned to Angela – his dead wife – and the

child they'd never managed to conceive, before a cruel and heartless god took her from him. The tears ran free, and the phone answered…

TWENTY-EIGHT

GUTTERIDGE LAY ON HIS FOLDED ARM, peering deep into the vibrant grey eyes looking back at him.

Intermittent smiles tugged at the corners of Eve's mouth as she tried to decipher the tranquil look in his exploratory gazes, and the possible thoughts behind them.

He stroked her face with such truth, brushing away coils of jet-black hair so he could better see his prize. Eve smiled at the attention. It felt good.

'What are you thinking about?' she asked, the soft placidity in her Polish accent matching her features.

He shrugged imperceptibly. 'Just stuff,' he said, with a lid-stretching flash of the brows, 'and of you.'

She shuffled slightly in the heat of the potency of his answer, but not uncomfortably. The bed felt warm; so did she. 'What *about* me?'

He smiled, nearly becoming a fond laugh, and his touch turned more affectionate. 'Of how lovely you are.'

'Am I?'

A nod. 'Yes.'

'Do you mean, beautiful?'

A shake this time. 'No – although you *are* that. I mean, *you, you're* lovely.'

She smiled, having never before had anyone speak to her with such soft sincerity. She resisted the urge to show him her appreciation; a carnal response would undoubtedly have cheapened the moment.

Gutteridge shifted slightly, a get-ready for delivering the question sat poised on his tongue. Eve sensed it, her eyes pinching quizzically, inviting him to present his query.

'Do you remember,' he said, 'you once asked, "Do you want me?" Do you remember that?'

Her eyes averted, then returned. 'Yes. I remember.'

'What exactly did you mean?'

Her eyes dropped away and appeared to dampen.

Gutteridge's brows flickered. He stooped his head to collect her attention. 'Did you mean physically, orrr…?' he asked, the word tailing off, becoming the core of the question.

Another imperceptible shrug, coy and laced with vulnerability. '…Orrr,' she replied.

DS Keaton's small, round face flashed into Gutteridge's jostling thoughts; he suppressed it. 'And are you *still* wondering if I do?'

Another pause, then a nod, meek and fearing of the answer that may possibly peel from his lips. 'Yes.'

Gutteridge adjusted his head on the pillow, resetting the moment. 'Then ask me again.'

Her eyes returned to his, and she held the look. Her lips paused, then parted. '…Do you want me?'

He delivered a thought-filled, distant smile, his sinewy hand lifting from the pillow and cupping her ear softly, his thumb smoothing away the creases in her worried brow. 'Yes… yes I do,' he smiled, then erupted from the moment. 'I mean, you might not want me? You might think, *Fuck that, silly sod, with his salt-and-pepper hair and his weird knees, and that horrible job hunting down crims and serial murderers. And who the hell does he think he is anyway? Me all gorgeous and him looking like that*!'

She laughed, affectionately.

He continued. 'But my hope is, that maybe, you might want to give me a chance, because you make me happy, Eve, even though you *are* Polish. But… you can't have everything, now, can you?'

She smirked. 'English git.'

'Polish strumpet.'

She frowned at the new word. 'What is "strumpet"?'

'Strumpet? Erm? Harlot? Tart? Hussy?'

She smiled, fondly. 'Bell-end,' she fired back – an English colloquialism that had always tickled her – before turning serious and pensive. 'Do you think you could ever love me?'

The word 'love' hit Gutteridge like a slap. Was he afraid of it? Of the concept? Or simply the word? He decided he shouldn't be if happiness was to be the ultimate goal, but he held fast the answer, deciding to keep it ambiguous.

'Anything's possible, I suppose,' he said, 'even something as ludicrous as loving you!' His eyes smiled into hers. 'And anyway, who's to say I don't already?' he quipped.

She decided she was happy with that, at least for now. 'Should I make tea?' she asked.

He smiled the most genuine smile his face had worn for a very long time. 'Please.'

She climbed from the bed, her limbs moving with a protracted elegance that reminded Gutteridge of the Lipizzaner horses he'd once seen on a visit to Croatia. Tall, slender, a sophistication to the way they motivated her lithe magnificence. She looked equally ethereal, and for the briefest of moments, he felt unworthy to be speaking of love to a creature so otherworldly.

'Use my shirt,' he suggested, pointing to the chair, her

nakedness dazzling the soft morning light. She slipped it on and slid from the room.

The taste of gyoza and chilli ramen still lined his mouth. They'd been to Wagamama, the first time they'd ever been out together in Gloucester, outside of that first drink after Eve's evening of troubles.

The night had been pleasurable, but an acute awareness that he might be seen out with her had undeniably existed, and he'd had to fight hard for it to not show. But he'd relaxed into the evening with a relative ease that had surprised him, and eventually – as usually happened – he'd succumb to her undeniable charms, and all that eventually existed was her, and him, and her killer eyes.

But he'd been unable to completely shake the feeling that they were being watched, no doubt fuelled by paranoia of gossip, but still, the notion had sat taunting him from the back of his mind, and he'd had to expel the idea from his thoughts on several occasions.

The door to the bedroom crept open, motivated by an elegant foot. Eve extended her sirenic limbs into the room brandishing hand-painted china cups teetering on matching saucers Gutteridge forgot he even owned.

'Where on earth did you find them?' he asked.

'At the back of the cupboard, behind the mugs.'

He laughed. 'I bought them years ago on a whim. This is probably the first time they've ever been used.'

'Maybe that means something, in a cosmic way?' she suggested, with a twee shrug.

'Yep… it means you're classy, and I prefer mugs.'

She giggled, carefully passing one over. She sat and shuffled to get comfortable. 'What does "whim" mean?' she asked.

'Erm, whim…? A fancy. An impulse. Whimsy.'

'Ah!' she exhaled. 'Whimsy, whim. The same, yes? I have heard of whimsy.'

'You've got it,' he said, stooping a sip from the cup. The fine edge of the porcelain felt dignified to drink from; he lifted his pinky in jest. Eve laughed...

*

O'Leary stared into the back of his van at the body of his dear, beloved Sophie, crudely and unceremoniously wrapped in blue plastic sheeting, dumbbell weights hastily tied along its length in coils of nylon rope.

Tears of disbelief misted his eyes. Another body of yet another life he was unable to recall extinguishing, but this time, along with the shock, came a plummeting sense of loss.

'Did *you* do this?' he sniffled.

'No, my child, this was your doing. A version *of* you,' said the voice of wisdom.

'But... I wouldn't... Would I? A version?'

'You would, and you did,' said the god. 'She'd found out about our work together, about our quest. What other choice did you have that wouldn't have threatened to cut short our ability to complete what we've started?'

A tear peeled free of O'Leary's eye, running the gauntlet of his quivering cheek, and dripped from his nose, splashing onto the shrouded body.

'Don't weep, child,' said the voice. 'Those that fail to comprehend what it is we attempt to achieve, by association of their reluctance to understand, *must* become our enemies.'

As repugnant as the thought may be to stomach, O'Leary attempted to recall the kill, but that part of his memory remained shrouded in darkness, the same as the time he'd discovered the body of the suited man on the kitchen floor of his workplace, knife buried deep in his chest, his feet baptised by an expanding lake of blood.

He'd also blanked out at the time he visited the church, and hadn't even remembered leaving, finding himself midway across a busy highway as a car swerved to pass him, horn and vocal cords blaring.

'Trouble yourself not, my child,' consoled the voice of wisdom. 'She too has become a martyr to our most worthy of causes. Her sacrifice was justified and shall not have been made in vain. You shall reunite together in the bosom of the light of heaven when our work here is done... There are those who seek to stifle our message, it is *they* whom we must focus our efforts. Close the doors. Learn to forget, as *I* have had to relearn unforgiveness. In the absence of contrition, my child, the only option left open to me is to force attrition.'

O'Leary complied, slowly pressing the doors closed. He swallowed back his grief and stumbling disbelief. 'What now?' he asked, his voice briefly cracking.

'Your phone. The pictures,' said the voice. 'He who is working to prevent us must be stopped.'

O'Leary took his mobile from his pocket and opened the photo file. He scrolled through an album of images of a man, with a woman, sharing food at the Wagamama in the Gloucester Quays. Laughing, grinning, looking to each other with a sinner's lustful eyes, unaware that, from just four tables distant, they were being watched.

O'Leary scrolled through the album of his mark: of the restaurant; of the couple leaving arm in arm, laughing, joking, not a care in the world; of the Quays' multistorey car park; of the blood-red tail lights of an ink-black Saab being followed; of a remote cottage a short distance past the village of Highnam; of sinners fucking in front of a flagstone hearth, swapping the expectorant flavours of the dead animals they'd consumed in the salivation of their lust, fire burning hot behind their intertwining copulation like the chastising flames of hell. And of DI Gutteridge, a man assigned to effect an early conclusion to the iron will of God, and that, and that alone, made him a problem that needed solving, and at any cost.

TWENTY-NINE

'WE'VE GOT A PRINT! THREE TO BE EXACT.'

The words sang down the phone like a delivering angel, warming Gutteridge's ear, giving Carl's normally clinically factual voice an air of excited optimism.

'You're shitting me?'

'Nope. The fucker's slipped up, *finally*,' gloated Carl. 'I've expelled anyone from the scene not critical to the investigation, pretty much leaving just me and Gustav, just in case he's been sloppy elsewhere. How quickly do you think you can get over here? Home Farm, on the A-road to Staunton and Corse, about two miles past the Over Roundabout.'

It felt weirdly odd to Gutteridge that the scene was in such close proximity to his own home, not that any of the other locations could exactly be considered distant, but this was within spitting distance, and that, somehow, made the incident more real.

He turned a look to Eve who was now sitting up in bed, leaning on one arm, listening with a hand pressed across her perfect mouth. Her features mirrored the concern in his face. 'Um…? I can be there in fifteen minutes if you could hang on that long. I won't bother showering.'

'No. Shower. Let's not risk contamination. We can hold off making our full sweep until you're here. We'll just potter.'

'Okay. I'll be as quick as I can. Twenty-five, thirty tops. Oh, and what are we looking at this time?'

Carl's audible excitement at finding usable evidence subsided. 'It's a girl… it's a little girl…'

'Shit,' Gutteridge sighed, his brief venture into optimism sinking through the mattress. 'All right, old friend. I'll see you soon.'

Gutteridge lowered the phone to his lap.

'Everything okay?' Ewelina asked, her voice caressing the words.

Gutteridge sat in reflection, lip pinched between thumb and forefinger, trying to untangle his thoughts. 'Hm? Oh, sorry.' He took a breath. 'Another body, discovered by a farmer just up the road from here. Hanging in the milking sheds.'

'*Another* one!' she said. '*Hanging?* Not another child?'

His expression was wan and woeful. 'Yes,' he whispered, voice flavoured with regret.

The colour emptied from Eve's cheeks. 'I honestly don't know how you do it.'

'…Do it?'

'You know. Deal with the hate and the malice of the world; it can't be easy.'

Gutteridge's brows flashed ironically. He was surprised she knew the word malice. 'It isn't, but you try to stay detached.' He turned and smiled ruefully. 'I have to go. Are you going to be okay? Are you working today?' His voice was soft and compliant.

She nodded. 'I am.'

Gutteridge's face turned serene. He pondered the night they'd shared, and the resultant question that sat poised on his lips. 'Why don't you stay here again tonight? We could drive to yours later and get some bits and pieces, you know, things you'd need if you ever stayed over. Then we could collect takeaway on the way back.'

Eve's face illuminated. 'Really?'

Gutteridge forced his expression to remain matter-of-fact, playing down the relevance of such a suggestion, but for reasons he really wasn't sure of. 'Yes. Well, why not? It'd be good. Wouldn't it? Good for us.'

Eve failed to hide her joy. The colour returned to her smiling cheeks and she looked coy, almost humbled, intrigued by the way life seemed to be unfolding. 'Okay,' she mewed, 'I'd like that.'

They exchanged a look, then Gutteridge leaned in to deposit a kiss on her grateful mouth. The words 'I love you' came to him, hanging in his throat, and his brow knitted within the kiss at his inclination to tell her. But he held the words fast on his tongue. *Not yet*, he thought, logic stepping in to dam the river of his emotions. *Not yet...*

*

Gutteridge's car was directed by a daisy chain of uniformed officers to a parking space being held for him under the instruction of Carl McNamara. He lifted a muted wave in thanks and pulled into the spot just shy of the yellow crime-scene tape that fidgeted and buzzed in the breath of the morning wind.

The sky was suitably grey and ominous. He saw Keaton's car parked on the opposite side of the lane but couldn't see her anywhere nearby.

The farmhouse ahead of him looked tired and in need of love, fading remnants of what looked to Gutteridge to be a woman's touch just visible through the jaded exterior, but looking decidedly neglected.

Gutteridge wondered what the story was of this particular home, of this particular life, then he spied Terrence Manly across the way being interviewed by a female officer, and at once, he knew.

Manly was nothing more than a mere passing acquaintance, whenever he visited the White Hart in Kingsholm. He knew him to be a farmer, but without ever knowing which particular farm. He also knew – but only from the hum of the pub's highly effective gossip machine – that his wife had passed away, and the state of his home reflected the fact.

The old feeling returned to Gutteridge, the feeling that he wanted out: out of this life; out of this career; out of constantly having to come to terms with how shitty the world and humanity could be. Certainly, he still found interest in the work – as he always had – but so often it happened, and with increasing regularity, that the thrill was being offset by the gut-dragging depression that being forced to face the ill will of the world gifted him…

He popped the door, exhaling a long, calming breath, and rose into the morning freshness. The buzz of the tape applauded his arrival, and Manly spied him from the far end of the lane, lifting a hesitant chin in recognition of their occasional friendship.

Gutteridge closed the door with a gentle nudge, resisting taking out his notebook and pen. Manly looked decidedly shaken up, and more in need of a friend than an official interrogation, and Gutteridge was more than happy to assume that role.

Gutteridge sauntered up the bank toward Manly wearing a weak, but understanding, smile. The female officer peeled aside to make way for his arrival. 'Thank you, officer. I won't keep him too long… Terry,' Gutteridge said softly with a nod. 'You okay?'

Manly took a deep breath and exhaled the knot in his stomach. 'Yeah. I'm okay.'

Gutteridge stooped an inquisitive look into Manly's fidgeting eyes. 'Was it you who discovered the body?'

Manly nodded, then loosed an unconvincing laugh. Gutteridge frowned at the unexpected mirth. 'The word "body" would suggest it, *she*, was still in one piece,' Manly said with an uncomfortable smirk, forcing levity, which instantly morphed into a stammering weep. A stilted, reluctant sob of a grown man who'd been raised to believe it masculine for others not to witness. 'I'm sorry,' he apologised.

'Hey, you don't have to apologise to me. I see this shit a lot, and I weep from time to time myself. It's natural.'

Manly loosed a saline smile in appreciation of the kind words. 'How could anyone do such a thing?'

Gutteridge flashed empathetic brows. 'Not anyone can. It takes a particular set of circumstances to produce life's monsters.' He suddenly realised he had no knowledge of what was waiting for him in the milking sheds. No information. No description. He was going into this one blind. In his haste to get to the scene, he'd neglected to ask.

But at least he now knew it must be something bad, but as bad as the spatchcocked Peek child beneath the viaduct?

Manly's eyes flicked towards the yard. 'I don't know if I'll ever be able to go into those milking sheds again…'

Gutteridge broke with protocol and lifted a comforting touch to Manly's shoulder. 'If there's anything I've learned over the years, it's that time *is* the healer people say it is.'

'Really?' Manly said, wanting to believe it. But the doubt remained. 'I hope so. Dear God, I hope so.'

Gutteridge spun sweeping looks about the farm. 'Is there someone you can stay with for a bit, while all this is dealt with and the crime scene's cleared? Don't I remember you saying you had a sister?'

Manly's front turned exasperated. 'No, well, yes, I do. And

of course I could. But the *farm*. The cows still haven't been milked. The crops need feeding, the top field needs scrubbing. I can't just walk away!'

Gutteridge dropped his eyes in contemplation. 'Isn't Ted Poole's farm the next one along from here?'

Manly's brows knitted, wondering where Gutteridge was going with this. 'Erm. Yes. Yes, it is…'

Could you not use his milking equipment for today, and tomorrow if needs be, if I arranged it? I know him well, and he owes me one.'

Manly coloured, exasperated, looking put out and reluctant.

'*Listen*, I *know* it's not ideal, but we have to do right by that child,' insisted Gutteridge. 'Please, Terry.'

Manly dropped the reluctant front and sagged into compliance. 'Okay, I suppose that could work, *if* he agreed to it. We haven't always got along.'

'Oh, he'll agree to it,' insisted Gutteridge. 'A possible driving ban being made to mysteriously vanish from his life will see to that.' Gutteridge took his phone from his pocket, scrolled to Poole's number, and tapped it…

*

Gutteridge stood in the core of the milking shed, contemplating the warped motivations behind the new addition to the building like a clueless punter in the Louvre.

'Dear God almighty!' he muttered under his breath at the lurid sight webbing the railings, hands cradling the sides of his face, peering through the protective mesh of his fingers.

The child's severed head stared out towards the farmhouse, bouncing to the harmonics of the whistling breeze in the web of bailing chord with the other body parts. 'I think you're right,' he said to Keaton, 'it's Sally Tweets... I recognise her from the photos... *Fuck it!*' he spat, mourning another failure to protect an innocent life.

Keaton stood beside him, still shaken by the sight that had greeted her arrival. 'I didn't realise it until I saw her in real life, but she looks just like my younger sister did when she was about the same age. It's horrible.'

'I didn't know you had a sister,' Gutteridge said, his eyes swimming over the details. 'What are the pieces of paper?'

'Carl says they're segments of one of those butcher's posters, you know, the ones that explain where the different cuts of meat come from.'

'Wow!' Gutteridge said. At that very moment, the message behind the 'art' choired loud and with crystal clarity. Finally, he could appreciate the repugnant brilliance behind each and every 'piece'. He turned to Carl who was milling around behind photographing the scene. 'You said there were prints?'

Carl finished photo-tiling the west side of the pens, then walked across to join the conversation. 'Yes. Two on her cheek, and one on her right forearm. There *are* others, but they're too smudged to be of any use. But the three that we have are clear enough to be logged and traceable. I've pinged pictures back to the lab already and they're being run through the database as we speak.'

Gutteridge allowed himself to harbour hope, however slight. 'Let's pray he's done something wrong in the past and is in the system.'

'We can only hope, old friend,' Carl agreed, opening the photo file of his SLR. 'Look,' he said, turning the viewing screen to face Gutteridge. 'See the triangular print below the actual fingerprint, a bit like a fold in torn cloth. I think he must have ripped through his glove without realising it and left us some nice sharp prints to help chase this fucker down.

They look to me like nitrile gloves,' he added, 'less stretchy than latex.'

A solitary drip splashed onto Keaton's head as she leaned into the camera. A viscous chill bled through her hair and onto her scalp. She lifted a hand to dab the cold wetness, lowering it again to eye level to examine a thick sock of deep cherry red now coating the tip of her forefinger.

Carl and Gutteridge leaned in to look, then all eyes lifted skyward to the rafters high above them.

Keaton's scream ignited the air. She sank to the ground at the sight of a child's emotionless face peering down at them from deep in the shadows of the roof space, staring with dry, empty, dollish eyes. It was a second body, suspended by its ankles, arms dangling, hanging face down from the timbers of the lofted roof space, mimicking the child depicted on the walls of Lidl, Llanthony Lock and the courthouse.

All attentions had been so drawn to the remains of the mutilated Tweets girl that no one had thought to look up.

It took Gutteridge a few moments to recognise the face through the swollen mulberry purple of the pooling blood discolouring the features, but he was certain, *this* was Thomas Leinster, the third child on the missing list. But no more; they'd just found him...

*

O'Leary watched from the top of the rise, crouched low behind the drystone wall running the perimeter of the adjoining field. He could see a soft, juddering image of Gutteridge milling about the yard through the lens of his binoculars, walking the scene, directing 'the troops', like some clueless dictator devoid of any real plan, but trying to style his way through his inept attempts at success.

O'Leary loosed a self-satisfied smile. 'What now?' he asked his mentor.

'You need to send the letter, then replace the items,' said the god. 'People will only listen if our actions directly affect them, as indeed, they shall.'

*

Gutteridge's phone began to buzz in his pocket. He respectfully left the scene to answer it. 'Gutteridge,' he muttered softly.

'Sir? It's McWilliams. Where are you at the moment?'

'I'm over at the Home Farm crime scene. Keaton's also here, and Carl. Why?'

'I've had a return email from Kerry Marston from the *Echo*. *She* is patient zero.'

'Patient zero?' Gutteridge replied.

'Yes. I've tracked the name Tick-Tock to her, or more specifically, a piece she wrote a couple of years back. It was just a two-paragraph… what's the term? A "back-of-the book" story mentioning the first ever artwork that appeared in the city. But in the piece, she actually referred to him as "Tick-Tock", so I emailed her, and she's replied. Pat… he called her on the phone. She *actually* spoke to him, and she's willing to talk with you. Can you get over there this morning sometime? She said the encounter was – how did she put it again? – "fascinating".'

THIRTY

GUTTERIDGE turned the nose of his Saab into the Peel Centre Retail Park and pulled into an empty space adjacent to the Gloucester Quays Shopping Centre. He shut the engine off and turned to Keaton. 'The *Echo* offices were recently relocated into there,' he said, indicating the Quays with a nod. 'Have you dealt much with Kerry Marston yet?'

'No. Not ever. Why?'

'Because she can be a pushy son of a bitch,' he explained, with a disapproving pinch of the brow. 'Typical hack, you know the type, sarcastic, difficult. She used to be a big name on the *Daily Mirror* staff, until she trod on the wrong toes and it all went to shit. She's made a good few enemies over the years, so was kicked over to the *Echo* as a take-it-or-leave-it offer she couldn't really refuse. Apparently, she has relatives in the area, so…' Gutteridge took a breath and reclined into the seat. 'In reporter terms, they're lucky to have her, but she can be a bit tricky to deal with, so let me do the talking, okay?'

Keaton felt slighted by the newbie treatment, but she strained to let it go, if only for the sake of the case. 'Okay. *Sir*.'

Gutteridge frowned at the 'Sir', and the slight pithiness hidden within the delivery. 'I don't mean to sound condescending, but I *do* know how to handle her, and after today, so will you, so don't take it personally, all right? You're a fine detective, Jane, no one else I'd rather be with, but she's a ballsy London hack with a good thirty years behind her of not giving a fuck how her incessant barracking might upset prominent people who *probably* deserved far more respect, so remember that.'

Keaton softened her stance and nodded. 'Okay... sorry.'

'That's all right... come on, let's introduce you to the concrete witch...'

Gutteridge approached the reception desk with Keaton following a step behind. The girl behind the counter lifted an unexpectedly genuine smile to greet their arrival.

'I'm here to see Kerry Marston, she's expecting me... *us*,' he said, spinning an apologetic look to Keaton. 'DI Gutteridge.'

The girl: young; bottle blonde; and synthetic in that way modern girls tended to be, raised a brow in recognition of his name. Her youthful prettiness shone through the needlessly but fashionably heavy layers of caked make-up as she smiled up at his minor celebrity. 'I'll put a call through, see if she's near her desk. Won't be a sec,' she chirped.

Gutteridge could hear a diluted West Country twang flavouring her voice, soft and pliant. Bristol was his best guess, judging by her dress sense, which had more than a hint of Essex woven in its execution than anything Gutteridge would have considered tasteful.

The over-made-up girl clucked into the phone, then returned it to its base. 'She's on her way down, won't be a mo. Is this about the Spatchcock Killer?' she asked, with a strange air of excitement in her voice.

'Erm... I can't really say too much about that now, can I? It wouldn't be very prudent for me to disclose such information in the foyer of a newspaper office, now, would it?'

The girl smiled, then laughed. Her face and manner were attractive. 'I guess not. But if you did, I'd promise not to say anything.'

Gutteridge crimped a regretful smile. 'Sorry.'

The girl turned her attention to Keaton. 'Is he always this secretive?'

''Fraid so,' Keaton replied. 'Professional is probably more the word.'

The girl shimmied in her seat. 'Oooo. I like a professional man.'

Gutteridge held an amused look into the girl's playful eyes… 'I bet you do,' he replied, with equal playfulness, the girl grinning like a naughty child. She was now, to Gutteridge's mind, about twice as attractive as the first impression had suggested.

Keaton rolled her eyes, the feelings of jealousy returning for a repeat performance. She shook the feeling away again.

Gutteridge was still making love to the girl with his toying manner.

'How is Eve these days?' Keaton prodded, dragging Gutteridge back from his flirtation into the foyer, just as a smartly dressed fifty-something lolloped down the staircase towards them. Superior headmistress eyes locked on the pair standing waiting, back straight, head high. *This* was obviously Kerry Marston, and she looked every bit as self-assured and formidable as Gutteridge had suggested.

'DI Pat Gutteridge, to what do I owe this honour?'

Gutteridge turned and sauntered to the base of the staircase to intercept her arrival. He nodded a greeting with distrust in his eyes. 'Kerry,' he said with a dip in his voice, 'I was led to believe you had knowledge of the reason for our visit, unless you're finally losing it?'

Marston loosed a laughed and extended a hand to shake.

'Not quite yet, but I do keep misplacing my glasses, which is a worry…' She flicked an obviated look to the case file clamped beneath his arm. 'Tick-Tick? You have questions?' She turned her eyes to drink in Keaton. 'And you must be Jane?'

Keaton baulked at the perceived familiarity. 'Erm. Yes. DS Keaton.'

Marston smiled at her with a hint of synthetic warmth. 'I hear you're the reason our DI here is still with us – in a professional sense, that is?'

Keaton baulked again, and her eyes spun to Gutteridge to see his reaction to what she felt was mild disrespect, but he was grinning, seeming to be enjoying the cat-and-mouse banter.

'Now, now, Kerry. Go easy on her,' Gutteridge said, 'we've just come to hear what you have to say about this encounter with Tick-Tock.'

Marston turned her supercilious gaze back to Gutteridge. 'And what's in it for me?'

'For you?' Gutteridge said, but hardly surprised by the question. Like in all their encounters, Gutteridge felt like he was in a verbal game of chess, and carefully considered his next gambit. 'How about I don't slap you with a charge for obstruction of justice?'

'And you really think you could make that stick?' Marston replied.

Gutteridge's lids pinched. He stepped forwards, leaned into Marston and lowered his voice. 'Or how about I make a call to the *Sun*'s chief editor, a very good friend of mine who I know not to be a fan of yours, and inform him that *you*, an ex-section editor of the *Mirror*, had important information regarding a child-mutilating serial killer, and chose not to disclose it?'

Marston's self-assured front visibly wavered, despite her vain attempts not to let it show.

Gutteridge leaned in further. 'And how about we try to

get this fucking freak off the streets, before any more innocent children are abducted and killed?'

Gutteridge stepped back again and furrowed a theatrical brow. 'How are your two kids these days? Won't the girl be about twelve now?'

Marston visibly wilted, sagging from her staunch position. 'Thirteen.'

'Well then, why don't we stop butting heads for five fucking minutes and see if we can't help each other out?'

Marston smiled weakly through her moderate humiliation, and quietly invited the detectives to follow with a reluctant flick of the head. 'Follow me. We can use one of the interview rooms upstairs.'

The watching receptionist winked up at Gutteridge with a sparkling look of awe in her eyes. It was the first time she'd ever seen Marston lose a haranguing match.

Gutteridge returned the wink, the girl with gemstone eyes now looking closer to a supermodel than the child that had raided its mother's make-up case that he'd encountered earlier.

*

The air in the interview room felt dead and suppressed, the heavily soundproofed walls absorbing the treble from the metallic clanks of rearranging chairs, giving the space a feeling akin to a womb.

Marston sat, then stretched up from her seat and leaned across to swing the door shut with the tips of her long, spidery fingers, then sat again into the core of Gutteridge and Keaton's crescent of attention. She shuffled to get comfortable, then froze to consider the guests. 'So, what do you want to know?'

Gutteridge leaned in. 'McWilliams told me you actually spoke to Tick-Tock?'

Marston's whole visage flashed. 'Yes. Well. I *assume* it was him in person, I mean.'

Keaton also leaned into the conversation. 'Did the man you spoke to have an Irish accent?'

A look of recognition lit up Marston's face. 'Yes. Yes, he did. Only subtle, mind.'

'Then it probably *was* him,' Keaton confirmed. She suddenly remembered what Gutteridge had said to her in the car about letting him lead, and darted an apologetic look his way, but he seemed unmoved by her interjection.

Gutteridge continued. 'McWilliams said that, in your words, you found the encounter "fascinating". What exactly did you mean? In what way, fascinating?'

Marston leaned back in her seat, lifting her eyes clear of the watching faces, and knitted her fingers around her crossed leg. 'The answer is, I don't know... Well, of course I *do* know, but it was one of those subtle things it's hard to put a precise finger on... It was more the *way* he was, over what he said, although that *is* relevant... He seemed, odd, strange, detached from reality – if you know what I mean.'

Her eyes lowered again to the watching visitors. 'Can I ask *you* a question, if I promise the answer stays in here?'

Gutteridge turned a searching look across to Keaton for a second opinion, who shrugged and nodded. 'Go ahead,' he said.

Marston leaned in. 'Is there any evidence that *he* might *not* be working alone?'

Gutteridge frowned. 'Alone? No. Why do you ask?'

Marston juggled her thoughts. 'Because I got the distinct impression that he was consulting someone in the room with him, someone who *seemed* to me to be calling the shots.'

Gutteridge considered her words, then fixed her a granite stare. 'This stays in this room, right? At least until he's caught?'

'Of course,' Marston agreed.

Gutteridge shuffled his chair forwards and perched on his elbows. 'We have an account from a witness who also encountered this man. This witness said he seemed to be manifesting multiple personalities. Does that sound like it could be what you heard?'

Marston gave the notion consideration, then her face brightened. 'You know, the other voice – although muffled – did seem similar in tone to his own. It was just – I don't know – calmer, more in control, if that makes sense? I'd always assumed it must have been his agent or something, for his art, I mean, but it did strike me as odd that the conversation never steered far from the resentment he obviously truly felt towards anyone who ate the flesh of animals.'

'He spoke of that, then?' Keaton said.

'Oh yeah. A *lot!* He got really quite vicious on the subject, which I admit, didn't feel very much like someone phoning in just to promote their art. The anger seemed genuine, vitriolic even, not just a vehicle for his creation, which, of course, we later found out was to be the first of many.'

'What kind of things did he say?' Keaton asked.

'Well, you must understand, this was two years ago now. But I did attempt to write down the last of his rant in my rusting, bastard form of shorthand as he was saying it.'

Marston took a pair of reading glasses and a folded piece of paper from her jacket pocket, and carefully opened it. She put the glasses on and began to scan her scribblings. 'He was talking about the murder of innocent creatures, and his message to the world. Oh! And he said he'd witnessed first-hand what it is to take the life of the creatures us sinners choose to consume, and that his creations are to be considered a direct and unquestionable response to that merciless and unjust killing. *His* message, if you like, to a cruel world that gorges on the flesh of others, and he said the pain *he* feels each time a creature's life is taken, others will feel too, *through* his art and actions.'

Marston took the glasses off again. 'I just thought he was being a self-absorbed dickhead, a typical artist, all fanfare and overblown reaction to compensate for a lack of any real talent… until the bodies began turning up, that is.'

'And you didn't feel this was something the police ought to know?' Keaton jabbed.

Marston darted a retaliatory look back to Keaton's rebuke, then softened again. 'To be perfectly honest with you, the call bothered me, and when the bodies began turning up, that bother turned to fear.' Marston shrugged. 'This guy was obviously unhinged, a total nutcase, so rightly or wrongly, I decided to keep out of it.'

Marston turned her attention back to Gutteridge with curiosity in her eyes. 'The man crucified in the tree, why do you think our guy murdered *him?* And are you sure it was the same man? And if so, why the drastic change in MO?'

'Off the record again?' Gutteridge said.

Marston nodded.

'We're pretty certain it was our guy. The experts say the same hand wrote the words scrawled at each site, but as to the reason, we're not really sure. But we *think* he was probably an innocent victim. A wrong-place-wrong-time unfortunate.'

'And what was he doing here?'

Gutteridge frowned. 'What do you mean?'

'Here. In Gloucester? The press release named him as a Malcom Hood from Chipping Norton, so what was he doing so far over this way?'

Keaton and Gutteridge exchanged looks.

'You mean, you haven't checked?' Marston asked.

'I'm not sure?' Gutteridge said. 'His wife reported him as

missing to the Thames Valley Police, and after an interdivisional search of current missing persons cases, we got a match to the body *we* found.'

The supercilious look returned to Marston's face. 'And on which day was he reported missing?'

Gutteridge began flicking through the case file. 'I'm not sure, why?'

'Was it a weekday, or a weekend? I'm pretty sure I read his body was discovered on a weekday if I remember correctly?'

'I think you're right?' Gutteridge confirmed. 'Hang on, here it is… it was a Wednesday. She reported him missing on the Wednesday, then the body was discovered the following day, on the Thursday.'

'And was he a working man, this Mr Hood?'

Gutteridge shrugged. 'I assume so.'

Marston leaned into the huddle. 'So. I ask again. What was he doing in Gloucester? I doubt he was out shopping.'

'Why wouldn't he have been shopping?' Keaton asked.

Marston shot Keaton a mocking look. 'Are you serious? If you lived in Chipping Norton? Surely if it's high-street shopping you needed to do, you'd go to Banbury, or Oxford, just twenty minutes away, not traipse all the way over to fucking Gloucester, over an hour's drive.'

Keaton and Gutteridge shared a second look. 'I'm on it,' Keaton said, erupting from her chair and making for the door with phone in hand.

Gutteridge slumped back in his seat and levelled a look at Marston as the door behind him closed. 'Have you ever thought about becoming a detective, Kerry? We could use more people like you.'

Marston laughed. 'Now, where would the fun be in that? Who would be left to give you shit if I did? Nah. I'm better off here. Keep an eye on you.'

Gutteridge smiled. His phone buzzed in his pocket. He took it out and woke the screen. It was a message from Eve —

'I really miss you. I love you. Is that so very wrong? X'

Gutteridge reread the message several times, then allowed himself a wry smile.

'Sooo…' Marston said, observing the muted joy in Gutteridge's face. 'DI Gutteridge has a love interest.' Her lids pinched in contemplation, licking at her vibrant chestnut irises, watching the contented serenity calming Gutteridge's face. 'Shame,' she sighed, 'I'd always hoped we could get together again, like old times, just to see if you're still the man you once were.'

THIRTY-ONE

FATHER DYLAN BEGAN TO TIRE FROM his day of confession, but took solace from the fact that they were held just once a month.

He'd had three adulteries; two shoplifters; at least four who'd felt guilt for feeling pleased that their marriages had ended; and a whole host of impure thoughts and urges to masturbate to contend with, and he felt decidedly sullied.

As the final sinner respectfully left the adjoining booth, Dylan slumped his back against the panelled wall and sighed… 'Who'd be a priest?' he muttered into the solitude, allowing his eyes to close, absorbing the quiet of an empty church from within the peace and tranquility of the lightless cabinet…

*

He woke with a start to the bang of the large main doors. He looked about him with confusion, not instantly recognising where he was.

He slipped his phone from his cassock pocket to check the time, the burning brightness briefly blinding him. It was 17:19. 'Oh Jesus,' he slurred; he'd been asleep for at least an hour.

Soft, tentative footsteps grew louder as they neared the adjoining booth. The door to the cabinet crept open; someone entered, sat, and closed the door behind them.

Father Dylan sat up from his slouch and wiped his eyes awake. 'Sorry,' he chuckled into the wicker mesh, 'I– I fell asleep for a brief moment there. It's been a long day, very long… Do you have something you wish to confess, my child?'

The shadow on the far side of the mesh sat still, and silent, save for the stuttered sounds of sobbing and the creaking of the seat.

'What is it that distresses you, my child?' the priest asked. 'I'm sure we're alone, you can talk freely. I'm here to listen, and I'll help in any way I can.'

The shadow drew a faltering breath. 'I don't know that what I'm doing is right?' the voice wept, the voice of a man.

'Can you explain more to me exactly what it is that troubles you?'

The sobbing intensified. 'It's… the killing. I question the killing. How, *how* can it be right? How can it *possibly* be right?'

Cold fingers slid down the priest's spine. He'd encountered this voice before. Gently Irish and talking of ultimate sin with words dripping with madness. He quaked to the memory of their first encounter and gripped his knees tight. 'Erm… k-killing…? Is this *you* you're speaking of? *You* who's been killing?'

The voice paused from its inconsolable sobbing… 'Yes!'

The priest contemplated slipping the lock off the door and making a run for it, but, no longer young, he wasn't sure he'd be fleet enough, especially clad in the leg-wrapping impedance of his robes.

He clutched a hand to his stomach, and inhaled a calming breath, trying to keep fear from showing in his voice. 'And, exactly *who* is it you've killed?'

The voice folded beneath the weight of the question and started to shed uncontrollable tears of guilt and remorse. 'Oh, dear Jesus. Sophie! It– it was my beloved Sophie. Dear Father, help me…!'

'And, wh-who is Sophie?'

'M-My partner. I killed her, and I don't even remember doing it.'

The priest took a moment to steel himself. 'And, is it *you*, my child, who is also responsible for the recent taking of the lives of children? I believe we've met before.'

The shadow fell still, the weeping briefly subsiding. 'Yes!'

The priest fumbled for his phone and began scrolling through his contacts until it flashed past DI Gutteridge's name. He carefully rolled the screen back until it appeared again and tapped it.

The voice continued. 'Is it really God that's in me?' the shadow pleaded, his voice now a whisper. 'How can I tell? How *would* I tell?'

'You truly believe God is in you?' the priest asked, opening up the message box, and beginning frantically typing:

> '*He's here! The man's here again! At the church. Please, come quickly!*'

He hit send and exhaled. His mind began to race. *You need to keep him here, as long as possible*, he thought, *you need to at least try. Try to keep him talking…*

'Do you think God would really ask you to take a life? Does *that* sound like the god you love, or who loves you?' he asked the shadow.

The shadow didn't respond, it just sat quietly in the core of its contemplation of the priest's question.

The priest's phone buzzed in his hand, sounding almost

deafening in the heart of the enclosed paneling. Father Dylan tried clamping the case tightly in his fingers to mute the vibration, pressing the device hard against his stomach, then peeked down at the screen. It was a reply. It was from Gutteridge:

'I'm on my way!'

'What are you doing?' The shadow barked abruptly, the voice now just inches from the priest's ear, face pressed hard up against the mesh, eyes turned down towards the illuminated screen.

Father Dylan flinched, nearly dropping the phone from his panicking fingers. 'N-Nothing! I– I w-w-was just checking the time.'

'You're lying to me! I can tell you're lying. Who were you calling?!'

The priest shrank from the window and sighted the latch to the door. 'It was really no one. Please, c-carry on, I'm listening, I promise,' insisted the priest.

The shadow began to rock and seethe, agitation engulfing the silhouetted figure like a cankerous parasite.

The priest looked on at the face in the uplit glow of his phone as waves of spitting rage filled the confessional.

The shadow's eyes rolled up beneath his lids as it slid away from sight, and began kicking around on the floor of the adjoining cabinet, spasming violently, splintering the door of the booth from its lightweight hinges.

The priest yelped to the sounds of cracking wood and the violent thrashing, and fumbled his panicked fingers at the lock of his own door, trying to effect an escape, when suddenly, all went quiet…

The priest froze, his face buckling beneath the weight of his fears. 'Please God, I don't deserve this. Please, please help me. Have I not always served you well?' he begged into the darkness.

He sat for what felt like minutes, but he really couldn't be sure; time seemed to have stopped.

His shaking thumb was still leaning on the latch. He held a breath, and quietly slipped it back from its staple, and slowly, pushed it open.

The door swung out into the nave with a dry-hinged creak that cut through the still air like a scalpel.

The door to the other booth lay splintered on the floor, but there was no sign of anything human, or inhuman.

'Sweet Mary!' the priest exhaled, the disbelief in his voice echoing around the timbers of the lofted ceiling and the stone of the rows of three-point archways.

Tentatively, he negotiated the shattered planking, and turned a look into what remained of the adjoining booth.

O'Leary stepped from the murk of the unlit box into the frame of the shattered doorway, his face a picture of resentment.

Father Dylan stumbled back from the looming figure, shocked by the relative youth in the face watching him with such malice in his young eyes.

The priest tripped over the splintered door and slumped to the floor, O'Leary following as the priest tried to shuffle back from his pursuer.

'Where do you think you're goin'?' O'Leary said, his rumbling Munster accent resonating throughout the hall. 'I feckin' told you what I would do if you betrayed the trust of moi boy, and the fool that you are, you didn't listen.'

The priest's fumbling retreat was halted by the back row of pews. O'Leary crouched down before him, considering the fear in the face pleading back at him with wide, beseeching eyes. 'You're no man of God. You're no man at aall. You're a serpent who dresses loik one, and Oi caan't be lettin' that live now, can Oi?'

O'Leary's hand thrust forwards, sending a sensation into the priest's body like fingers slithering through his internal organs.

The priest winced at the pain, and looked down as O'Leary withdrew his hand again, and saw the handle of a knife protruding from his gut, then turned disbelieving eyes up to meet O'Leary's cold, levelled gaze.

'This is the point where you realise you fucked up,' O'Leary said. 'How does it feel? Knowin' you're going to die, simply because you're a no-good wanker who doesn't know roit from wrong?' O'Leary huffed a dismissive smirk. 'Actually, I don't rightly care. I told you what I would do to you if you betrayed moi son, and as a man of moi word, I'd better be getting on with that, before whoever it is you called arrives…'

*

Gutteridge abandoned his car in the street and sprinted down the path to the church entrance. He made a grab for the wrought-iron handle, shouldering the heavy oak door aside with a bang that shook the stillness, stumbling into the vestibule.

'Father Dylan!?' he called into the echoing chambers, hurrying inside and looking about the hall, beads of sweat rupturing from his dampened hairline.

He breathed deep and clamped a hand to the stitch in his side. 'Father Dylan, are you here?' he called again, but there was no answer.

He made his way further in, then noticed the shards of shattered door to the confessional strewn across the marble flooring.

'*Father!*' he screamed, striding towards the booths. Then he stopped, noticing ribbons of coagulating blood staining the purity of the mottled white slab.

'Oh shit!' he slurred, his dreading eyes following thick, crimson tracks made by a dragged body as it arced around the pews, past his hesitant feet, and down the aisle towards the altar.

Gutteridge drew a breath as his eyes met the priest's, his carefully severed head sitting centre of the altar, looking out over the absent congregation, the word 'JUDAS' smeared across the frontage in blood.

The priest's headless body lay draped across the steps in inverted cruciform, the cleanly cut, open neck facing Gutteridge, leeching fluids into the aisle like an upended bottle.

It was like Cynthia all over again, reigniting the horrific memory as if it was yesterday.

The sound of running footsteps approached along the footpath outside. Keaton burst through the entrance, breathing heavily and looking hopefully about the nave. 'Are we in time?'

The look on the face twisting back to witness her arrival said it all. She clocked the head watching them from atop the altar with a mewl and a shudder.

Gutteridge sagged. 'No… no we weren't…'

THIRTY-TWO

THE CARESSING, EASTERN EUROPEAN tones of the voice drifting across the table of the Coal House Inn did little to soothe Gutteridge's mounting frustrations, but Eve took it upon herself to persevere.

'I can tell you're shaken up, *and* frustrated, but that's understandable.' She cocked her head, inquisitively. 'Why don't you run it all past me?' she suggested. 'I'm not saying that I'd *personally* be of any real use, but I often find just talking about things I'm stuck on in life helps me reorganise them in my *own* mind, and through that process, a path to effect a solution often just appears.'

An unconvincing smile displayed Gutteridge's doubt. 'We're not really supposed to talk about the case to the public, not even those we're closest to.'

The use of the words 'those we're closest to' didn't pass Eve by, but she resisted smiling. She lifted a shrug and held it. 'Is there really that much to tell that hasn't already been in the news?'

Gutteridge mirrored the shrug. 'Some, but in reality, not a lot. Truth is, we've still no real, *solid* leads to work with.'

'Well then. Talk to me. Let me be a wall to bounce your thoughts off.'

Gutteridge levelled a look into the misty grey eyes pinching back at him and twisted in his seat to look about the bar for unwanted ears. They were seated in the corner of the snug by the log burner, and very much alone.

'Fuck it,' he said, turning back to front the quizzical gaze urging him to spill all.

A glowing sense of companionship briefly tugged at the corners of Eve's mouth, but she tried to mask it with a look of cool, calm interest. 'So then, why don't you tell me what you have so far?'

Gutteridge shut his eyes and allowed himself to subside into his thoughts. 'Our guy: he's Irish, or of Irish descent. Mid-thirties or thereabouts. He's vegan or vegetarian. An artist, possibly trained, maybe studying art, or studied art? According to Carl, extremely adept at using a knife, and – if the forensics report is anything to go by – seems to favour a chef's or carving-style implement. He possibly drives an off-white, mid-size van, possibly a Vauxhall Vivaro, which we believe to be clean, displaying no markings or sign writing.' He took a breath and turned his eyes to the ceiling. 'What else…? He's methodical, calculating, but also seems able to turn frenzied for brief moments, as anger takes him over. He used a captive bolt pistol on at least two of his kills, Thomas Leinster and Jayden Peek.'

'So, just the boys then,' Eve said.

Gutteridge paused from his thoughts… 'What?'

'The gun… he used that gun thing *just* on the boys, not the girl? If you discount the man you found hanging in the tree, that is, who I think you said was probably a… a… what is the word? Collateral kill?'

Gutteridge considered the relevance of the observation. 'Yes… the boys… just the boys? Hmmm… could that be relevant?' he asked the empty snug.

'Maybe he hated his father?' suggested Eve. 'Or stepfather?

Or a brother? But a man for sure.' Eve's whole demeanour softened. 'My father used to beat me, and I spent years persecuting all the men I ever encountered because of it. But I soon realised – in time – that he was the few, not the many.'

Gutteridge's brow wound in sympathy. 'I'm sorry, I didn't know. You've never talked about that.'

'I know. But why would I when it hurt so much?'

'We're not all like that, you know?'

'I know,' said Eve.

Gutteridge clutched her hand tight, then huffed a smirk.

Eve's brow flickered. 'What is it?'

Gutteridge's temperate smile warmed the air between them. 'Nothing,' he said. 'It's just sometimes, I think your English is better than mine.' He chuckled softly at the observation and looked on at her beauty with fondness in his heart. 'You amaze me.'

'I do?'

'Yes…'

Eve blinked a smile in response to Gutteridge's admiring gazes.

'Anyway. Where were we? Oh yeah, so the captive bolt gun, you think that might be relevant, at least in the way he *chose* to deploy it? Hmmm… you might be right. And his father, you say…?'

Another shrug from Eve. 'It's possible. And *how* is he choosing them? The children I mean?'

Gutteridge sucked in a breath and reeled back from the conversation, lacing his fingers behind his head and reclining in the seat. 'Now, that we *don't* know. At first, we thought he might be scouting fast-food joints; the autopsies found remnants of junk food present in the stomachs of all but one of the children. Chicken nuggets; fries; burgers; those weird fish things smothered in tartare sauce.'

'And which one *didn't* they find any in?' Eve asked.

'Jayden Peek. They found a lot of crap in there, unhealthy shit that did little to keep him svelte, but nothing that might have suggested he'd recently been to some burger joint, something later confirmed by the parents.'

'Could that not just be the exception that proves the rule?'

'Fuck me!' Gutteridge said. 'Your English *is* better than mine.' He laughed it off. 'Anyway, maybe. But if that *is* the case, that begs the question of exactly *how* he was chosen?'

'Jayden Peek? Wasn't that the boy that was abducted from outside of his home?' asked Eve.

'Yes, that's right. But *that* then raises questions of how our perp knew the kid was a meat-eater, simply by looking at him? Which then leads me to conclude that he *must* have encountered the Peek kid before.'

'Could the killer not have observed him at a fast-food joint, *then* followed him home?'

Gutteridge shook his head. 'No. Well, we don't believe so. The last time they all ate out was the day before, and it was no fast-food joint, and that correlates with the findings of the autopsy. And besides, according to the interview sheets, they continued shopping for a good half-day *after* they'd eaten. Pretty brazen to follow a family around a busy city centre for half a day and risk being noticed. And anyway, we checked all CCTV from the area, and there wasn't a single person anywhere that was obviously following.'

'Hm...' Eve pondered. 'And exactly how is it you know that he was abducted from outside of his house?'

'Twofold: the mother spoke to him from the front door not long before he disappeared; and SOCO found traces of bleach that had been sprayed over what they believed to be blood-evidence just a few yards up the street.'

'And that destroys it?'

'Utterly. It renders the DNA completely untraceable.'

'No idiot then,' said Eve. 'Right. So, what do we have. A man; mid-thirties; Irish – so may possibly have an Irish surname; has access to, and is adept at, using kitchen-style knives; must have encountered, or at least observed Jayden Peek at some eatery or other, and in all probability, had some means of learning where he resided.' Eve sat motionless, pondering the details. '*Could* he be a chef, this guy? Good with knives; sees them eat; knows what they ordered. Do you have a list of *all* the places where the Peeks last ate, and not just the day before?'

Gutteridge's eyes narrowed at the proposition. 'No. I don't believe we do. That might be worth pursuing though?'

Eve smiled across at him as a waitress arrived with their food. 'Did I help?' she asked, leaning back to make way.

Gutteridge sat silently, lost in thought. Eve cleared the drinks to make room for the plates. 'Yes… yes, I think you did.'

His phone rang out in his pocket. He lifted apologetic eyes to the waitress as he stood to answer it.

He made for the door and swiped his finger at the screen. 'Gutteridge.'

'Sir. It's Keaton. He was FSA.'

'FSA? Who was?'

'Our Martyr. He worked for the Food Standards Agency, and get this, he was in the Gloucester area for two days making random checks of local pubs and restaurants.'

'Shit!' Gutteridge whispered.

'Sir?'

'It fits. It fucking fits… our guy, I think he might actually work in a food joint. He might even be a chef. Can you contact the Peeks, see if they're available to come in for a further interview, I've got more questions.'

'Okay, sir. It's late now, I'll try and arrange something for tomorrow.'

'Thank you. And good work. Oh, and knock it off with the "sir" shit, we're off duty.'

Keaton laughed. 'Okay, *Pat.*'

'That's better. Now have a nice evening, *Jane.* See you tomorrow…'

*

The fatigued, lusting eyes of the security guard on the door of Asda tracked two teenage girls as they left the store, favouring the straight-backed girl on the right with the platinum-blonde curls. 'Goodnight, ladies,' he called, turning to follow them out into the fresh, evening air, but the only response he got was a clandestine giggle as they hurried off towards their car.

A hooded figure slipped unseen behind his lusting into the bright, fluorescent glow of the store, bleeding out into the blackness of the night air like a beacon to the hungry.

The hooded figure hurried into the warren of aisles, head held low to obscure his face from the cameras, a fully laden cross-body bag draped across his shoulder.

The store was close to empty, just a few stragglers remaining at the tail end of a busy day.

The figure slipped a hand beneath the flap of his bag and drew out a polyethylene drinks bottle, half-filled with jagged chunks of dry ice. He screwed the loosened lid down tight, and with a swift, well-rehearsed move, extended an arm and slipped the bottle onto a shelf behind neatly stacked rows of condiment jars.

He rounded the end of the shelving and made his way towards the refrigerated aisles, counting in his head.

He'd done multiple timed tests with the same brand of drinks bottle, varying the amounts of solidified carbon-dioxide and logging the results, and knew the integrity of the bottle should relent sometime between 120 and 150 seconds.

He arrived at the aisle displaying the meat products and began feigning interest in the neatly stacked rows of dissected animal, whilst still keeping his mind on the count.

A smart, suited woman walked up behind him, her gait tall and elegant, lip pinched between thumb and forefinger. He turned his face away as she stepped in, extending an arm to take a fillet steak down from the shelf, and placing it carefully in her basket.

'Fucking cunt!' he muttered under his breath as she turned to continue her shop.

A sharp crack from the far side of the store sliced through the calm, sending shards of shattered glass spinning into the condiment aisle.

Screams from the handful of shoppers lit the air as the guard and the manager sprinted from the door to investigate.

Diversion in place, O'Leary leapt into action, scooping tubs of peppercorn sauce from his bag and neatly shelving them. His head spun like a nervous bird as he filled the shelf.

He shuffled a few feet left, taking a cautionary look around to check he was still alone, then began re-shelving pre-packed steaks he'd lifted the day before.

Carefully, he filed the last tray of meat, stepping back for a final look, then he turned to leave, flicking a glance down aisle five at the duty manager and the bewildered guard as he hurried past.

He grinned through his mounting insecurity that the will of his god was justified, and dissolved into the night.

'I can sense the doubt in you again,' said the voice of wisdom.

'No. It's– it's not doubt, n-not really,' said O'Leary. 'But… is poisoning really going to have the effect we seek? Doesn't it seem… I don't know? Inelegant?'

'Ahhhh. Now I see what it is that grieves you,' said the voice. 'The artist in you does not consider my closed-fisted approach worthy of our efforts? Does he not comprehend the effect it will have on the will of those who choose to feast on the flesh of the slaughtered?'

'You're right. You're always right. I know you are, and yes, it will, for sure. But—'

'*You* are a fine man, and indeed a fine artist, and I feel pride to have been instrumental in creating such a being. I wish all of my subjects could be as loyal and true as you are to me. Your work, your *creations*, have forced a sinful world to sit up and take notice, but now must come the consequences.'

O'Leary shed a tear that meandered down his cheek.

The voice continued. 'We need to make the world pause for thought, to wake them from their torpid ignorance of what it is they do... and to those who deny my will, I bring forth my eleventh plague... I gift to them death, and they shall reap it for the abhorrent seeds that they have chosen to sow. They will shed bloodied tears of regret, and choke and drown in the sorrow of their uncaring hearts.'

O'Leary popped the door of his van and climbed inside. 'I will question you no more. Thy will is mine.'

'Have faith, my child,' said the voice. 'We have a long journey ahead of us, it grows dark. There is one who transpired to stifle our message, and for that, he must be punished.'

THIRTY-THREE

TOBY JACKSON rolled onto his hip and began feeling around the plush upholstery of the couch for the cluster of remotes to the home-cinema system. 'So, *The Thing*, what did you think?'

Asha – the Polish beauty lounging by his side – stretched her exaggerated limbs awake and turned tired eyes towards him. 'You were right, an awesome film. Perhaps a tad gory for my liking, but other than that, prrretty awesome.'

Jackson joined her in the stretch. 'I can never tire of watching it, must have seen it at least fifty times,' Jackson proclaimed. It's still a classic. Effects are incredible.'

Jackson finally found the remotes nestled down the side of the seat cushion and began pointing them one at a time at the wall.

The scrolling film credits flickered off, the surround-sound fell silent with a gentle pop, and the screen began to spool away into the ceiling.

He checked his watch. 'Shit!' he said, his face brightening at the time. 'It's 2:27! I didn't realise it was so late.'

'Let's go to bed,' said the Polish beauty, still holding the stretch, lying submissively open on her back, arms draped over her head seductively. 'Or you could just fuck me right here, right now?'

The response in the face looking back at her sultry, grey eyes spoke volumes.

The doorbells chimed, loud and intrusive, waking the stillness, echoing around the house.

Asha sat from her recline and curled into an insecure ball, wrapping herself around her folded knees. 'Wh-Who could that be?'

Jackson sat upright and turned to face the sound. 'I– I don't know? The main gates, they should be shut by now,' he said, checking his watch again. 'The time-locks are supposed to kick in at ten…'

He turned to the girl. 'Are *you* expecting anyone?'

She frowned at the suggestion. 'At this hour. Of course not!'

The doorbells chimed again, seeming louder this time in the core of their unease.

'You'd better go and answer it,' said Asha. 'It might be someone in trrrouble.'

Jackson rose uneasily to his feet. 'Okay,' he said, his voice uncertain.

His legs felt soft and reluctant as they carried him into the entrance hall. He hooked the security chain through its staple, snapped the deadbolts back, and slowly opened the door…

Jackson presented an eye to the slither of night sky peeking through the frame. The cold air chilled his skin, but he could see no one.

A foot suddenly stamped the door open, ripping the chain off the surround and sending its latch hurtling across the hallway.

The door clipped Jackson's shoulder, spinning him around and smashing open against the wall.

Asha's scream filled the air as O'Leary strode into the house, barefoot and naked, save for the layers of clingfilm crudely wrapping his entire body, a letterbox opening torn from in front of his manic stare so he could witness the fear in the faces looking back at him.

He had a cross-body bag draped across his shoulder, his gloved right hand clutching what looked to be at least a ten-inch knife.

Jackson staggered back from the blow and slammed against the opposite wall.

The mile-long girl screamed a second time and spun a panicked look towards the side table where one of the three guns they kept in the house was stashed.

Being a tech-millionaire, Jackson had spoken with Asha of an event such as this on many occasions, imagining they were prepared, but faced with the reality of their fears becoming flesh, they both froze, paralysed by the savagery of the moment.

O'Leary thundered towards Jackson who now lay slumped against the wall; he hooked the point of his knife beneath his jaw. He used upward pressure to force Jackson to his feet. '*Get up!*' O'Leary insisted. 'I said, *get up*!'

The point of the blade pierced Jackson's skin. He complied, softly begging, his demeanour humble. 'Please, I'll give you any amount of money, just don't hurt us!'

'Just get up, and get over there!' O'Leary hissed, flashing thunderous eyes in the direction of the cinema room.

Asha sat perched on the edge of the seat, hesitating in the direction of the gun, pondering the feasibility of making a dash for the side table, opening the drawer, finding the gun, sliding the safety off, taking aim, and firing shots into the intruder, all before the assailant could react. He was, after all, only armed with a knife, but she wasn't sure she could, and the opportunity to attempt it was trickling away fast.

'You! Back in the seat!' O'Leary spat, snapping a look in her direction.

She complied, giving the side table one last desperately longing look as she sank her reluctance back into the embrace of the upholstery.

'Please, don't hurt him. You can take anything you like, just don't hurt him,' she begged.

'I don't want none of your shit,' O'Leary said, a mildly Irish accent flavouring his words.

'What *do* you want?' Jackson asked.

O'Leary spun him into the seat next to the girl. 'Shut the *fuck* up,' he fizzled.

O'Leary strode to the adjoining room, grabbing one of the balloon-backed chairs from around the ostentatious dining table, and strode back into the cinema room, sliding the seat back beneath the couch right behind the girl.

He grabbed a roll of duct-tape from his bag, clamping his hand beneath the girl's chin, and wrenched her head back towards him, cranking her neck over the rear of the couch.

He began coiling the tape around one of the chair legs and up over the dome of her forehead, binding her firmly in the seat. Asha's body arced under the force like an archer's bow, and she felt certain her neck would snap like a dry twig.

She lay helpless and prone, her supine neck stretched over the back of the seat, eyes to the ceiling.

Her throat lay exposed, her delicate fingers clawing at her taut neckline. She began to weep tears of fear for her young life, the tightness in her windpipe making the glint of the knife above her as it caught the light impossible to ignore.

'Don't hurt her!' Jackson pleaded. 'She's all I've got. Just tell me what it is you want, and you can have it. *Anything!* Just name it!'

O'Leary tore the last coil of tape from the roll and spun his hateful gaze to Jackson. 'Unfortunately for you, what I want, *you* can't give me!' he seethed.

Jackson's confusion displayed loud and clear in his tear-drenched face. 'But… I don't understand? There must be something?'

But O'Leary failed to hear him, far too distracted by the sight of the Polish angel in her humbled state, lying beneath his perverting eyes.

The girl's skittering pupils pleaded up at him as he looked down upon her vulnerability with impure malice illuminating his face. She could see it in his flickering eyes: the sight of her elegant, sweat-beaded neck stretched long and open excited him.

His loins began to swell as he looked upon her fear with excitement, hypnotised by the intense, rhythmical pulse of her carotid artery beneath her smooth, perfect, delicate skin.

Becoming lost in his fantasies, O'Leary carefully presented the blade of his knife to her slender windpipe. *One cut*, he thought. *Just one, swift cut, and she'd be gone.*

'Can't you see this is wrong!' O'Leary said. But his voice was now deeper, calmer, softly spoken and almost comforting in its transitioned tone. 'I sense sin in your heart, my child, you must fight it.'

O'Leary stumbled from the moment, seeming surprised by his own voice, lifting the blade clear of the girl's throat like a scolded child. 'S-s-s-sorry! I'm so sorry! Oh God! Forgive me! I… I didn't mean to… Oh Lord. Please forgive me!'

O'Leary's frantic demeanour softened again, appearing to dissolve away like salt crystals in water.

The hostages looked on through widening, paralysed eyes.

'Apologise not to me, my son,' said the softer voice, 'for it is *I* that gifted man the capacity to sin. But you must learn to fight it, fight that will, fight those desires, fight the urges that manifest inside of you. And if in this one simple endeavour you can succeed, only then can you consider yourself worthy of the title, "a good man".'

O'Leary's personality pushed through again. 'I will try. I will. But the temptation grows stronger in me each time I kill. But I will try.'

Jackson's pinprick pupils shook in the reddening discs of his panicked stare, gazing back at the insanity unfolding before him. At a man negotiating with himself not to take the life of his future wife.

O'Leary's apologetic front melted away again, visibly transforming. 'Remember why it is we are here,' said the calmer, wiser voice. 'Someone took something from you, from *us*, and for *that* they must be punished.' The calmer, passive eyes remained, turning to drink in Jackson. '*This* man took from us our message, took it away from eyes that need to see it. Bought it with a sinner's wealth, depriving the world of the purity of its message.'

Jackson crumbled beneath the force of the perceived psychosis as O'Leary's personality morphed to the fore once more like a man stepping through a curtain.

Asha whimpered, mourning her defiled innocence. Jackson's breath quickened. 'I– I don't know what's happening,' he wept.

O'Leary peered out through the rip in the clingfilm, resentment cementing his gaze. 'Don't you know who I am? Haven't you worked it out yet?' he said. O'Leary huffed a dismissively mocking smirk. 'I once read in an interview that you desired to meet me, and yet, you claim not to know me.'

Jackson attempted to recall the interview.

The girl's eye sockets filled with tears, drowning her vision.

Jackson sagged. 'I don't know. All I know is I want to live. I want *Asha* to live.'

O'Leary's gaze hardened to the pleas and the pathetic sobbing. 'You *want* to live! You steal from me, my creation, and you want to live! I hardly know if you're being serious, or if you're intentionally intending to mock me?'

Jackson winced at the threat. 'I don't know what you mean! Please! I don't know anything,' he sobbed.

O'Leary leaned into him, demeanour dripping with contempt. '*I* am Tick-Tock, and you *stole* from me my art. *Bought* my art!' O'Leary's face began to contort with ultimate loathing. '*You* were instrumental in causing the world to focus not on the message, but the *value* of my creations, substituting gratitude and appreciation for gluttony and greed. *You* started a trend that devalued the word of my gift, until the world that needed to listen could no longer hear, and no one knew to care anymore, until all they could see was the pound signs of their avarice, and not the beauty in the relevance of what I bestowed upon them.'

He leaned further in, levelled his gaze with Jackson's and lowered his voice to a whisper. 'Because of you, *I* was forced to kill to make them hear again, to create my message in ways that could not be bought. Bought by the likes of *you* and your meaningless ilk, with your sinner's wealth and your inability to appreciate *who*, or *what* I am.'

All Jackson could think about at that moment – as the grim realisation finally hit home like a kick to the gut that the Spatchcock Killer was crouched before him – was to get the threat away from his beloved Asha.

'I'm sorry, you must believe me, I didn't understand. I– I never realised that what I was doing was wrong. Can you not find it in your heart to forgive me my ignorance?'

Jackson darted a look towards the room where the section of wall was displayed 'We could take it back, back to Gloucester. I know people, *important* people. I could arrange to have it displayed in a prime location for all to see, so the *whole* world can marvel at its brilliance, the way *I* do. Let's go, now, and take a look at it, it's just through there,' he said, indicating the adjoining archway. 'I only bought it because I admired it, admired your work, like I admire *all* of your work.' His beseeching eyes pawed at O'Leary. '*Please!* I'm just an ignorant fan, you can't blame me for not having what it takes to comprehend your incomparable genius, I mean, how could I... But we can right the wrong. It's not too late!'

O'Leary's softening gaze turned to follow Jackson's, curiosity at the chance of seeing his long-lost work again dousing his anger.

He'd titled it 'Animal Cruelty', and it was one of his favourite pieces he'd created.

He turned back to Jackson, and lowered the knife to Asha's throat again, pressing it firmly against her flesh until the skin either side of the blade flashed white. He squinted threatening eyes at Jackson. 'Get up!' he barked. 'And if you try anything clever, I swear to God, I'll kill her!'

Jackson rose nervously from the seat and nodded his understanding. 'You have my word.'

O'Leary lifted the blade clear of Asha's throat, leaving a crimson indent in her alabaster skin. 'Show me,' he said. 'You first.'

Jackson rounded the couch and skulked past O'Leary who traced his movements with the knife.

'Don't worry, my love,' Jackson called to Asha, her moist, reddened, unblinking eyes following him across the room. 'Everything's going to be okay,' he assured her, uncertain of the truth in his words.

He flicked O'Leary a distrusting look. 'It's through here. Follow me.'

O'Leary followed, knife pressed between Jackson's shoulder blades.

Jackson extended a cautious arm to flick on the cluster of spotlights he'd had installed to show the section of wall off to its best. O'Leary's resultant gasp was audible, the sight he beheld exciting his eyes.

The section of wall looked much larger in the context of the space it now graced. O'Leary had to reacquaint himself with its details; so much time had passed since he last saw it, he barely recognised it as his own work.

But details did slowly begin to emerge that aided memory: the soft edges where the breeze had lifted the stencils; the spray-can drips he'd made into details with the use of a fine brush; and reliving the rage he felt when crowning the finished piece with the message he'd scrawled beneath, punctuated by the anger present in the sweep of the brush.

Jackson stepped graciously to one side, allowing O'Leary an unfettered view.

*

Asha dug her freshly manicured thumbnails frantically at the ribbon of tape binding her to the couch, trying to pierce the restraint, but the multiple layers were proving too thick to puncture.

She *knew* from experience that, if she tried to tug at it, it would more than likely consolidate the flat ribbon into a thick rope of glue, thread and plastic that her slender arms would then have little chance of breaking.

She began to saw the nail across the surface, trying to compromise its integrity.

Her nail finally began to dig in, catching the reinforcing threads, fraying the tape until a stress-riser appeared along the front edge.

Asha noticed the break through the glistening corners of her eyes, and began sawing frantically at the nick, her tearing cuticles burning to the force as she sliced, and cut, and hacked at the fraying edge…

*

O'Leary lowered the knife and stepped up to the framed section of wall, presenting the flat of his hand to the cold surface of the mural, allowing himself a moment to marvel at the steelwork cradle built specially to house and transport the masterpiece, *his* masterpiece.

'You see,' said Jackson, sensing the placidity in O'Leary's demeanour, 'we can put it back. Back where it belongs. Or better still, place it somewhere where *everyone* will see it to appreciate it. That area around the docks, maybe? It would be perfect. Every person who passes that way couldn't help but—'

Jackson's schmoozing ceased; his fixed stare locked on the adjoining doorway. O'Leary turned to see what had arrested his attention, and saw Asha standing in the doorway, her whole body quaking at the pressure of having the upper hand.

Blood from her torn nail dripped from the handle of the pistol she held, aimed directly at O'Leary's head.

'*Kurwa ciecie!*' she hissed. 'How fucking dare you, you–you… fucking *cunt*!'

O'Leary stuttered in the crux of the threat, cowering before the muzzle of the gun, a pleading hand held out towards her, eyes begging for mercy he didn't deserve.

The boiling resentment welled in her gut, the indignity and humiliation she felt tugging her finger against the trigger.

The pistol fired, kicking in her slender fingers. The *crack* of the shot shattered the tension as the bullet scythed through the palm of O'Leary's insistent hand.

Blood, fat and splintered bone blew through the hole,

peppering O'Leary's shocked expression as a hot, searing pain sliced up his arm.

O'Leary howled in agony, dropping to his knees and cradling his hand.

Jackson's hesitant front appealed across the divide to Asha. 'Asha! Again! Shoot him again!'

Asha's shaking hands raised the pistol a second time, attempting to take aim, just as O'Leary struggled to his feet and made a desperate dash for the door, dropping his knife in the process.

O'Leary swung a parting elbow hard into Asha's jaw as he rushed past, snapping her head back against the frame of the door with a sickening thud that shook the timbers of the building.

She slumped to the floor where she had stood, dropping to the ground like a wet towel and blacking out.

O'Leary stumbled out into the night, charging for the section of perimeter fence he'd cut away to gain access, leaving an intermittent trail of blood in his wake like Morse code to his pain.

Jackson dashed across the room and sank to the floor. He fumbled his hands around Asha's unconscious body, cradling her in his arms, rocking in his relief that he was still alive. That *they* were still alive.

'Asha!' he begged, cupping her emotionless face in his adoring hand. '*Asha!*' he pleaded, delivering a love-loaded kiss to the crown of her lolloping forehead, cradling her swelling jawline in his hand.

Her lids flickered momentarily, then with a groan, she simpered awake. He could feel her breath on his face, and tears broke free of his relieved eyes as he searched in his pocket for his phone.

His shaking thumb swiped the screen awake, and he dabbed '999'...

THIRTY-FOUR

'ARE YOU GOING TO BE OKAY?' Gutteridge asked, over the sounds of carpenters installing a new door, as he sat opposite Jackson and the Polish muse at the dining table of their home, but directing the question more to Asha and her heavily bruised jawline than the man clinging to her arm like he'd nearly lost her.

She nodded, coyly. 'Yes. Thank you. I'm fine. *I'll* be fine.'

'The wanker clocked her as he fled; she was out cold, poor thing,' explained Jackson. 'She's slightly concussed, and twisted her knee in the fall, but she's doing great now.' He turned and smiled at her ruefully, but with gratitude and fondness warming his gaze. 'You should have seen her, she was amazing. She saved our lives, I'm sure of it.'

But Gutteridge could sense something missing from the girl's demeanour, something he'd seen the very first time he encountered her. The subtle, self-assured confidence at knowing she was one of God's finest creations that he'd witnessed before, was gone, humiliated out of her by the humbling nature of the night's ordeal, and he prayed that, one day, it may return, because it elevated her beauty to something verging on ethereal, rather than just a physical sublimity that made the heads of passers-by turn to look.

Gutteridge joined in bolstering her timid facade with temperate smiles. 'You'll be okay, no permanent harm done, eh? Does it hurt?' he asked – cocking a look at the bruising on the side of her face.

She stretched her mouth wide with a grimace. 'A bit. It's not nearly as bad as it was, but at least it isn't brrroken,' she replied, the gentle way she rolled the 'r' in 'broken' – once again – reminding him of Eve… *Eve*, he remembered… He must call Eve. He scrutinised the angel opposite, then turned to more important matters.

Gutteridge took his flip-pad from his pocket and opened it to a clean page. 'So, I think you said on the phone he was *naked*?'

'Yes. Well? Kind of, but not really,' Jackson said. 'He was covered head to toe in clingfilm – for some fucking reason? But you could certainly see everything.'

Gutteridge lowered his eyes to make a note. 'We think he does that so he won't leave evidence behind,' he explained. 'Hair; skin; fibres; fluids. That sort of thing. Clever really.'

'*Fluids?*' said Jackson. 'Oh… I see…Of course… Well, the bastard did have a fucking boner when he was holding that knife to Asha's throat,' Jackson said. 'Fucking freak!'

Asha visibly folded in on herself at the reminder of how close she was to having her young life taken from her. Gutteridge noticed, lamenting her lost confidence.

He ceased writing, lowered the pad, and quietly folded it shut. 'Listen. People like him are rare, few and far between. In my twenty odd years on the job, I've only ever come across two like him, and *he* is one of them. So don't let your imagination run away with you, convincing yourself that the world is full of crazies, because that's painfully easy to do, and on the whole, it isn't true.'

He extended a compassionate hand and placed it atop Asha's fidgeting, interwoven fingers. 'I wouldn't lie to you, not about something like this. Okay? I promise.' He removed the hand again with a parting squeeze and smiled back at her look of appreciation for his words of comfort.

He looked to Jackson again. 'Cheshire police are placing officers on twenty-four-hour surveillances,' he added. 'You'll be just fine, and we'll catch him.'

'When?' Jackson asked, attempting not to sound impatient, and failing.

Gutteridge fought to maintain the facade of supreme confidence he'd been wearing for the last week. 'Soon… very soon – well that's the hope, especially with the new leads we have to follow.'

Jackson took a pensive sip of his tea and lifted sombre eyes to Gutteridge through the curtain of rising steam. 'Did he really behead that priest?'

Gutteridge closed his eyes and nodded mournfully. 'Yes.'

'*Jesus!*' Jackson responded, his voice now a whisper. 'I can't believe he was here, standing just over there, he even touched us… I'm not sure I'll ever be the same again.'

Gutteridge reopened his pad. 'Tell me about the two manifestations you saw. You *did* say two, right?'

Jackson hugged Asha's arm like a favourite pillow, looking to her for confirmation that what they'd witnessed was real.

'Yes. Two… *one* of them was definitely him,' he said, 'that much I do know. But as for the other, fuck knows.' He sat back in his seat, uncoiling himself from Asha's arm, and began toying with the rim of his mug. 'Saying that, I did at one point – and I know how this is going to sound, so try not to judge me – but at one point, I was convinced the other voice was that of God himself, as if *God* was in him, sharing his body, sharing his mind.' He looked across at Gutteridge with questioning eyes. 'Does that sound mad?'

Gutteridge loosed an ironic laugh. 'Yes, but no… The

priest you mentioned – Father Dylan – told us a similar story, that our perp proclaimed God was inside of him, in his mouth; in his stomach; behind his eyes. So, no. No, it doesn't sound mad, not at all – although, obviously, it is.'

Gutteridge made a conscious decision not to disclose the third personality the priest had encountered; the couple seemed unnerved enough.

Asha leaned forwards to join in the discussion. 'We got the feeling that the God character that was inside of him, was– how do you say it? *Calling the shots*? If I've said that right?'

Gutteridge laughed. 'Yes. That's right. So you *think* he was being guided by this other personality? By the *God* side?'

'Yes. At least that's the way it seemed,' agreed Jackson. 'Saying that, when he *was* himself, the agenda he was following *did* seem to be driven by his *own* mind, by *his* agenda. As though the war was his own, but the God he was harbouring was somehow the General.'

A workman appeared in the doorway, politely hesitating by the entrance to the room. Jackson addressed him with a raised-brow smile.

'Sorry to disturb you, boss. That's all done. Did you want to come and check it before we leave?' he said to Jackson.

None of them had even noticed the commotion had stopped, and Jackson briefly excused himself from the table. 'I'm sure it'll be fine, Gary,' Jackson said as he left the room. 'The work you've done for me in the past has always been to a high standard. What do I owe you…?'

Gutteridge watched them as they left, then his eyes returned to Asha's. They both exchanged coy smiles in the lull of the conversation.

'Are you *sure* you're going to be all right?' Gutteridge asked, softening his voice to a caress. 'You can always seek counselling, if you needed it. You'd be surprised how many in similar situations to yourself find it helps.'

Asha responded with an appreciative, but declining smile. 'I am a strrrong girl, I will be okay,' she assured him, rolling the 'r' again in 'strong'.

Eve's face flashed momentarily into Gutteridge's mind. He nodded his understanding, and took a sip of his tea without his eyes ever leaving Asha's. 'You know, you remind me of someone,' he said, lowering the mug again and holding the stare.

Asha cocked her head, her brow flickering her intrigue, but she didn't seem surprised. 'I know,' she said, 'I've seen it in your eyes whenever you look at me.'

Gutteridge huffed a laugh. 'Is it that obvious?'

She too laughed. 'Yes.'

Gutteridge allowed his thoughts to drift away to Eve. 'She's beautiful, like you. And *kind*, the way you are.'

'What is her name?'

'Ewelina. *Eve.*'

'Ahh. So, she is Polish. Like me?'

'Yes.'

'Prrretty name,' she said, now sounding more Polish than ever – as if she'd purposefully been stifling her accent. 'A nice girl?'

'Yes. Very.'

'Do you have a picture?'

Gutteridge frowned at the request, then remembered the one picture he had in his phone. 'Yes. Yes, I do.' He opened the file and handed his phone across the table to an eager hand.

Asha scrutinised the image. 'Wow… she is beautiful, and tall, like a goddess. Her face, it is similar to mine. Yes?'

'Perhaps. Well, maybe not quite as—'

Asha halted his sentence just with a look. Neither berating, nor exultant, just a look. She handed him back the phone. Her piercing grey eyes narrowed. 'When you look at me – the way you do – is it *her* you are thinking of? Is it *her* you see? See in me?'

Gutteridge squirmed, more used to being the interrogator than the interrogated.

His hot cheeks flushed cerise, feeling discomfort at being quizzed about his personal life by a stranger, and yet, on some deeper, emotional level, he felt able to confide in her, be open with her, perhaps because, in some childlike way, he was madly in love with the woman sat facing him.

'You can't possibly be a stranger to men looking at you,' he said.

She smirked. 'No. But with you, it's somehow different.'

Gutteridge sighed. 'You're right. And yes… yes, it is. You're so very much like her, it's difficult not to see her in you. In fact, *you* are the reason I contacted her again. Encountering you is the sole reason she's once more in my life.' He warmed her with a smile that lit his eyes. 'You… you're really very lovely, the way Eve is – *if,* that isn't wrong for me to say.'

The girl popped a dismissive shrug. 'Maybe it is? Maybe it isn't? Either way, it can be our little secrrret.'

She winked, delivering a smile across the divide as genuine as any he'd ever received.

His heart swelled for a beat, and for that briefest of moments, he felt envy for Jackson and his perfect life.

A sudden desperation to speak to Eve enveloped him, a desire to admit to her his feelings, feelings he'd been denying, feelings ignited by the presence of the girl sat opposite.

But he naturally shied from the word 'love', and for far too long now he'd been afraid to use it again, afraid of its power. He feared feeling it, only to lose it again.

He also had his undeniable feelings for Jane Keaton to contend with, wishing to clear away the confusion they birthed deep within him.

But arguably more important than any of those things was that he had a killer to catch, and that fact alone created a barrier to his own avenues for happiness.

Asha looked on as Gutteridge floundered in his feelings.

'What is it that holds you back?' the angel asked.

Gutteridge re-emerged from his thoughts. 'Holds me back? Back from what?'

'From telling this girl how you feel?'

Gutteridge's lower lids licked at his coronas. 'But— how?'

The girl laughed. 'I can read it in yourrr face. You are a very emotional man, a sensual man. The turmoil of your confused feelings displays in your eyes, like a book, it's very loud, and besides, if there wasn't a prrroblem, then you wouldn't look to me with such conflict in yourrr face.'

Gutteridge flushed with abashment, dropped his gaze to the tabletop, hands cradling his lukewarm mug.

Asha craned her slender neck down to level her eyes with his. Her brows knitted. 'There is another?'

He stared back at her, his face a picture of surprise. 'How did you know that?'

'I didn't – not for sure – but I do now. Tell me about her?'

Gutteridge shook his head. 'No, it– it couldn't possibly be not that one, it's too complicated. That one, the *other* one, could never happen.'

'Why?'

'No. It– it just couldn't. It would create too many complications, I just—'

'But you have feelings for her, this girl?' asked Asha.

'Yes. Yes, I do, but not the same.'

Asha twisted a look into his eyes. 'You have perhaps been

intimate with her – this other girl – and this is what causes the confusion?'

'No. No we haven't. We *nearly* did, but no.'

Jackson's voice approached from the hallway; he finally returned to the dining room with DS Keaton in tow.

Gutteridge and the angel sat back out of the conversation, each taking a breath to reset themselves.

'Sorry about that,' Jackson apologised. 'They've done a lovely job of that door,' he said to Asha, 'extra locks and *three* weapons-grade chains.'

Keaton rounded Jackson and entered the room. She took a seat two to the left of Gutteridge and smiled in his direction.

He responded with his own, tentative smile as the Polish angel watched their interaction. Her face lit up, her feminine instincts tugging at the corners of her ruby-red lips.

'So, how did you get on?' Gutteridge asked.

Keaton stowed her bag at the side of the seat. 'Good. They're going to do DNA analysis on the blood they've collected, but it's type A-negative – fairly rare. Only about 8% of the population – if I remember my figures correctly? So, it'll be useful in ascertaining if it was our guy.'

'It *was* him, going by what Mr Jackson and Asha have told me, almost certainly.'

Keaton frowned at the overfamiliar use of the girl's Christian name but concluded Gutteridge probably had difficulty pronouncing her surname.

'Have they gone?' Gutteridge asked, referring to the SOCO team.

Keaton nodded. 'Yes. Just. It's pitch black out there now.' She checked her watch – 22:47. She turned her wrist over to show Gutteridge.

'*Jesus*,' he said. 'We'd better get going. Sorry for keeping you both up for so long, and thank you for your time, *and* the tea.'

They all stood from the table, collecting coats and jackets from the backs of seats.

Asha took Jackson's arm and pulled him to one side. A clandestine conversation ensued, with Jackson listening intently, darting looks in the direction of the waiting detectives.

Jackson's face brightened agreeably, and he turned to address the watching visitors. 'It's getting late. You wouldn't be getting back to Gloucester until the early hours. Why don't you both stay here the night? We have two guest rooms ready: clean linen; towels; both en suite. It would be our pleasure; it'd be no trouble?'

Gutteridge made motions to gratefully turn down the offer, when Asha piped in. '*Please*, you'd be very welcome, and if we're being trrruthful, we're still a bit shaken up after last night's ordeal. It would be comforting to know someone else was here, even if it is just forrr one night – if that doesn't sound too selfish.'

Gutteridge turned to Keaton, who lifted why-the-hell-not shoulders in response to his telepathic query.

He turned back to the anxious couple and their expectant faces. 'Well, if you're sure, that would be much appreciated, and I can't deny, the prospect of that long drive in the dark wasn't sitting well.'

Asha's brightening face lit the room. 'Good! Well, that's settled then… Toby, why don't you get… I'm sorry, I don't know your first name?' she said to Keaton.

'It's Jane.'

'Jane. Pleased to meet you, Jane. Why don't you get Jane a drrrink, while I show our Detective Inspector here where their rooms are located.'

She rounded the table and looped her arm playfully through his, acting like an excited teenager on an impromptu sleepover, and towed him towards the spiralling wooden staircase that climbed from the entrance hallway.

Jackson observed her coquettish energies leading Gutteridge away, and laughed, then remembered his instructions. 'What can I get you, *Jane*?'

Keaton placed her coat and bag back down again, and shuffled uncomfortably at the attention of the stranger. Outside of work, when not shielded by the power of her badge, her confidence could falter.

'Erm? Gin?'

'Gin it is,' he sang. 'We have Silent Pool, with tonic? A slice of lemon, or orange? I recommend orange?'

Keaton smiled her gratitude. 'Okay. That sounds lovely.'

'Coming right up, oh, and please, relax. Our home is your home, at least for tonight. Oh, and call me Toby,' he beamed. He was charming, and Keaton could see the attraction.

*

Gutteridge was towed to the top of the staircase and led onto a thickly carpeted landing that stretched the entire length of the first floor.

A lattice of exposed beams looped the lofted roof space high above them, feeling more like a cathedral than a home. The smell of the oak and Axminster wool hit his nose, and the envy returned.

'Fuck! This is lovely,' he said, his head spinning to all the details like a meerkat's.

She took his hand in hers and led him along the landing. 'I will put you here,' she said, indicating a door, 'and Jane, here,' she added, indicating the door next to it. 'Follow me, this is your rrroom,' she chirped – opening the first door, and leading Gutteridge in by his arm.

She leaned a furtive look down the landing and closed the door behind her. She turned to face Gutteridge face on. 'Both these rooms have queen-sized beds,' she explained, looking about the large space, then lifting a finger to the far side of the room. Gutteridge's eyes followed, '*There* is an adjoining doorway. It leads directly into Jane's rrroom.' She drilled Gutteridge with a look. '*If* you needed to see her for any reason – to talk about the case, perhaps – or perhaps not,' she added, looking knowingly into his soul with deep, sensuous eyes, 'you could access her rrroom that way, and no one would ever know, only you, and her.'

She paused to consider him. 'It is not my business to say, but you are a very nice man, a hard-working man, and you should have someone… someone to share your life with, someone to hold you at night. *Maybe* you need to get this *other* girl – whoever she may be – out of your system,' she said with a wink, 'and only then can you finally make the decision that will give you the happiness you seek. Clear away the dead wood.'

She smiled into his eyes. She looked more beautiful than she ever had in the soft light of the room. Gutteridge's breathing became laboured by the tightening in the pit of his stomach as she stepped nearer, eyes beyond human in their beauty, staring deep into his boiling desires.

She leaned into his ear. 'And you need to forrrget about me,' she whispered. 'It's Eve, *Eve* is the girl for you. She is a goddess. She is perrrfect, and you need to look after her.' She leaned out again, paused, then twisted her sultry features and placed her lips against his.

His whole soul shifted at the taste of her breath, and for a moment, he felt fifteen again.

The scent of her perfume and perfect skin washed through him like a biblical flood, and he felt light-headed and lost in the moment.

She loosed a parting breath into his lungs and released the kiss. Gutteridge hovered in the aftermath, floating around inside of his fantasies, until finally, he returned to the room.

Asha cupped an affectionate hand to the side of his face. 'After tonight, go to Eve, look after Eve, *take* Eve. Think only of her, and not of me...' She smiled. 'Come on,' she said, 'let us join the others. You look like you could do with a drrrink...'

THIRTY-FIVE

'TELL ME, DID WE DO THE WRONG THING?' Gutteridge asked, as Keaton stood facing him, adjusting his tie like an overly supportive wife, the early morning sun burning through the window and warming her shoulder.

'Depends how you define "wrong",' she replied.

A shrug. 'Could we end up regretting last night?'

She finished squaring the knot and dropped her hands to her sides. 'Well, I don't regret it, and I'd be lying through my teeth if I said I hadn't ever wanted you to fuck me… Why, do you?'

Gutteridge lifted an affectionate hand to the side of her face. Her skin felt soft and pliant, like the skin of her inner thighs he'd been stroking just a few hours earlier. She closed her eyes and rolled her cheek against the caress of his fingers. 'Haven't *you* ever wanted *me*?' she asked.

'Of course… of course I have. You know I have.'

'Well then. Didn't you like it?'

Gutteridge exhaled a chestful of pent-up desire. 'Of course I did. It was like a dream.'

Her lids parted again and she looked to him with eyes drowning in socially realistic tears of truth. Her voice began to crack. 'A dream that was, but that must never be again. You have a girl now, a girl that needs you to make her happy, that makes *you* happy. A girl who's perfect for you, and her name... is Eve...'

Keaton's soft features delighted his searching eyes as he dabbed her eyes dry.

'You're right,' he said, 'but I'm glad we did this. You're wise beyond your years, Jane.'

'I am?'

'Yes.'

She peered into his guilt-ridden face. 'So don't regret last night. I wanted it, and I think you did too.'

'I did.'

'So then... you and me aren't meant to be – except as colleagues. And no one need ever know.'

She then loosed a grin through the tears like a cat that got the cream. 'But you sure did a number on me last night, I won't forget that in a hurry,' she chuckled.

She stepped back and stooped to grab her bag, and looked about the room to check she hadn't left anything behind. She presented herself to Gutteridge again. 'How do I look?'

He smiled wide. 'As always, Jane, beautiful.'

'Thank you... Means a lot... Come on then. Back to detective mode,' she fizzed, erupting to life, 'we have an arsehole to catch.'

She walked to the door, opened it, and turned to give the den of their night of intimacy one last look... Her brows crimped quizzical. 'Did *she* – Asha – set this up?'

Gutteridge laughed out loud. 'Ohhh you have no idea.'

*

The guests sat at the breakfast bar, finishing the toast and coffee that had greeted their arrival downstairs. They stood to bid their hosts farewell.

'Again, thank you,' said Keaton, 'that was really a very nice evening.'

'Our pleasure,' Jackson said. 'And if you're ever in the area again, feel free to drop by, anytime,' he added, as his eyes flitted from one grateful face to the other.

Jackson and Keaton sauntered out of the door into the morning warmth, exchanging information about Knutsford.

Gutteridge pocketed his phone, grabbed his jacket, and turned to follow, only to be intercepted by Asha. She checked behind her, then fronted him. The feminine sweep of her eyes searched his soul for answers. A theatrical raise of the brows. 'Aaaand, did you? If it's not too impertinent to ask?'

A wry smile. 'Put it this way, there's only one set of bedclothes to change.'

'And… is she out of your system? Do you now feel ready to tell the goddess how you feel?'

Another smile. 'Yes. Yes, I do. Thanks to you.'

Asha smiled warmly, and wrapped her slender arms around his broad shoulders, before lifting a kiss to his lips on pointed toes.

She dropped onto her heels again. 'Now go… Go make her happy. Go make *yourself* happy and catch that killer.'

He fixed her the most sincere of looks. 'I will, and again, thank you. If I never get the chance to see you again, I want you to know, you're amazing.'

She smiled, almost mournfully. 'Goodbye, Detective.'

'It's Patrick. My name, it's Patrick.'

'Patrick.' She smiled. 'Then goodbye, *Patrick*. Take good care of yourself.'

'And you, Asha.'

Gutteridge brushed her cheek tenderly with the backs of his fingers, then turned, and left through the door into the rays of the low-hanging sun…

*

The M6 motorway was surprisingly empty so close to rush hour. Gutteridge drove. He handed Keaton his phone. 'I had messages come through when I turned it on, could you read them out for me?'

Keaton woke the phone and began scanning the incomings.

'There's one from Eve,' she laughed, 'but I'd better not read that.'

'Oh… erm… okay. I'm sorry.'

Keaton turned a censorious look into his ear. 'Oi! What did we just say? As far as we're concerned, last night didn't happen.'

'You're right. I'm sorry.'

She turned her attention back to the phone. 'Although, saying that, walking has been an issue for me this morning. I've been stumbling around like a newborn deer!'

'Will you just read those messages!'

Keaton grinned, scrolling through the phone. 'The Peeks have made contact; they've been away for the funeral for Jayden. They say they'll be returning sometime this morning; they can come in this afternoon, if you're still wanting to see them?'

'I do. Can you organise that?'

'Of course. I wonder where they've been?'

Gutteridge shrugged. 'My guess – Chester.'

'Why Chester?'

'Their accents – especially the mother's – have a subtly soft drawl that verges on Scouse, but they sometimes clip the end of their words, especially those ending in a "t", like the Welsh do, so my guess would be central Chester. They may have originated from there, and *moved* to Gloucester?'

'How do you know this stuff?'

'I take interest in the world. I observe it, then try to work out why it is the way it is. Chester is smack in the middle of Wales and Liverpool, so both those pronounced accents tend to bleed into the city, colouring the natural Cheshire accent into its own thing, but with elements of both still discernible.'

Keaton smiled, and shook her head.

'What else?' Gutteridge asked.

She opened the next message. 'Oh shit!'

'What is it?'

'Another body! But it might not be related to our case. It's a woman, thirties. They want you to call in.'

He turned his face to Keaton, but his eyes remained on the road. 'Where was it discovered? Does it say?'

'Hang on, let me look…' She mouthed the message as she read it. 'It seems to be a body-dump that's gone wrong. She was found by the side of the River Severn bridge that crosses the M50?'

'I know it. It's near Tewkesbury.'

Keaton carried on scanning the message. 'Seems the body was probably thrown from the bridge, but it landed in a flooded section of field, and not the river itself?'

Gutteridge checked the mirrors to change lanes. 'Yeah. The grasslands either side of the river at that particular spot are floodplains; it's shallow when the water table's high, but it looks every bit like part of the river. Whoever dumped the body probably didn't know that, and assumed it was deeper.' Gutteridge sat in thought, aided by the monotonic drone of the car. 'So it must have been dumped at night.'

'How do you figure that?'

'Well, apart from it being too busy during the day, he probably tossed the body off the bridge and heard the splash, but it was too dark to see that the body was still visible.'

'Riiiight. Makes sense… Could it have been a woman?'

'I doubt it. If I'm remembering right, there's a fairly high railing to contend with, and steel crash-barriers in front of that. You'd have to be a pretty strong woman to negotiate those with any speed, but it's possible, I guess. Anything else?'

'Just one. Bryant says the station has received a letter, not addressed to anyone in particular on the envelope, but when it was opened, it was marked for your attention.' She scrolled down the text. 'Oh hell! They think it's from the Spatchcock Killer, it says something about the eleventh plague? But they don't want to disclose too much information over text.' She turned horrified eyes to Gutteridge who was mulling over the message. 'Doesn't that bother you? Freak you out? That he's addressing you in person? And what does "eleventh plague" mean?'

Gutteridge took a breath. 'It might be a reference to the ten plagues of Egypt, from the book of Exodus, if my memory serves me right.'

'What's that?'

'It's a passage from the Bible. According to the book, the incumbent Pharaoh refused to allow the Israelites to return to Canaan, so God inflicted ten plagues upon his lands and his people as a demonstration of his divine power and displeasure. It's an interesting book, you should read it sometime – cover to cover. I don't believe any of what's in it, of course, but it's still worth a read.'

He turned to Keaton. 'Are you religious in any way?'

She shook a defiant head before he'd even finished presenting the question. 'Nope! Not one iota. As far as I'm concerned, religion's toxic.'

Gutteridge smirked at the display of divine anarchy, before turning serious, focusing on the road ahead to aid thought. 'So what the hell could he be referring to – "eleventh plague"…?'

His phone began to buzz in Keaton's hand. 'It's Bryant,' she said.

'Can you answer it?'

She swiped to answer the call. 'Hello sir, it's Keaton. DI Gutteridge is driving at the moment, shall I put you on speaker…?' She listened, then dabbed the screen, and Bryant's voice filled the cabin.

'Morning, sir,' Gutteridge said.

Bryant bypassed the social pleasantries and cut straight to the chase. 'Have you seen the news?'

'The news? No, not yet. Why?'

'Whereabouts are you?'

'M6 southbound. We stayed over at Toby Jackson's house last night, after he invited us to stay. I accepted because it was getting late, and it gave us more time to quiz them further about the events of the previous night.'

The phone fell silent. 'And I imagine it was a very fine wine he served? And lots of it?'

Gutteridge spun a smile that collided with Keaton's. 'Yes, sir, very. But Jane here, she hit the gin bottle…' Keaton elbowed him in the side. 'So, tell me about this news, what's happened?'

'Some crazy bastard has been shoplifting meat, lacing it with poison, and placing it back on supermarket shelves. There are eleven hospitalisations already, and one of those is in a critical condition, kidney and liver failure, and they don't hold out much hope that she's going to pull through.'

Gutteridge sat silent in the drone of the engine. 'The eleventh plague,' he murmured.

'So you've worked that out too,' Bryant said. 'That's what we think. I mean, holy shit, this fucker's poisoning people now!'

'Do we know what kind of poison it is?' Keaton asked.

'Not yet, but the doctors and pathology are guessing some

diluted form of rat poison, judging by the symptoms: retching; spasming; agitation; bleeding from the gums.'

'My God!' Gutteridge slurred. 'Oh, while you're on, can someone contact the Peeks and see if we can set up an interview for two o'clock this afternoon?'

'Ah. Yes. Hold on... We've had a message through. Now where was it... Here we are. They called to say they won't be returning now until late today. Do you want me to set up a meeting for first thing tomorrow morning?'

'Please, sir.'

'New leads?'

'I wouldn't go so far as to say new leads. New questions really. I have an idea, a hunch if you like, but I don't want to say too much until I've had a chance to talk with them.'

'Okay, leave that with me, I'll get Tamara to set that up. Oh! And forensics have come back with a preliminary report on the two bodies that were found in the milking sheds. *Many* similarities to the Peeks' case.'

The sounds of papers being shuffled filled the car. 'Here we are,' Bryant said. 'The implement used, again, seems to have been a chef's-style knife.' Gutteridge smiled inside. *Eve might possibly be right on this,* he thought, *clever girl.*

Bryant continued. 'They found minute particles of high-grade stainless steel on the surfaces of the dissected areas, indicating the blade had recently been sharpened. There's also evidence of frost damage to both the girl and the boy's skin tissue, suggesting they may have been stored in either a refrigerator or freezer for some considerable time before they were found. Samples are being taken to try and establish a timescale.' More shuffling of papers. 'Thomas Leinster's body, although intact – like Jayden Peek – had been genitally mutilated. His dismembered penis and testicles were found in his mouth again, sewn to his tongue.'

Keaton exhaled her disgust. Gutteridge's groin winced at the thought. 'Don't you think it odd that he only mutilates the boys?'

The phone sat quiet. 'I wouldn't call being cut into cubes and suspended in a shed *not* mutilated?'

'What I mean is – unless it says something to the contrary on that report you have in your hands – that it only seems to be the boys that are being harmed in ways that could be considered sexually demeaning. The girl, she was only cut up to effect a comparison, to *sell* the idea of that particular art-piece. But the genitals of the two boys being removed and sewn into their mouths seems unnecessary, except to be vindictive and degrading, as if he has some specific vendetta against men?'

Eve's theories about 'the father figure' began reciprocating around Gutteridge's contemplations of the case. He thought of Eve's soft features smiling across the table at him, and guilt manifested in his gut as he turned a look to Keaton.

But the Polish angel was right, he'd needed to get Keaton out of his system, and he could only hope that, finally, he had.

Gutteridge continued. 'I believe there's a chance our perp had a bad upbringing, and may even have been abused by his father? That would certainly fit the profile, and could be *why* he consciously, or *sub*consciously, mutilates the genitals.'

'It's a theory,' Bryant said. 'It won't help us find him any quicker, but it would certainly be something for the profilers to work with when we do, *if* we do.'

'We will,' Gutteridge assured him, 'I can smell we're getting closer.'

'I hope to God you're right. I'll arrange that interview, and I'll text you the time.'

'Thank you, sir.'

'Oh, and I hope your hangovers clear up real soon, *slackers*,' said Bryant, with a smile they could only sense as the phone rang off.

'What's this theory?' asked Keaton.

Gutteridge took a thoughtful breath. 'Just that, a theory. Eve came up with it. Between you and me, she's a smart girl that one. Turns out, *she* was abused as a child, and as a consequence, persecuted every man she encountered for years afterwards because of it. She reckons that's why our perp mutilates the genitals.'

Keaton felt uncomfortable that she – with her psychology degree hanging proudly on the wall at home – hadn't seen through that. 'Smart, *and* gorgeous,' she muttered.

'Oi!' Gutteridge snapped. 'So are you.'

An appreciative smile floated across the cabin to soften Gutteridge's chastising stare, punctuated by a jaunty squeeze of his knee. 'Come on then, *Romeo*,' she chirped. 'Let's you and me go and catch this fucker!'

THIRTY-SIX

CAREFUL HANDS METICULOUSLY measured grains of rat poison into a scoop, expertly levelling each with the blade of a knife, adding them to a container of water, precisely one litre – no more, no less – carefully counting the amounts like a laboratory technician.

O'Leary had done extensive testing on dogs he'd abducted from gardens, to find the perfect ratio of poison, to weight of food. Too much in too little, and the animal could taste it, rejecting each morsel. Too little in any amount, and the dog didn't die, it just lay on the floor, panting, retching, spine corkscrewing in spasm, leeching vomit from a mouth biting wildly at the air, until he'd had to intervene and put the pathetic creatures out of their misery.

Killing the dogs had felt counterintuitive, but guided by his lord and master, he had been convinced it was a worthwhile sacrifice for the greater good.

He'd taken his findings and figured quadrupling the amounts should be effective at translating the experiment to human proportions.

He measured; and mixed; and stirred, loading syringes with the tincture of his 'Eleventh Plague'.

'All done,' he said, finally taking a breath, snapping the gloves from his fingers and binning them. The palm of his left hand was heavily bound in bandages. He winced as he flexed his fingers. It was staring to smell bad, but he couldn't risk a visit to a hospital.

He unscrewed the lid from a bottle of antiseptic, and poured it behind the gauze. O'Leary collapsed with the pain, clenched teeth grinding to the tune of his agony. He held the crouch until the crippling burn became just tenderness again, and stood.

He took a moment to gather himself. 'Will this be the final batch?' he asked.

'Why would it be the final batch?' said the voice of wisdom. 'What would be the reason for stopping our good work now?'

O'Leary took a second to absorb the relevance of the words of his God. 'But— we can't do this forever? And how do we eventually gauge the effectiveness of our efforts? Can we really, *truly* convince the world that the slaughtering of beasts is against your will? Can we *really* end the pain and suffering by the taking of lives?!'

'I flooded the world out of anger, killed all the beasts and mankind, except those few that were chosen to survive. There comes a time when actions, not words, are what the world needs... As *I* ignited the bush with the flames of my love to convey my message to Moses, and to make known my presence to those who knew not of me, *you* gave to the nescient world your art, to show them the error of their ways, and to guide them away from the darkness they follow into the light of my desire. But the time for words and symbolism has passed. Actions are what is needed now. Sometimes death is the only way. Without their compliance, comes the retribution for their sins.'

'But, what happens if I'm caught? Are they not *all* blinded by the darkness of which you speak? Can you not see, they won't understand? Won't comprehend what it is I'm… *we're* trying to do?'

'My child, fret not. We will cross that bridge when we come to it. You know what you need to do, we have spoken at length of an insurance policy for an event such as this, and now, that time has come…'

THIRTY-SEVEN

CARL McNAMARA carefully drew back the sheet from the corpse of the woman found dumped from the bridge. Gutteridge and Keaton looked on, clad in full suits, gloves and masks.

'See here,' explained Carl, rolling the body onto its side. 'There's extensive pooling around the area of the back, but you can still see – if you look closely – post-mortem bruising from intermittent, longitudinal ridges running the entire length of her body. My guess is, she's been lying in the back of a van, or maybe even a pickup, and for quite some time before she was dumped.'

He lowered the body respectfully onto its back again and turned to Gutteridge. 'Most vans these days come lined with timber, but if that timber was removed for any reason – say, because it's become soaked in incriminating evidence – then that would expose the stiffening ridges pressed into the steel floor panels. It would be a fairly simple process to match them up, *if* you managed to find the vehicle.'

'And what are these?' asked Keaton, indicating diagonal ligature marks across the arms, legs and chest with her gloved pinky.

'She was wrapped in a tarpaulin, a very cheap, lightweight, low-quality affair. The heat-sealed, woven plastic variety. She'd then had barbell weights – five in total – tied her entire length in coils of blue nylon rope. That's what left those tracks, and these circular bruises.'

Carl moved to the head end of the corpse. The detectives repositioned themselves either side of the table to better see.

'Here's how she died,' he said, indicating deep purple bruising either side of the windpipe and to the back of the neck. 'She was strangled, by a very strong individual, so almost definitely a man, judging by the span of the hands. See,' he said, rounding the table and hovering his clawed hands above the marks.

He removed them again and stepped back. 'Her windpipe has been sheared by the force, snapped, if you like – not an easy thing to do. I also found a mixture of aspirated blood and vomit in her windpipe. She'd effectively drowned in it, poor creature.'

Keaton's hand rose involuntarily to her throat. She swallowed back her empathy. 'Do we have an ID yet?' she asked.

'No. Not as yet. The lab are working on a DNA profile as we speak, in the vain hope she's in the system.' He lifted strangely confident eyes to the watching pair. 'But what I *can* say is this – I think this was done by our killer.'

'Really?' Gutteridge exhaled.

'Yes.'

'How would you know?'

McNamara flashed his brows. 'Those longitudinal marks I showed you? I found similar markings on the Peek boy, less pronounced maybe, but definitely visible. His were *across* his back, lying widthways. I took photos not thinking they were of particular use at the time, until I saw these,' he said, pointing beneath the corpse lying in the stainless-steel tray.

'And I assume you've already done a comparison?' Gutteridge said.

'Yes! And it's a match.' He stepped away, and began pacing, visibly selecting his words with care. 'I think this girl... *woman*... knew him, and somehow got in the way. Perhaps she found things out about him and had to be taken out of the picture?'

He tilted a compassionate head and looked down upon her chalky, ashen face. 'Hell of a thing, strangling a person. Watching their life ebb away to the force of your will, and having the conviction to ignore any compunction for pity and not let go. It takes either an iron resolve, or extreme passion. More often than not – in my experience – it seems to be passion that triumphs.'

Carl broke from his foray into pity and raised his guard again. He re-covered the body. 'Any theories yet on our killer?'

Gutteridge didn't feel anywhere near as self-assured as he wished he did, but he hid it well. 'I do have one. I think our guy works in a food joint. I think he's possibly even a chef, or at least someone adept at preparing food. I think that's how he's choosing them – his victims I mean.'

'What happened to the idea that he follows them from fast-food joints?'

Gutteridge rolled his head. 'I know, and that might still have legs. But it leaves a gaping hole when it comes to Jayden Peek. Could it have been nothing more than a post-hoc-ergo-propter-hoc assumption?'

Keaton piped up. 'Have you considered it could be both?' she asked. 'Maybe he is... *was*... scouting burger joints, and that would make sense. Those places ship animals from abattoirs by the truck load. Wouldn't he then feel a hatred for anyone that fuels that need to keep killing? And maybe he does work in a food joint; it would certainly explain his adeptness with a blade, and could very well be how he singled out the Peeks' kid?'

Gutteridge looked doubtful. 'But how would he have known where he lived, the Peek kid I mean? Ahh *fuck it*! I'm afraid this one's got me well and truly stumped, old friend.'

'Hey. Keep on it. You'll get there... so what now?'

'We're re-interviewing the Peeks tomorrow morning, see if there isn't anything we've missed.'

'Then, good luck. Stick at it. This chump's getting sloppy, we'll catch him, and *soon*.'

But Gutteridge looked more pessimistic than ever, his optimistic front crumbling like the walls of Jericho. 'Let's hope you're right, old chum, and thanks,' he said, turning to leave, then spun a look back towards the autopsy table. 'Oh, and cheers. Those ridges, it's a good lead,' he said, indicating the shrouded body. 'I'll put feelers out to missing persons, see if we can't find who she is. You never know, it might lead us to him.'

He parted on an unconvincing smile, and made for the door, swinging an arm to invite Keaton to pass through first. He followed her out, turning his wrist over to check the time. It was 19:06. He needed to see Eve. He *desired* to see Eve. He had a declaration of love to get off his chest. A declaration that threatened to be long overdue, and finally – for once in his lonely, solitary existence – he felt ready to voice it...

THIRTY-EIGHT

GUTTERIDGE STOOD AT HIS CHOPPING BOARD, orchestrating the veg for his bolognese into neat cubes with the sweep of his conductor's knife.

He lifted the board and scooped the results of his handiwork into the pan, before adding another splash of Merlot to the soup of ingredients for good measure.

He leaned over the hob, savouring the fumes of the wine as the alcohol boiled away.

Eve swept silently into the kitchen with a supernatural elegance that made her look as if she was floating. Gutteridge's eyes roused to the sight of her. Her onyx-black hair was curled at the ends, coiling around the sweep of her shoulders like a bramble. Glossed black lips popped from within the backdrop of her alabaster skin, and Gutteridge felt that if he couldn't say, 'I love you' tonight, then he never would. She looked every bit as breathtaking and irresistible as she was.

He replaced the lid as Eve arrived by his side. She turned him towards her with a gentle tug on his arm until they were face to face. 'When are you going to come and join me?' she asked, affecting a subtle childlike tone to her voice to get her way, leaning her pert body against his. 'I miss you; I haven't been seeing you much lately.'

He smiled apologetically. 'I'm sorry, Eve, it's just been so busy. This case is taking a lot of my time, but I know, that's no excuse.'

She smiled into his eyes. 'That's okay, I forrrgive you.' The roll in her 'r' carried his mind away to the Angel of Knutsford. Her advice rang loud in his mind.

'Eve. I have something I wish to say,' he said, placing the tea towel gently to one side.

A look of concern darkened the joy in Eve's face.

'Oh! No. It's nothing bad,' he assured her.

She allowed a semblance of relief to calm her concern, but she wasn't used to seeing Gutteridge so serious. 'What is it, this thing you want to say?'

He opened his phone and scrolled to one of her old messages. He held the phone up to show her. 'Do you remember this?' he asked.

Eve squinted at the screen and read the text out loud – 'I really miss you. I love you. Is that so very wrong?'

'Do you remember sending that?'

'Of course.'

'And… did you, perhaps – I don't know – send it as a joke?'

Eve's entire aspect coloured offended. 'I wouldn't joke about such a thing. I'm not one to toy with people's feelings, that would be crrruel, and that's not who I am.'

Gutteridge's stance turned apologetic. 'I'm sorry, I didn't mean it to come out that way, believe me. You see, the truth is, I was hoping you weren't.'

She paused from the moment… 'You do?'

'Yes. Of course.'

Her inquisitive pupils flicked from one eye to the other. 'So, do you think, one day, you *could* ever love me?'

Gutteridge stepped to her, clutching her shoulders in his robust hands. He stooped a look deep into her eyes. 'I already do. I've just been too blind to see it.'

A single tear broke free of her eye, quivering lips flinching a succession of insecure smiles. 'Really? Is that trrrue?'

He peered into her effervescent face. Soft. Unblinking. 'I love you, Eve, and I have done for a long time. You fill me with happiness every time I see you, and I dearly want you in my life.'

Eve beamed, elated by the force of Gutteridge's declaration. Her breath wavered, and she engulfed Gutteridge in her shaking arms. He could feel the stutter of her happy tears through his abdomen, and he smiled inside. He'd been wondering how he would feel if he ever managed to tell her the truth of his feelings, and the answer was, 'amazing'…

*

The sink lay filled with the evening's dishes, lights turned down to something more romantic, the air pungent with the aroma of a perfect dinner.

Eve sat high in Gutteridge's vision, straddling the chair where he sat. Her perfectly formed, immaculate breasts were at rest at eye level as she lowered onto the physical manifestation of his appreciation of her beauty.

Her elated face choired to the ceiling above them as she glided onto him, his splayed fingers gripping her taut, svelte torso in the cradle of his hands, her waist so small his fingers nearly touched.

His exploring eyes watched, fascinated, as he felt her around him, her healthy, able body reciprocating to the rhythm of his fantasies.

Eve's fluttering eyes left the ceiling as she lolloped her sweat-jewelled face forwards to meet his. Their lips touched, and she exhaled her desire into him with a rapturous groan that filled his head.

He opened his eyes a sliver. He could almost imagine it was the girl, Asha, he was sharing breath with. Their face, their eyes, their lips – soft-focused by the interwoven fingers of his lashes – looked so similar in aspect they were one and the same.

Eve engulfed him in her arms, his face pulled hard into the pit of her neck. The saccharine scent of her perspiration filled his nose, and he'd never felt more alive.

*

O'Leary knelt by the window sill, gazing through misted panes of glass, feeling detached from what he was witnessing to the point that he could imagine it was a television he was watching.

His hand descended to his loins at the sight of the slender beauty riding Gutteridge. Her body looked perfect in the diffusing haze of the window pane.

He suddenly remembered he wasn't alone, and the words of warning from his mentor rang loud in his mind. He snapped his hand away from his swelling genitals and attempted to purify his thoughts.

'Better,' said the voice of his guiding light. 'You see, you *are* able to resist, that makes you stronger than most in this corrupted world.'

'I'm sorry,' whispered O'Leary, 'I was weak.'

'Apologise not, my child. You have resisted, and that is all that matters.'

O'Leary's attention returned to the copulating couple. 'Is he still a danger?'

'Indeed.'

'But, how do we stop him, in a way that won't bring unwanted attention?'

'You cannot negotiate with evil, but there are other ways

to convince them of the error of their ways. *He* is a mere child, and how do you punish a child?'

O'Leary hovered in the core of the question, fighting to extract an answer, but failing. 'I don't know?'

'You punish them.'

'How?'

'You take from them something of meaning, something they covet, something of value to their corrupted lives. You take from them their favourite toy. *That* is how.'

THIRTY-NINE

GUTTERIDGE ESCORTED Karen and Rodger Peek through the warren of corridors to interview room 3, inviting them in with a matadoresque swing of the arm. 'Please,' he said with a sombre smile, 'take a seat. Thank you for coming in at such short notice. I understand you've been away and only just returned, so we're grateful for your time.'

He began to close the door behind him just as DS Keaton arrived, trotting up the corridor to intercept their arrival. She rolled her face around the frame. 'Before we begin, would anyone like tea, or coffee?'

Rodger Peek turned saddened pessimist's eyes towards the question. 'Do you have anything a bit stronger? Absinthe maybe?'

Karen Peek burned his inappropriate levity with a look of crippling disappointment that seemed well rehearsed.

He sagged beneath her stare. 'Sorry,' he mewed, 'tea would be lovely.'

Karen Peek nodded in a rare moment of solidarity. 'Please,' she said, forcing a smile that projected no further than the end of her nose.

Gutteridge also lifted a nod as he took to the seat opposite, flashing appreciative eyes. 'Me too,' he mouthed.

Keaton quietly closed the door behind her, and the room descended into uncomfortable silence.

Gutteridge began unwrapping the sealing film from two cassette tapes.

'Tapes?' said Rodger Peek. 'You still use tapes?'

Gutteridge forced a smile towards the mocking tone woven into the comment as he logged the details of the interview on the labels. 'Afraid so… believe it or not, these are still considered more reliable than a digital copy. Those can get accidentally wiped with a careless press of a key; *these* are analogue.'

He inserted the tapes into the recorder, adjusted the position of the mike, and after checking the visitors were ready, simultaneously depressed the record buttons.

'It's Monday, the eleventh of May,' he said, checking his wristwatch, '10:13am. Interviewing Karen and Rodger Peek. The interview is taking place in room number 3 at Gloucester Police station. DI Gutteridge presiding, DS Keaton also in attendance.' He pressed the buttons to pause the recording. 'Before we begin, do any of you have any questions you'd like to ask?'

Karen Peek sat coiled in on herself, visibly struggling to hold it together, then melted, her imploring eyes seeming to scold Gutteridge for his clinical efficiency. 'When are you going to catch the man who killed my son!?'

Gutteridge's stomach sank to the floor of his pelvis at the sight of her tears. 'We're doing all we can, Mrs Peek, but these things take time.'

'How much time?' Rodger Peek interjected, his voice blurting the question, allowing his anger to feed off his wife's grief.

Gutteridge tentatively raised a hand. 'Please, try not to get upset. We have a whole team of fine detectives on this working night and day. We *will* catch him.'

Rodger Peek settled again. 'We just want him caught.'

'I understand. We *all* do. If you can help me with answers to my questions, it may bring us closer to finding the man who took your child from you.'

'It'll never end for me,' Karen Peek wept, 'our boy is gone. He's dead, and nothing you can do can change that.'

'I know,' Gutteridge said, massaging his words, 'I understand your pain, believe me.'

'Do you!?' snapped Karen Peek, fixing Gutteridge a bellicose stare designed to belittle him. 'Do you really…? Do you *really* understand how I feel? How *we* feel?'

Gutteridge countered the look with a face lit with ironic serenity. 'In fact, I do…' He dropped eyes to the desktop, then lifted them again. 'Do you remember the Masterson case, roughly nine years ago now? It was all over the news at the time. Jerry Masterson murdered at least twelve people. Well, twelve that we know of.' His whole aspect sagged. 'And my wife – Cynthia – was one of them.'

Karen Peek's scolding eyes softened. 'Your wife?'

Gutteridge nodded. 'Yes… he took her from me, simply because I'd had the audacity to work out who he was. To work out that, out of all the likely suspects we had on file, *he* was the killer. He'd gone underground by then, but his picture was all over the television, the papers, the news channels, and sat at the very top of every wanted list in every county. He was on the run, in hiding because of me. So, as payment for my job well done, he killed my wife. L-Left her at home for me to find.' Gutteridge ran out of steady breath, and took a moment to regroup. 'So, you see, if there's anyone in this entire building who knows what it is you're going through, it's me…' His and Karen Peek's eyes met in solidarity, sharing their sadness. 'I'll catch this man who took your son from you, I promise, but you have to help me.'

Karen Peek dropped her shame to her lap. 'I'm sorry,' she said, desperately trying to keep it together, 'it's just hard, isn't it, knowing they're gone? I've not been handling it too well.'

Her weary husband placed a reassuring arm around her shoulder, feeling very much on the periphery of it all.

Gutteridge looked on at their suffering. 'I know it is. And as I say, I know how you're feeling, so no apology needed.'

He slowly opened his folder, clicking the nib of his pen out in readiness.

There was a soft knock at the door, and an apologetic Keaton entered brandishing a tray of cups. She placed the tray down, dealt the drinks to appreciative hands, placed the sugar bowl to one side, stowed the tray and sat to join them.

Keaton noticed the reddening in the whites of Gutteridge's eyes. Her brow furrowed, and she placed an inquisitive hand on his leg beneath the table. He smiled past his shoulder to let her know everything was fine, and they were ready.

Gutteridge depressed the record buttons again. 'Resuming the interview at…' he craned a look up at the clock on the wall, '10:27am. Now, we're going to be asking questions about your son, are you sure you're going to be okay with that?' he asked.

'Will it help catch him?' replied Rodger Peek.

'We think so, but there're no guarantees. We understand this can be hard, especially so soon after your loss.'

Rodger Peek turned to his wife. She nodded in response between gulps to swallow back her fraying emotions.

'Go ahead. We'll try to help in any way we can.'

'We appreciate it. We'll try to detain you for as short a time as possible…' Gutteridge consulted his notes. 'It's my understanding that during your last interview – I believe with DSs Stanton and Banks – that you were asked if you and your family had visited a fast-food restaurant anytime in the last – say – week before your son's disappearance. Is that correct?'

'Yes,' said Karen Peek, 'we've already answered that, and the answer was no, we hadn't.'

'Why is this relevant?' Rodger Peek asked.

Gutteridge wasn't sure at that point if he should disclose too much of his theorising and turned eyes to Keaton for support.

'The thing is, Mr Peek,' interjected Keaton, leaning into the conversation, 'the one hole we have in all of this, is how Jayden was, for want of a better word, chosen.'

'Chosen?' said Karen Peek.

Gutteridge rejoined the conversation. 'Yes. Chosen. You see, we had a theory that the victims may have been observed at fast-food joints, arguably the world's largest consumers of meat products – purely in a business sense. We believed it possible that our perpetrator could have observed the children eating at any one of these places, ingesting what – in his twisted mind – would be considered sinners' food, then followed them home after. As a theory, it fitted all but one of the victims – your son.'

Karen Peek crumbled again and began dismantling her tan leather handbag in search of a handkerchief.

'Jane,' Gutteridge whispered, lifting a chin towards the door.

'Of course,' she replied, standing from the desk. 'I'll get you some tissues.'

Karen Peek's shaking fingers found and fished her handkerchief from the core of the spillage. 'I'm fine, I've found it. Please, it's okay.'

Keaton released the door handle, and slowly took to her seat again. 'Are you sure? Or would you perhaps like some water?'

Another strained smile, a shake of the head. 'No. Please. I'm fine now.'

Gutteridge gave her a minute to collect herself. 'Are you sure you're going to be okay to carry on?'

Karen Peek nodded, almost enthusiastically. 'I'll be fine. Please, continue...'

'What's your point in all this?' her husband barked. 'Exactly what is it you're trying to find out?'

Keaton rocked into the huddle again. 'We need to know how he was chosen. *How* our perpetrator knew your son not only ate meat, but how he could have known where he lived?'

'Well, he must've followed him home, like you said.'

'No,' Gutteridge said, 'we checked what CCTV footage there was from the day he went missing; no one followed you anywhere.'

'He must have obtained your address somehow,' explained Keaton, 'but we need to know how.'

Gutteridge sat in thought. The air in the room felt pregnant. 'Okay, forget fast food. Was there *anywhere* you ate that day? Or maybe the day before?'

The Peeks looked to each other, searching in each other's eyes, trying to assemble their memories.

'There was just one place,' said Rodger Peek, 'a little teashop on Westgate, about halfway down the bank.'

'What did you have?' asked Keaton, leaning in.

'Have?'

'To *eat?*' Gutteridge said. 'What did you *eat?*'

Rodger Peek's brow furrowed. 'Just tea. Oh, and toast, with jam. All three of us. Why?'

Gutteridge wanted to curse and spit. 'No. Nothing. That's erm... that's not it.'

'And that's definitely the only place you'd been?' asked Keaton.

Mr Peek nodded. 'I'm sure of it. We were away on holiday for three weeks before that. In Portugal. We'd only just come back.'

Gutteridge's heart sank. He slid down the smooth plastic

of the seat. He had to face it – he had nothing.

Rodger Peek allowed himself a soft, ironic laugh to lighten his mood. 'We certainly won't be going there again in a hurry, bloody weird sodding place,' he muttered into the awkwardness.

Keaton twisted her interest towards the comment. 'Why?'

Rodger Peek emerged from his musing. 'What?'

'Why *wouldn't* you be in a hurry to go there again?'

'Because it was weird... One of those bizarre *vegan* places that you see cropping up all over the damn place. It didn't even say so on the sign. It was just called some bloody silly name I couldn't even hope to pronounce.'

Gutteridge woke from his cloud of dejection. 'Sorry, how did you know it was vegan, if you say it didn't say so anywhere?'

Peek looked confused by the intensity of the question. 'Well, you could tell by what was on the menu. Or more accurately, what *wasn't* on it.'

Karen Peek's insipid voice edged into the conversation. 'Jayden wanted sausages, that was his favourite thing to eat, but they didn't do them, except those pretend ones made of soya.' Her face crumpled and she inhaled stuttered breath. 'He was so upset, we promised to take him to McDonald's afterwards, but we never did. It was his favourite place to eat and we never took him.' She folded in on her tears again.

Gutteridge shuffled his seat to the table and fixed Rodger Peek with an intense stare. 'I want you to think very hard for me. *Did* you pay with a cheque? Something you were maybe asked to personalise, you know, write your details on?'

'A cheque? No. I never pay with cheques.'

'Are you sure? Are you absolutely certain?'

'Yes. Yes, I'm sure... why?'

Gutteridge reeled in frustration, cupping his brow in the pit of his thumb. 'I thought we had something there. I *really* thought that may have been it.'

His frustrated eyes flitted around the scattered detritus spilling from Karen Peek's bag, trying to regroup his scrambled ideas.

His eyes pinched, locking on a sliver of paper peeking from beneath a silver compact. He rotated his gaze to better see what was printed on it – *Gan Feoil Tea Rooms.*

He extended a tentative arm. 'May I?' he asked, presenting his hand to the slick of random objects, hovering his fingers above the ticket.

Karen Peek gulped back her sobs and finished drying her eyes. Her brow creased. 'Um... yes. Of course.'

Gutteridge extended his middle and forefinger and pulled the slip of paper clear of the chaos. He rotated it around to face him. 'What's this?' he asked.

Rodger Peek twisted a look. 'What? Oh... it's a raffle ticket. In fact, it's from that bloody silly tea shop, the one with a silly name. It was to win a weekend away, or something.'

'A weekend break in a country cottage,' Karen Peek corrected. 'I don't even know if they've drawn it yet.'

Gutteridge's eyes cemented with a look of urgent interest. 'And how would you know if you'd won?'

Karen Peek looked bemused by his question. 'Well. We filled in the other half of the slip – with our details. But *he* keeps that half.'

'Who does?' Keaton asked.

'The man. The young man who runs the place?'

Gutteridge snapped a look to Keaton. 'Oh shit!' he slurred.

DS Keaton levelled a look into Karen Peek's eyes. 'This man, did he have a... a *Scottish* accent?'

Karen Peek dropped a pensive look into her lap. 'No. No he didn't. In fact, I think he was Irish?'

Jane Keaton's whole face dropped. 'Oh dear God in heaven!'

FORTY

RODGER PEEK'S EYES flitted between the two detectives. 'What is it? What's happening?'

Cogs were working overtime behind Gutteridge's eyes, he leaned into the mike, checking his watch. 'DI Gutteridge, terminating the interview at 10:43,' he said, clicking the machine off and extracting the tapes.

He turned a counterfeit smile to the bewildered visitors. 'We're really very sorry, we need to conclude the interview. Thank you again for coming in.' He stood from the desk. 'If we need to speak to you further, you'll be contacted in due course.'

Gutteridge snapped up his pad, pen and the two tapes from the desk and strode to the door. He held it open with an affected smile for the Peeks to pass through.

Rodger Peek spun a dazed look to his wife, then complied. He followed Gutteridge's lead, then stopped and turned to front him. 'Would someone like to tell me what's going on here? What exactly is happening? What is it you know?'

'It's nothing, Mr Peek,' he assured him. 'Please, go home, grieve. You'll be contacted if we need anything further. There's something important we need to attend to.'

'Is it about our son?' Karen Peek added. 'Is that man in some way involved?'

Keaton stepped in to try and quell their incessant questioning. 'No one said he was. There's just something we've remembered we need to address, that's all...'

Gutteridge spied the desk sergeant walking past. 'Sergeant Milburn, would you please be kind enough to show Mr and Mrs Peek the way out.' He spun a smile back towards their shared, osmotic confusion. 'Once again, thank you for your time, and have a safe journey home,' he said, before striding off towards the incident room with a measurable sense of urgency.

'Is Bryant in?' Gutteridge asked, hurrying along the corridor, Keaton having to break into an intermittent trot to keep up.

'As far as I know.'

'Holy fuck, Jane, is it him?'

She tried not to let hope reign supreme in her optimistic mind. 'I don't want to be guilty of counting *that* particular chicken, only to be disappointed by the outcome.'

Gutteridge stopped mid flow and paused, turning to front Keaton. 'I'm not sure what to do? I don't want to go barrelling in there with search warrants, stomping through his life if he *isn't* our guy. Besides, a warrant would take time to obtain, time we can ill afford to piss away.'

'But what if it *is* him?'

'Yeah, I know. But the reality is, we don't actually have any real, hard evidence that it *is*, at least not enough to convince a judge to issue a warrant... All we really have is a ticket stub, and a hunch... *Fuck it!*' he spat.

Keaton joined him in the contemplation of their limited options. 'What if we just paid the place a visit to check it out, to check *him* out? We could just pop in like punters, for tea and a slice of cake, pretend we're office workers on a break or something, check the lay of the land, see what's what?'

Gutteridge chewed a lip, mulling over the suggestion. 'That might be our best option, but I don't want to run the risk of alerting him of our interest, only to find out later that he's destroyed evidence because of it, or worse still, run! But at the same time, what if it *is* him, and we have a real chance to put an end to this?'

He paced the corridor in front of Keaton's attentive gaze. 'Sod it!' he said. 'Let's you and me go and check him out. *If* we suspect there's something in this, then we can apply for that warrant, based on our observations, *and* that ticket stub. We know what we're looking for, we've read the profile, hell, we helped compile it. And if it's him, I'm thinking it'll be pretty obvious. But we *must* tread carefully, he can't know he's being watched.'

'Understood.'

'Who's in at the moment?'

'I'm not sure about the others, but I know for sure that McWilliams is. I saw him when I was making the drinks.'

'Go find him. Have him contact the council and/or the Land Registry, find out who owns the property this "Gan Feoil" place is on,' he said – reading the stub he still held in his hand, 'see if he can find a name of who owns it, or is leasing it. And tell him to let us know *immediately* when he finds out. I want a name!'

The pop of excitement returned to Keaton's belly. 'On it, boss.'

'Meet me back here in ten. We'll go and check this guy out. But Jane, we need to be guarded; a lot rides on this! Let's keep this to ourselves – for now – at least until we know more.'

An understanding nod, and Keaton trotted off in the direction she last saw McWilliams…

*

Gutteridge parked his car at the bottom of the rise on Westgate Street, opposite the row of loading bays. They alighted the car and began making their way up the bank towards the location displayed on the app on Keaton's phone.

'So,' said Gutteridge, 'we're office types on a break, griping about the shitty pay rise that's just been announced at wherever the fuck it is we're supposed to work.'

'That won't take much acting,' said Keaton, with a sneer.

'Be serious,' he snapped, 'we've got to look utterly engrossed in what we're talking about. And *be* animated, so we can flinch looks out of the conversation and check this guy out without it looking like we are.'

'Okay. I'm sorry.'

'That's all right,' he said. 'But you're right, the pay sucks!'

They both spied the Gan Feoil Tea Rooms looming large and surreal ahead of them to the right. It looked deafeningly normal, but it still amazed them both that neither of them had noticed it before.

It had a trendy, artisan, old-world look. A forced, country-cottage feel that seemed at odds with the rest of the neighbourhood, located so near to the outer fringes of the shopping district, where the rents were cheap because the businesses usually failed.

'Are you ready?' Gutteridge asked with barely a movement of the lips as they neared the door, slowing their pace to a crawl.

'As I'll ever be,' she replied, leaning a look up at the sign, and typing the name of the establishment into her phone's search engine.

'Come on then.'

With a breath to calm the fizzle in his gut, Gutteridge stepped up to the door, grasped the handle, then stopped...

The place was empty, no one inside. The lights were on; lightly billowing steam rising from the coffee machine; cakes lying in wait beneath covers along the countertop; a chilled, glass cabinet sat filled with neatly stacked, pre-made sandwiches, but no punters, and no one behind the till.

Gutteridge took a second calming breath and quietly opened the door…

They both entered, attempting to cut a balance between treading silently, but not looking like they were trying to.

Keaton took the handle from Gutteridge and silently closed the door behind her.

Gutteridge sauntered nonchalantly to the counter. He could hear voices emanating from the kitchen, two of them, and the clattering sounds of obvious agitation.

Keaton joined his side, and they both listened…

'Another one! Dear heaven, will this never end?!' said the first voice, desperate, despondent, irked.

'It will end when the world is once again educated to my ways, and complies with my wants and my will,' the second voice said. 'The mass slaughter of the beasts must end. *We* must work to stop it.' This second voice was calm, controlled, patient.

'But the killing *won't* stop! Will it? Just look…! Will you just look!'

The second, softer voice drifting from the kitchen seemed to be the only one able to remain composed. 'Every cause worth fighting for has its martyrs. *He* is but one of them, and *you*, my child, shall eventually be another.'

The agitated clattering ceased… 'What do you mean – I'll be another? I thought you said… that people will talk of my deeds for centuries to come, and that they will hold me aloft for being the bearer of your message, and saint me for doing so?'

'And they shall, my son. But mouths, they tend to speak only of the deeds of the dead, not the living. But your sacrifice shall loosen their tongues, spreading the word and highlighting the truth of their sins, so eventually, they shall *know* of the actions they took that dishonoured my name, and through the crippling shame they'll be forced to wear, they shall change.'

Keaton's widening eyes spun a manic look to Gutteridge. 'It's him!' she whispered, her breaths staccato. 'Oh God, Pat! It's him!'

Gutteridge's face mirrored the stunned expression glowering back at him, pleading to him for guidance. He froze – what to do?

The door to the kitchen suddenly crashed open with a petulant kick, and the slab of wood swung free of its frame, replaced by a backlit silhouette of a man: mid-thirties; average height; a heavily bandaged hand catching the door with a wince on its backswing.

The silhouette's face looked aghast at finding he wasn't alone. His features – soft and gentle – looked almost teenage in their years in comparison to their expectations, an innocence in their form that caught them off guard. If it was a monster they were expecting, they were destined to be disappointed.

A message chimed loudly on Gutteridge's phone. In the swirling mist of his shock, he glanced momentarily down at the screen. It was a text from McWilliams; it was just one line long. A name – '*Kieran Conor O'Leary*'.

Gutteridge lifted his disbelieving eyes again. They met the panicked look of recognition gazing back at him. *This* man *knew* who he was and seemed to fear his being there.

The three of them stood, triangulated in a self-awareness stalemate, O'Leary visibly attempting to regroup.

'Kieran O'Leary?' Gutteridge asked, his voice, guarded.

O'Leary's eyes flashed at the sound of his own name. 'Erm... yes... I'm Kieran O'Leary?' He hesitated in the moment. 'Oh. Would you please excuse me just one moment,

I have something boiling on the hob.' He threw out a forced smile that failed to land, then turned, and hurried back into the kitchen.

Gutteridge reaching an involuntary hand to try to halt him. 'Mr *O'Leary*!' he called.

He and Keaton shared a fleeting look, stunned by the realisation they were in the presence of the myth, the legend, before Gutteridge set off to round the counter to give chase.

'*Kieran O'Leary! Please! Stop!*' he yelled, shouldering the door aside.

He entered a kitchen strewn with the debris from what looked to be a scuffle or a fight, then noticed the fire door ahead of him swinging shut with a metallic *clack*.

'*O'Leary!*' he screamed, sprinting for the exit as Keaton entered the kitchen behind him.

Gutteridge suddenly stuttered out of the sprint and stumbled to a halt like he'd tripped on a wire. The floor and walls to his right were decorated with a carnival of blood. Fans and splashes of ejected crimson clashed with the canteen-sterility of the kitchen.

Rodger Peek's body lay slumped against the wall in the core of the explosion of colour, head resting on his shoulder, knife protruding from behind his clavicle like a second neck, eyes beading within a vacant stare devoid of verve, looking out across the last view he must have seen in his receding vision.

Keaton simpered at the sight as she rounded the counter to join Gutteridge's side. She'd seen this man alive not thirty minutes ago.

Gutteridge took to his heels again, leaving Keaton to deal with her shock.

He crashed through the door in time to see a cream Vauxhall van speeding off down a single-track side road then turn onto Berkeley Street.

He ran back in time to see Keaton exiting the shop, her face pasty white and anaemic.

'Call it in,' he shouted. 'Get uniform down here as quick as possible to secure the premises, I'll run and get the car.' He set off, then stopped mid-flight to turn back. 'Try to see if there are any keys lying around to lock the place up, we don't want a member of the public wandering in and finding *that* fucking mess!' he said, walking backwards towards where he'd parked the Saab. 'I'll pick you up out here. Be quick. I'll call McWilliams, see if we've got an address for this psycho!'

He set off for the car again, sprinting for all he was worth. It was only 150 yards away but it felt like a mile. He slowed long enough to scroll to McWilliams' number and dab it, then continued his sprint.

The phone rang once, then answered. 'Ian! It's Gutteridge. I need an address for this O'Leary guy. He's running!'

The line hung silent for a beat, until the silence was broken to the tune of a Glaswegian accent steeped in disbelief. 'You're fucking shitting me! It's never him?'

'Yes! It's him. He's running. Get me an address, *any* fucking address, and quick, before we lose him!' he puffed, his voice jarring to the thump of his urgent footfall.

'I'm sure I came across what must be his home address while I was searching? I'll text it to you, give me five minutes.'

'You've got two!' Gutteridge insisted. 'As quick as you can!'

The line rang off just as Gutteridge reached his car. He fired at it frantically with the fob on his keyring until it flashed awake. He popped the door and leapt inside, sliding the key in the ignition and turning it in one swift motion. The engine fired. He checked the mirrors, threw it in gear, and sped off up the pedestrian-only zone to collect Keaton.

Disgruntled shoppers shot disapproving looks his way as they leapt aside to avoid being hit. Keaton padded around at the top of the rise in readiness for his arrival. The car juddered to a halt, the anti-lock brakes thrumming through Gutteridge's vice-like grip on the wheel.

Keaton dropped inside and shut the door just as both their phones sang out simultaneously. The same message flashed up on both their phones. An address...

'Farley's End!' Keaton barked, as she clipped into her seatbelt. 'Make for Over Farm, then drop down on the A48 towards Calcott's Green. I'll direct you from there.'

Gutteridge punched the throttle, and the car began reeling in the horizon.

'Call the station, tell them we need an armed response unit sent to that location, and tell them it's urgent!'

'I'm on it.'

'And phone Bryant, let him know what's happening. But call armed response first... Did you get through to uniform?'

'I did. They're sending cars over now. I told them just to secure the scene, but not to go inside.'

'Good!' said Gutteridge, drifting onto the road towards the Over Roundabout junction, which led onto the A40. The back wheels clawed for grip. He gunned it!

Gutteridge leaned into the wheel, foot flat to the floor. 'The glovebox. Open it,' he said.

Keaton complied, struggling to grasp the lock in the violent swaying of the car. She popped the catch and it fell open.

'Take all that crap out,' Gutteridge said, nodding towards the eclectic mix of junk spilling out of the unit. 'Just throw it on the floor. There's a false bottom in the glovebox with a tab at the front; lift it,' he said.

Keaton frowned at what he'd said, then began scooping the detritus from years of ownership onto the floor: maps; tissues; pens and CDs rained into the footwell, until she saw a tab made from a folded length of ribbon poking from a gap at the front.

She pulled it… 'Holy shit!' she said, looking down at a Glock 17M semi-automatic pistol stowed in a secret compartment. 'You've got a gun!'

As team leader, Gutteridge had to choose his explanation with care. 'Officially, I *am* an Authorised Firearms Officer. But I shouldn't really have that, not in here, not like that, but I'm fucked if I'm following this lunatic without it, not after the last time. Not after…' he choked, 'after losing… Cynthia.'

Keaton scrolled through her Rolodex of their previous conversations but could recall no mention of a 'Cynthia'. 'Cynthia?' she asked.

Gutteridge turned placid within the clamour of the screaming engine. 'She was my wife, many years ago, before I moved to Gloucester. I lost her…'

'You *lost* her? How?'

'A guy called Jerry killed her.'

Keaton turned to her side window to aid thought, then returned her fascinated gaze to Gutteridge. 'You mean, Jerry Masterson? The killer in the Masterson case? The one you were instrumental in solving?'

'Yeah, the one I solved – for my sins. And not a day goes by when I wish I hadn't.'

Keaton had only loosely browsed the Masterson case notes during her time in training. It suddenly occurred to her that his last victim's surname was also Gutteridge. 'But… why?'

Gutteridge's whole demeanour turned ironic. 'Revenge. For working out it was him.'

'*Jeeeeesus!* I'm so sorry, Pat. I had no idea.'

Gutteridge thundered onto the slip road that bypassed the Over Roundabout and drifted the car onto the A40. The rear end caught again and he floored it. 'That's okay. It's in the past now. I think people at the station try not to gossip about it out of some bizarre form of respect?'

Keaton sat uncomfortably in the howl of the engine. She now understood his need for Eve, and maybe even his fascination with *her* – such that it was – even if it was just for her lips and her body – lips and a body she'd been more than happy to relinquish for their single night of shared ecstasy.

'Take a left here!' she barked, nearly missing the junction, lost in her thoughts. 'The A48.' She braced herself for the bend, then placed a comforting hand gently on his thigh. She smiled across at him apologetically. 'You're not alone, Pat… you've got Eve now. And you've got me…'

FORTY-ONE

'YOUR DESTINATION IS ON THE RIGHT,' announced the app on Keaton's phone, the soothing, female voice sounding jarringly passive in the midst of the considerable excitement.

They both sighted the house 150 yards ahead, semi-hidden by a thick cluster of trees. Gutteridge pulled the car off to the side of the road and parked in the entrance to an adjoining field.

They both exited the car, serenaded by the ticks and pops of an overexerted engine cooling.

'Be vigilant,' Gutteridge said, stowing the pistol in his belt and removing his jacket. He tossed it onto the back seat and quietly nudged the door shut with his hip. Keaton followed suit, copying him.

'Stay close, but keep behind,' he said, trotting to a break in the hedgerow where the gravel driveway started.

Two sweeping dunes of pebbles fanned into the road indicated a vehicle had entered at speed, and by the fact the gravel in the road hadn't been displaced by a succession of passing tyres, Gutteridge assessed it must have been recent.

He peeked around the corner, using a rogue fan of leaves to hide his presence. There was a red-brick farmhouse sitting roughly seventy yards back from the street, the door hanging off its hinges.

'The door's been kicked in!' he whispered.

Keaton leaned in to look, then extended her arm displaying a weighty bunch of keys hanging from her index finger. 'These are what I used to lock up with. I found them by the side of the till. He must've had his van keys on a separate fob? Probably couldn't fit them all in his pocket,' she said, jiggling her discovery's considerable mass. 'I bet the keys to *that* house are on here.'

'You're probably right,' Gutteridge agreed, lunging a fleeting look further down the drive. He saw the cream van abandoned outside of a run-down outbuilding, the door left wide open. 'He's here!' he hissed. 'I see his van…'

He rolled a look back to Keaton. 'Where the fuck are Armed Response?! How long does it fucking take?'

Keaton raised empathetic shoulders, sharing in his frustration.

Gutteridge leaned back in and studied the windows, burning each one in succession for signs of life, but could see no movement – except the peripheral trips fuelled by his growing paranoia.

Half of the windows he could see had the curtains drawn closed, with no obvious signs of twitching.

He took to a knee, flitting eyes studying the ground beneath him, stewing in his frustration for a moment, then broke from it with iron resolve. 'I'm going in!'

'You're *what?*' Keaton fizzed. 'But you're not even wearing a vest! Why take the risk? What would you be gaining over just waiting for ARU to arrive?'

Gutteridge stood again and spun to face her objections. 'But we're so close, so near to ending this! And what if he's in there destroying evidence? Or worse still, committing suicide!'

Keaton threw him a dismissive scowl. 'So what? Let the fucker die!' she stabbed.

Gutteridge reeled at the honesty of her response. 'That wouldn't be right, he should be paying for what he's done, not allowed to take the easy way out! And what if he's abducted another child, one that we don't know about yet, and is in there with it now? I don't think either of us could live with the knowledge that we could have saved a life, and did nothing, could we? So, no. I'm going in!'

Keaton sagged, unable to find a solid argument against his reasoning. 'Okay. But it's *we*. *We're* going in – together,' she insisted. 'You lead, I'll follow close behind. I can keep an eye out for blind spots, watch your back – so to speak. And before you argue, I won't take no for an answer.' She fixed him with an insistent stare. 'I'm your partner, Pat, like it or not, so let's do this.'

Reluctantly, he nodded, looking strangely thrilled, but appreciative of the support.

He peered through the unkempt foliage one last time to check the coast was clear, taking the gun from his belt and dropping the clip out; it was full. He pulled back the slide to check the chamber was empty, then snapped the magazine back into the grip and shuttled the slide to load the chamber. He took a deep, calming breath to pacify the jitter in his gut, and slid the safety off.

'Come on,' he whispered, urging her to follow with an arcing toss of the head.

She complied, stooping behind his considerable frame as he sprinted for the shattered door, the muzzle of his Glock aimed at the ground as he crunched across the no-man's-land of gravel.

Keaton was desperately trying to recall her training, and secretly hoped ARU would suddenly arrive and take over. But she too had a fizzle of excitement coursing through her whole body like the initial pulsating rush of an orgasm, and she felt alive to her own mortality.

They reached what remained of the door, which had been kicked with considerable force. Way more force than either of them would have estimated the physique of the man they'd encountered could exert. Whoever kicked this, wasn't alive to their own perceivable limitations, and that unsettled them.

Gutteridge wasn't sure if he should make their presence known or continue inside unannounced. Looking down at the component parts of the door lying at his feet, he came down on the side of 'unannounced'.

'Ready?' he mouthed to Keaton. She nodded, her eyes ablaze with perverted excitement.

Gutteridge sank to knee level, then flicked a look around the doorless frame. The coast looked clear.

He rose again and rolled in through the opening, tiptoeing around the fragments of panelling, straightened arms holding the muzzle of the Glock to the ground, occasionally lifting it to address blind corners.

Keaton followed close behind, double-checking every cleared corner, crevice and doorway as they moved methodically through the building.

The decor surprised her: unexpectedly tasteful. Again, not the decrepit grief-hole of a psychotically deluded monster she was expecting. A feminine touch to the detailing that made her think that the woman lying in one of the polished steel drawers back at the morgue at one time lived here.

She gripped the back of Gutteridge's shirt tightly, ready to pull him clear of anything she saw that his sweeping gaze failed to see.

She could feel the tepid perspiration soaking the fibres of the cloth, reminding her of the night they were weak, relenting to their shared desires, gifting themselves to each other in a sweat-soaked haze of liberated expectation.

Gutteridge entered the living room, addressing every nook and corner with the muzzle of the gun. He darted looks behind the couch and the curtains while Keaton kept watch at the door. The room looked clear.

He assumed his position at the head of the procession again and nodded two pistoled fingers at Keaton to continue the sweep.

They both moved down the hallway back to back and slid into the kitchen. It was neat and tidy, save for one drawer that had been ripped from its cabinet, spilling its contents across the floor like a rainbow of polished steel.

It looked to be mostly cutlery, and Gutteridge stood for a moment examining what was there: knives; forks; spoons; potato peelers; cob-holders; three fruit knives; a bread knife; a cheese knife; four butter knives; and a wooden-handled ceramic rolling pin that was now cracked. He looked over by the sink, and then scanned the countertops.

'He's armed,' Gutteridge whispered. 'He's got a knife!'

'How do you know?'

'There are no chef's knives,' he replied, lifting a chin towards the drawer's arc of detritus. 'At least we know he doesn't have a gun.'

'He might?'

'If he had a gun, why would he need a knife?'

Once again, the feeling of inadequacy returned to Keaton. She nodded.

There was a woody thud from above that shook the ceiling. They both shied from the sound and backed towards the perimeter of the room. 'He's upstairs!' Keaton mouthed.

Gutteridge nodded, the gut-knotting anxiety showing in his face. 'Come on,' he said.

He lunged for the door and spied the base of the staircase ten yards ahead at the far end of the passage. It looked to have a thick-pile carpet running its entire length, held in place with polished brass stair rods that Gutteridge thought would be effective in silencing their approach, a tasteful Mario Buatta-esque design he reckoned would suit his own cottage.

He took a breath, and rushed across the divide, eyes and muzzle locked on the stairwell as he approached it.

There was another muffled thump from the floor above, and by the lack of stealth, Gutteridge thought it a fair bet O'Leary wasn't yet alive to their presence.

He squatted by the base of the staircase, eyes turned to the top of the ascent through the upright rows of barley-twist spindles.

Keaton darted across to join his side. They could hear multiple voices emanating from one of the rooms above, but had to assume they were being made by the same mouth. The speech was far too quiet to discern what was being said, but the agitation in the voices was palpable.

'What are you thinking?' Keaton asked.

'I'm thinking this guy's fucking mental!' He knelt in contemplation of his options, half expecting O'Leary to arrive at the top of the stairs at any moment. 'I'm going up,' he whispered with conviction, already standing to do so, brow beaded with sweat.

He darted across to the wall side of the staircase and began slowly making his way up, one step at a time, trying to place each foot as close to the outsides of each tread as possible to avoid making sound.

As he reached halfway, he could begin to make out snippets of the conversation, something about being caught, and martyrdom...?

The next tread Gutteridge stepped onto groaned under his weight, a sharp, woody crack that cut through the tension.

The conversation upstairs ceased, and the house fell into an eery, leaden silence you could have sliced with a knife.

Gutteridge held his position, raising the sight of his gun to the head of the stairwell. He knew he'd been heard and was being listened for. The chance that one of the other treads would emit a sound was high, and he froze.

Gutteridge stared at the wall at the top of the rise through the sights of the Glock. 'O'Leary,' he called, his voice echoing around the well of the staircase, 'stay where you are. We're armed, but we mean you no harm.'

Sounds of panicked movement echoed down the stairwell. Keaton placed a primed foot onto the bottom step in readiness...

Gutteridge set off in the direction of the voices. Keaton followed, covering the ascent two treads at a time.

She rejoined Gutteridge's rear and re-gripped his shirt as they edged methodically through a long, door-lined landing area, Gutteridge swinging the gun into every room he encountered, until he reached the last door on the left just past an ornate Elizabethan side table and froze...

Gutteridge began to shake; Keaton could feel it through his back. She watched the grip on the pistol softening, along with his resolve.

'Oh God! P-Please! No! You– You don't want to do this!' Gutteridge said, lowering the weapon, then hesitating, before cautiously stuttering into the room.

Keaton stepped in and peered around the doorframe... O'Leary was standing over by the window, the glare of the sun behind bleeding around his silhouette, making him look like he was immolating. His arm was held out to his side, holding a polished metal object that looked like a gun, but that wasn't a gun – not in the ordinary sense.

The end of the device was being held to the head of a woman, a woman Keaton had seen before, watching through the bedroom window of Gutteridge's home. It was *Eve!* Gaffer-taped to a chair and looking as petrified as those watching.

Her mouth had also been taped, framing bloodshot, tear-soaked eyes shaking in terror, pleading across at Gutteridge as he stood in checkmate.

Gutteridge began to weep, simpering words of fear. 'Oh Eve! I'm sorry.... please, don't hurt her! She has nothing to do with this.'

O'Leary thrust the captive bolt pistol hard against her scalp, the end of the striking pin pointed straight to the top of her head. 'You! You fucking made her part of this! You give me no choice!' he barked.

'How did I make her a part of this? This is your doing! Can you not see all of this is wrong?'

'It's *not* wrong. How can the will of God be wrong? The god – may I remind you – that created all of this,' he said, looking about the room in an exaggerated manner. 'A god that gave me life. That gave *you* life!' He shook a berating head. '*You... You* should be helping me in his quest, not trying to prevent it!' His whole demeanour turned angered and resentful. 'You think you know so much, but you know nothing! *Nothing!*'

'I know that taking the lives of innocent children and– and mutilating their bodies can't be right.'

O'Leary's eyes slowly filled with malice, resentment and tears, briefly rolling up under his lids, then recentring. He jabbed the pistol hard against the crown of Eve's head, his finger tugging at the trigger. 'What the fuck would someone loik you know of roit or wrong?! You no-good sinning bastard! I've seen you copulatin' with this– this... *whore*!' he spat, teeth grinding his loathing, thrusting the pistol down onto her bleeding scalp with every resentful word he hissed, his hate and frustration pulling at the trigger.

Urine began to rain through the seat as Eve cowered beneath the threat, quaking at the very real possibility that life was about to end.

She closed her eyes and waited for the moment to come. For the sound, and the hit, and the jolt to her skull. *Would it hurt? Or would it be too instantaneous to even register anything had happened?* she wondered – finding herself hoping for the latter but feeling it would be demeaning to go out without any kind of fanfare. An ungracious full-stop to a life lived and loved.

'*Kieran!*' Gutteridge pleaded. 'Listen to me. None of this is your fault. You're not well. You need help, can you not see that? We can get it for you. We can *help* you! *Please*, just put the weapon down. You don't want to hurt anyone else.'

'He's right,' interjected Keaton, stepping slowly into the room, 'we can get you the assistance you need. But this has to end.'

Gutteridge took a cautious, unthreatening step nearer. There was a bed in the corner, and boxes stacked against the left side wall. It was very much a spare room.

'Kieran, I need you to look deep inside yourself. Do you really think the god you worship would urge you to do the things you've done? Or do you think there's even the remotest of possibilities that you've created this god yourself, for reasons I couldn't even hope to understand. Reasons that I'm sure are the fault of others?' He recalled Eve's hypothesis. 'Your father for instance?'

O'Leary's eyes fluttered, briefly rolled up under his lids, then centred again. A new voice filled the room. 'Don't listen to them, my child. What you have done, you did for me. You have done what has been asked of you. You are the instrument of my wrath, the conveyor of my displeasure, and *all* who oppose you, shall—'

'*Kieran! Stop!*' Keaton screamed.

O'Leary rocked on his heels and returned to the room. '*This* isn't you! *You* are manifesting this! Look deep, *deep* inside your heart. You know it to be true.'

Guttering took another passive step closer. 'We know you've questioned it yourself. We spoke to the priest you went to see, so we *know* you have doubts and that what we're saying has truth, and *we* can help. But you need to stop this.'

'Please, Kieran,' Keaton begged, holding up her hands, showing them empty.

'Ask yourself one thing,' Gutteridge asked. 'Is there anything that this supposed god that lives inside of you knows, that isn't knowledge you already possess from your own reading of the scriptures…?'

O'Leary's eyes dropped away from the conversation. Keaton could see him fighting with his conflicted emotions, considering Gutteridge's words. 'But… he said… he was…'

'I know,' Keaton interjected, her brow wilting, 'but don't you realise, it was you all along, you doing these things? Know it. *Feel* it. Understand it. We can get you the help and assistance you need. I wouldn't lie to you, believe me. You *must* believe me.'

Thundering footsteps began to infest the house, calls of 'Clear!' and Gutteridge's name echoing around the stairwell.

The footsteps began to climb the staircase, flashes of torchlight painting the walls.

Attentions momentarily turned towards the advancing commotion, then back to O'Leary, who now had the captive bolt pistol pressed firmly beneath his jaw.

'Please… forgive me for what I have done!' he said, looking drained and forlorn, his saline tears filling his quivering mouth.

Gutteridge lunged towards O'Leary, open hands extending towards the weapon in desperation. 'No! *Kieran!* Don't!' he cried.

An explosive *crack* shattered the silence, and O'Leary's body dropped to the ground like wet cloth, misting fans of blood spraying from his mouth.

Eve began to scream through the tape, rocking in her humiliation. Gutteridge lowered his weapon and ran to her, dropping to his knees. He took his penknife from his pocket, cut her hands free, and carefully removed the tape from her mouth.

She began to shed inconsolable tears at the indignity of it all as she thanked him in humbled tones. He wiped the drips of blood curtaining her hairline aside with a compassionate thumb, and she threw her arms around his relief. He could smell the fear in her sweat as she shivered in his requited embrace.

Keaton looked on, dazed by the whole grim experience as Armed Response began filling the room, checking O'Leary's vital signs and placing comforting hands to Gutteridge's back.

Keaton slumped, allowed herself to breathe again, forcing an anaemic smile, and shed her own, single, solitary tear…

FORTY-TWO

JANE KEATON twisted a look behind her towards the open doors of the chapel, dressed head to toe in duck-egg-blue tulle and chiffon. She'd always dreamed of being a bridesmaid, but maybe not at a wedding where her feelings were so conflicted.

A lime-green Lamborghini arrived at the base of the steps, a beaming Toby Jackson at the wheel. He blipped the throttle of the Huracan, sending a turbine V10 howl resonating around the pillars of the nave, exciting the waiting congregation who felt a desire to applaud the outrage.

A suited man stepped in, opened the door, and began scooping carefully packed armfuls of silk and satin from the tiny cabin, then extended a gracious hand to heave Ewelina Kaminska and her abounding skirts into the clement weather that God felt fit to provide.

The gem-encrusted bodice of the dress was sleek and tight-fitting, and Keaton had to hold the gasp that sat poised in her throat begging to be heard at how beautiful she looked in the glow of the midday sun, a sun that seemed to burn to honour her arrival.

The music started, and her attention returned to the front. She caught Gutteridge's eye. He smiled at her with a perceivable amount of sorrow and apology. She smiled back. 'It's okay,' she mouthed. 'You look great.'

She'd seen him mostly in suits the whole time she'd known him, but this was somehow different. He looked dashing, and handsome, and happy, and that was the part she found herself struggling with the most.

Eve arrived at the altar on her father's arm. Gutteridge had paid to fly him over from Poznan to give her away.

Keaton stepped in with the other maid to gently lift Eve's veil. This time, she couldn't hold it in, and the gasp was audible. Eve's features glowed within the subtly tasteful make-up, ringlets of onyx framing her feline beauty, and no one there – not even Asha Zielinska, sitting near the front – could compete…

Eve had managed to get over her ordeal with surprisingly little intervention from therapists. Jane Keaton had heard that the Poles were a resilient race, and going by the evidence, they – whoever *they* were – were right.

She worked to straighten the train and resumed her position respectfully by Eve's side.

Just two months had passed since Kieran O'Leary took his own life, and the images of his suicide still haunted Keaton to this day. But she drew solace from the fact that it was over, and that there were others – like Karen Peek – who had way more to contend with in the wake of his insanity.

Karen Peek had lost everything: her husband; her child; her entire life as she knew it. A woman no longer young, having to start all over again, building a new life, a new love, and with the nightmarish shadows left by the Spatchcock Killer to contend with.

No. Jane Keaton couldn't see herself as badly off, not in the light of the crippling misfortune of others…

The music ceased, the service began, and Jane Keaton couldn't take her eyes off Detective Inspector Patrick Gutteridge…

*

Jane Keaton stared at her reflection in the hotel bathroom mirror. She'd changed into her evening clothes, and the party was due to start. Guests had already begun to arrive, and she felt she should be there to help greet them.

She leaned on the sink, desperately trying to quell the tears that had been flowing freely for the last half-hour. For once in her normally decisive life, she was at a loss.

Her eyes left her confounded reflection and its streaked, mascara tears, and dropped to the pregnancy test sitting on the side of the sink, displaying two strong, vivid lines.

A sombre tear abandoned her eye and splashed onto the strip. Would she have it? Would she not? She loved the man, but didn't want to risk ruining his happiness. But it *was* his baby, and her love for him – by osmosis – translated to the new life gestating in her belly…

She dried her eyes, took a faltering breath, and fixed her make-up. She had a short window within which to make a decision that she knew would – in some way – affect her life forever, but tonight, she wanted to be there for him.

She walked to the door and took one last, long look at herself in the mirror, hand poised on the light switch…

Perhaps she'd have it, say it was another man's, and hope upon hope that it didn't look too much like him?

She could hear muffled music echoing from the ballroom downstairs. She forced a smile she didn't feel, cupped an affectionate hand to her abdomen, and switched off the light…